Victoria
REBELS

ALSO BY CAROLYN MEYER

Victoria REBELS

CAROLYN MEYER

A PAULA WISEMAN BOOK

SIMON & SCHUSTER BFYR

NEW YORK LONDON TORONTO SYDNEY NEW DELHI

For Leah Norod, Vankelia Tolbert, and Sydney V. Trebour,

who suggested that I write a book about Victoria

SIMON & SCHUSTER BFYR

An imprint of Simon & Schuster Children's Publishing Division
1230 Avenue of the Americas, New York, New York 10020

For information about special discounts for bulk purchases, please contact Simon & Schuster
Special Sales at 1-866-506-1949 or business@simonandschuster.com.
The Simon & Schuster Speakers Bureau can bring authors to your live event. For more
information or to book an event, contact the Simon & Schuster Speakers Bureau
at 1-866-248-3049 or visit our website at www.simonspeakers.com.
Also available in a SIMON & SCHUSTER BFYR hardcover edition
Book design by Laurent Linn
The text for this book is set in Minion Pro.
Manufactured in the United States of America
First SIMON & SCHUSTER BFYR paperback edition May 2014
2 4 6 8 10 9 7 5 3

The Library of Congress has cataloged the hardcover edition as follows:
Meyer, Carolyn.
Victoria rebels / Carolyn Meyer.
p. cm.
"A Paula Wiseman Book."
Summary: Through diary entries, reveals the life of Britain's strong-willed and short-
tempered Queen Victoria from the age of eight through her twenty-fourth birthday, up to her
third wedding anniversary with her beloved Albert in 1843.
Includes bibliographical references.
ISBN 978-1-4169-8729-1 (hardback) — ISBN 978-1-4424-2246-9 (eBook)
1. Victoria, Queen of Great Britain, 1819–1901—Childhood and youth—Juvenile fiction.
2. Great Britain—History—1800–1837—Juvenile fiction. 3. Great Britain—History—
Victoria, 1837–1901—Juvenile fiction. [1. Victoria, Queen of Great Britain, 1819–1901—
Childhood and youth—Fiction. 2. Great Britain—History—1800–1837—Fiction. 3. Great
Britain—History—Victoria, 1837–1901—Fiction. 4. Kings, queens, rulers, etc.—Fiction.
5. Courts and courtiers—Fiction. 6. Albert, Prince Consort, consort of Victoria, Queen of
Great Britain, 1819–1861—Fiction. 7. Diaries—Fiction.] I. Title.
PZ7.M5685Vic 2013
[Fic]—dc23
2012023255
ISBN 978-1-4169-8730-7 (pbk)

Author's Note: Queen Victoria's diaries have provided much of the inspiration for
this book. Victoria frequently used capitalization and underlining in her diary for
emphasis, and I have kept that style throughout the text. These passages are fictional
representations and are not meant to be direct quotes of Victoria's.

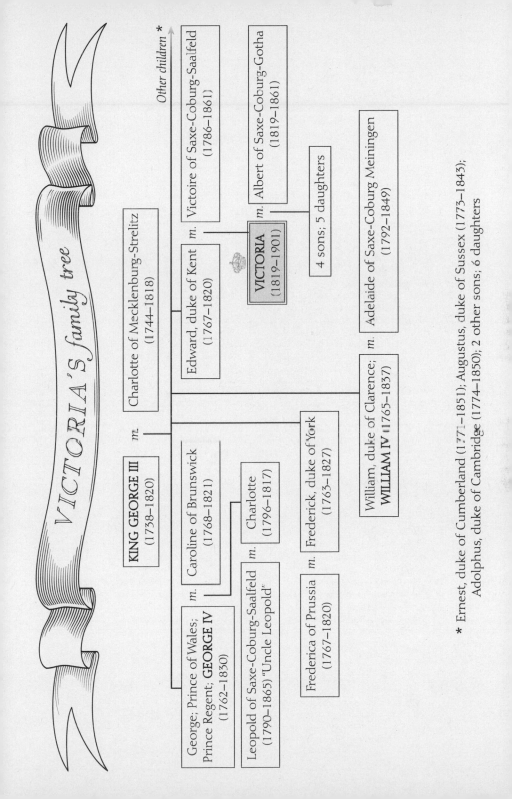

VICTORIA'S family tree

KING GEORGE III
(1738–1820)

m.

Charlotte of Mecklenburg-Strelitz
(1744–1818)

Other children *

George; Prince of Wales;
Prince Regent; GEORGE IV
(1762–1830)

m.

Caroline of Brunswick
(1768–1821)

Frederick, duke of York
(1763–1827)

William, duke of Clarence;
WILLIAM IV (1765–1837)

m.

Adelaide of Saxe-Coburg Meiningen
(1792–1849)

Edward, duke of Kent
(1767–1820)

m.

Victoire of Saxe-Coburg-Saalfeld
(1786–1861)

Leopold of Saxe-Coburg-Saalfeld
(1790–1865) "Uncle Leopold"

m.

Charlotte
(1796–1817)

Frederica of Prussia
(1767–1820)

VICTORIA
(1819–1901)

m.

Albert of Saxe-Coburg-Gotha
(1819–1861)

4 sons; 5 daughters

* Ernest, duke of Cumberland (1771–1851); Augustus, duke of Sussex (1773–1843);
Adolphus, duke of Cambridge (1774–1850); 2 other sons; 6 daughters

Part I

The Princess

Chapter 1

KENSINGTON PALACE, ENGLAND, 1827

I hate Sir John Conroy.

Mamma knew that I was never fond of him, though she did not suspect <u>how much</u> I despised him. "He has been a good friend to us since your papa died, Vickelchen," she reminded me often. My father, the duke of Kent, had died when I was an infant. "I do not know what I would do without Sir John."

He may have been a friend to Mamma—<u>too</u> good, in my opinion—but he was never a friend to me, though he pretended to be. And I had to pretend that I did not loathe him.

Sir John was very tall and did not trouble to bring himself down to meet my eye, so that I always had to tilt my head to gaze up at him. He often spoke to me in what he seemed to consider a jocular manner, once telling me that I reminded him of Dickey, my pet donkey. "Stubbornly resistant to being guided in a new direction," he said, and burst into a loud guffaw. I was not at all amused.

But that is not why I despised him.

It was Sir John's fault that Feodore, my half sister, left England.

I loved Feodore, whom I called Fidi, more than almost anyone except dearest Daisy, my governess. (I always called her Daisy, though her name was Louise Lehzen.) And except Mamma, of course.

We were preparing to celebrate my sister's twentieth birthday, on the seventh of December, when Fidi told me the news. I had returned to our apartment in Kensington Palace from an afternoon walk with dear Daisy. Promising to be absent only a minute or two, my governess left me alone to practice the sums assigned that morning by my tutor. I heard Fidi's special knock and rose from my writing table, thinking how pleased she would be with the gifts I had for her—a pair of pearl earrings and a drawing I'd made of myself, though I <u>had</u> placed the eyes too close together.

Fidi flung herself into Daisy's empty chair. My sister was very beautiful, with dark hair and a pretty mouth, but now her lovely brown eyes were puffed and reddened. She burst into sobs. I had never seen her in such a state.

"Dearest Fidi, what's wrong?"

"Tonight at dinner Mamma will announce that I'm to marry Prince Ernst of Hohenlohe-Langenburg." Her voice was thick with tears. "Perhaps you remember him? He came to visit this past July. This is all Sir John's doing."

<u>Prince Ernst?</u> I did recall a tall, thin man with bulging eyes and a large, blond mustache. Mamma had introduced him as a friend from Germany. I knew Fidi was of an age to marry, but I had not expected this. "He looked very old," I said rather severely.

"Not so *very* old." She attempted a quavering smile. "But old enough. Just thirty-four. And he *is* handsome, I suppose."

I had not found Prince Ernst handsome, but I didn't mention that he reminded me of a toad. "I suppose I shall learn to care for him," I said, though I wasn't at all certain I could. "Will he come to live here at Kensington Palace with us, or shall you move with him to a palace nearby?" We sometimes visited Uncle Leopold, Mamma's younger brother, at Claremont, his lovely mansion south of London. If Fidi were to live in such a pretty mansion, I believed I might find the situation tolerable.

Fidi traced the pattern on the carpet with the toe of her slipper. Her lip began to tremble, and her eyes welled again with tears. "No, dear Victoria, he will not, and neither will I. After the wedding in February, the prince and I leave to begin our life in Germany."

"Germany!" I wailed. "But you can't leave England! You cannot! When shall I ever see you again? I shall miss you so dreadfully!" With a sob I crept into my sister's arms.

"And I shall miss you too, dearest Vicky," she murmured. She rocked me as the two of us wept. We both knew it was useless to protest, once Mamma—and the dreadful Sir John Conroy—made up their minds.

I worried that my governess would return and find us in such a state. Daisy rarely left me for more than a moment; it was against rules set by Sir John and Mamma that I was never to be alone. I slid off my sister's lap and tidied my dress and sash. Fidi stayed sprawled in Daisy's chair with her face buried in her hands. "Oh, I cannot bear the man!" she cried.

I was as surprised by this outburst as by her tears. "Prince Ernst?" I asked carefully. "You truly can't bear him?"

Fidi peered at me from between her fingers. "No, no! I

scarcely know Prince Ernst, and I have no idea whether I can bear him or not."

"But who, then?"

"Sir John, of course! He controls everything that happens in our lives. Whatever he does is designed to gain him influence, and Mamma allows it! Our mother seems unable to draw a breath unless Conroy approves." She spat out the words as though they had a bitter taste.

Fidi sprang up and began to pace distractedly from one end to the other of the small sitting room. "I'll tell you a secret, Vicky," she said. "I know it's safe with you. My heart is bursting, and I must talk to someone, though you're too young, certainly, to understand—"

"I am *not* too young!" I protested. I disliked being treated like a child.

Fidi stared at me, her pretty face crumpled miserably. "I'm in love with someone else!" she whispered. I nodded sagely, though she was quite right, I did not truly understand. "You must promise never to speak of this again, Victoria."

Thrilled that she would confide in me, I solemnly promised.

"I'm in love with Captain d'Este, the son of Uncle Sussex."

I frowned. "Captain d'Este?" The duke of Sussex was one of Papa's younger brothers. He lived alone in a suite of rooms in another part of Kensington Palace, surrounded by thousands of books and dozens of clocks. Mamma described him as "eccentric." But I had never heard of a cousin named Captain d'Este.

"I met Augustus nearly two years ago when I was riding in St. James's Park," Fidi said, her cheeks flushing rosily when she spoke his name. "My horse became unruly, and dear Augustus came to my rescue. I was immediately attracted to him, and he to me. We began to meet secretly and soon fell deeply in love. I took our dear Baroness Späth into my confidence, and she agreed to carry our messages to arrange our trysts."

Baroness Späth was Mamma's old friend, even before Mamma married Papa and became duchess of Kent, and she adored my sister and me.

"What happened?" I whispered, dreading the unhappy ending I felt was sure to follow.

"We became incautious—reckless even—and rumors spread. Our secret meetings were no longer secret. Mamma learned of it. She forbade me ever to see Augustus again, because he is illegitimate. That's why you've never heard of him. The old king refused to recognize Uncle Sussex's marriage to Augustus's mother, which took place without royal approval and therefore wasn't legal. We believed we could bear a separation until we found a way to marry, perhaps even to elope. But of course Sir John was informed of 'the situation,' as Mamma called it, though I begged her not to speak to him about it. He persuaded Mamma that I was becoming troublesome—'willful,' he said— and the best solution was to marry me off at once."

Of course Sir John would interfere! I understood that very well.

"Sir John had several candidates in mind. There was even a rumor that King George himself was showing a great deal of interest in me."

"Uncle King wanted to marry you?" I shuddered at the very notion. King George IV was a gouty old man who wore a thick layer of rouge plastered on his flabby cheeks and a corset to hold in his fat stomach. Uncle King was very kind to me and once gave me a lovely diamond badge, but I could not imagine my beautiful sister wed to him.

"It was only a rumor, but Mamma and Sir John were taking no risk that it might be true. They settled on Prince Ernst, though he has no wealth to speak of. I was told about it only after everything had been arranged. Now, in just two months I will marry a man I scarcely know and do not love, and be sent away to ensure that I will never again see the man who has my heart."

"Dear, dear Fidi!" I cried, my heart breaking for her. "How *very* sad!"

"Sad for me, but sad for you as well, dearest sister! I fear that Sir John will do the same to you some day, and I can do nothing to prevent it! Oh, Victoria, I'd take you with me if I could, but that's impossible!"

"But surely—"

Suddenly a voice startled us. "Surely it is time for you to dress for dinner, Victoria."

Daisy had appeared at the door. How much had she heard? "And you as well, Feodore," she added briskly. Daisy had been Fidi's governess before she became mine.

Fidi leaped to her feet, kissed the top of my head, and rushed away.

Daisy closed the door and leaned against it. She was tall and thin with a stiff, straight back and sharp features. It was her duty as my governess to instruct me in matters of deportment. She corrected me when she thought I had been naughty or stubborn or had behaved in any way she did not approve. Yet beneath her stern manner was the warmest heart in the world. Daisy had always been devoted to me, and I returned her devotion without limit.

"So Feodore has told you her news," she said. "We must be happy for her, Victoria."

"It's so unfair," I complained. "Just because Mamma disapproves of Captain d'Este's parents."

"The duke of Sussex has defied moral standards," my governess said firmly. "Your mother is quite right to disapprove."

"But Fidi is leaving!" I wailed. "She's not at all happy, and so how can I be happy for her? How can Mamma allow it?"

"The duchess believes it's for the best," she said. "Sir John has convinced her of it." Daisy touched my cheek gently. "Now, come, we must wash your face—all that weeping!—and choose which dress you shall wear to Feodore's celebration."

Daisy took my hand as we went down to the Red Salon—I was not permitted to descend the sweeping marble staircase without holding the hand of a trusted adult—and pages in royal livery opened the double doors with a flourish. The walls of the salon were covered in red silk, a trifle faded. A steward cried, "The Princess Alexandrina Victoria!"

"Smile, Victoria," Daisy murmured as we prepared to enter, and everyone turned to watch.

Sir John and the entire Conroy family were already present: his round-faced wife, Eliza, their three sons, and their two daughters: Victoire, who is just my age—she was named for Mamma—and her older sister, Jane. I found both girls rather tiresome.

Several of my papa's brothers arrived, among them William, duke of Clarence, and his kind wife, Adelaide, who it turned out was a cousin of Prince Ernst. Naturally, none of Uncle William's many children by his former mistress had been invited. I acknowledged several other uncles and aunts and those few cousins who were fortunate enough to have the proper parents.

I was happy to see Uncle Leopold, my very favorite uncle. He had married Uncle King's only child, Princess Charlotte, but poor Charlotte and her newborn infant had died before I was born.

How very sad that was! *Does he know about Fidi's broken heart?* I wondered. Surely Uncle Leopold, who had himself suffered great loss, would not insist that my sister give up the man she loved to marry a man she did not—merely to satisfy Sir John!

Fidi and Mamma made their entrance. My sister was lovely but very pale. Mamma was dressed in the fur-trimmed blue velvet gown that she claimed gave her confidence. We sat down to dine, and after many courses had been served, Mamma rose and the company fell silent. She always felt uneasy about speaking in public. Her German accent was heavy, though she had lived in England since just before I was born. Sir John had written a little speech for her with the pronunciation of each word spelled out.

"It is with great pleasure," she said, *with* sounding like *vit*, "that I announce the engagement of my daughter, Princess Feodore of Leiningen, to Prince Ernst of Hohenlohe-Langenburg. The wedding"—*vedding*—"will take place here at Kensington Palace on the twenty-first day of February." Mamma paused, glancing at Fidi, who wore a brave smile that I knew was utterly false. Sir John jumped to his feet and began to applaud, a signal to everyone else to do the same. I could not bear to look at my sister.

"How excited you must be, Victoria," murmured Jane Conroy close to my ear. "It will be a splendid wedding. I do so look forward to it."

"I am not in the least excited, Jane," I told her sternly. "Feodore will be leaving. I do not look forward to that."

And it is all your father's doing, I thought, turning away, my lips pressed tightly together. *I hate Sir John Conroy.*

FIDI'S WEDDING, 1828

Ten days before the wedding Prince Ernst and his family arrived from Germany, along with Fidi's older brother, my half brother, Prince Charles of Leiningen. Prince Ernst made it a point to speak to me very kindly. I wanted to loathe him as much as I loathed Sir John, but in truth I did not. He seemed an amiable person, though no more handsome than I remembered, and Fidi was beginning to seem at ease with him. I saw them walking together in the garden, talking with their heads close together. He even succeeded in making her laugh! She appeared to like him, or at the very least not to find him odious.

As the day of my sister's wedding drew closer, I tried to shut her departure for Germany from my mind, but could not. Fidi was leaving, and I had to stay at Kensington. I would have no one close to my age but that dull and insipid Victoire Conroy. Dear Daisy, sensing my unhappiness, gave me a gift: a little wooden doll she had dressed in a tiny costume made of scraps of lace left over from my sister's wedding gown.

"She will fit into your pocket," Fidi said when I showed her the doll. "You can carry her everywhere, or tuck her beneath your pillow. She will listen to you when you whisper your secrets to her, and you can be assured that she will never speak of them to anyone else."

I named the doll Fidi. She was my secret, and so she remained, even during the time when I was permitted to have no secrets.

The night before Fidi's wedding Mamma entertained guests at a large dinner in the Red Salon. The menu included two soups, two kinds of fish, two roasts, several entrées, numerous entremets (my favorite was the maraschino jelly), and a variety of desserts. After the dinner—I fear I ate too much—Daisy accompanied me upstairs to the bedroom I shared with Mamma. My maid, Bessie, removed my velvet dress and helped me into my nightgown. She bustled about, laying out my stockings and undergarments for the next day. After she had banked the fire and snuffed out all the candles but one, Bessie made a curtsy, wished us good night, and left. I sometimes wondered about Bessie, what her life was like, but I was not allowed to have a conversation with her. "A princess must not speak personally to a servant," Daisy said. It was against the rules. I did not need to ask whose rules. Sir John's, of course. He made all the rules—too many to remember.

Daisy sat beside me, hands forming a pious steeple, and listened as I recited my prayers. I was not allowed to speak privately even to God! When I had said "amen" and was lying in my bed with the satin coverlet pulled up to my chin, Daisy settled in her usual chair close by. She opened a book and began to read silently by the light of the single candle left burning.

I closed my eyes, but thinking of the wedding the next morning, I was too excited to fall asleep. Dear Daisy began to snore gently. I heard the door open quietly. I kept my eyes closed, believing it was Mamma. Someone was standing close by my bed, but I sensed that it was not Mamma. I opened my eyes the merest slits. It was Fidi!

"Shhhhh," she warned. "Mamma is still with her guests. They're speaking German and having a fine time." Wearing only a thin shift, Fidi was shivering. "Let me come in next to you," she whispered, and I lifted the coverlet and made room for her. "I wanted to have just a few minutes alone with you," she said, curling up cozily next to me. "This is the last night I'll spend here at Kensington. Tomorrow we'll be at Claremont. Uncle Leopold had a suite of rooms prepared for us. We're to stay there for a few days, and then we will leave for Germany."

"We," I heard her say. "Us." In a few hours Prince Ernst would become her husband. "When are you coming back to Kensington?" I asked.

"I don't know. But I'll write to you as often as I can, and you must promise to write to me, as well."

"I promise. But oh, Fidi, what shall I ever do without you?" I had forgotten to whisper. Daisy stirred slightly. Fidi placed her finger on my lips. Daisy sighed and resumed her snoring.

"I wish I could go to Germany with you," I said, for perhaps the tenth time, or maybe the twentieth.

"Darling Vicky, let me tell you a story—the last I shall tell you, for you're getting too old for my stories."

"I will never be too old for your stories," I insisted.

Fidi began her story with the part I already knew: There was once a duke named Edward, a son of the king of England, who married a German princess named Victoire. When the princess learned that she was with child, the duke brought her to England so the baby would be born here. I was that baby.

"This is the part I haven't told you," Fidi continued. "A gypsy fortune-teller had once told the duke he would have a child who would grow up to rule England, and Edward believed it. He wanted the baby to be English enough to inherit the throne."

"And you believe it, too?"

"I do," Fidi said. "The king's only child died before you were born. The rest of your papa's brothers are old and fat and gouty, and not a single one of your older cousins is legitimate. As Mamma is fond of pointing out, they are all *bâtards* and cannot succeed to the throne. It's very likely that you will someday become queen, Vicky. Your papa planned on it. Mamma wants it. Sir John counts on it, and that's why he wants to control you."

I listened silently to what Fidi was telling me. *Can it be true that I shall be queen?* Fidi would not lie. Yet the idea was so astonishing that I could scarcely grasp it. *I, queen of England?*

"I shall miss you terribly," Fidi was saying. "But I'm also very glad to be leaving Kensington. I've felt like a prisoner from my first days here. I can escape—I'm not important to their plans. But I truly fear for you, dear Vicky, for you're now a prisoner as well."

Her words shocked me.

"You will have the title of queen," Fidi went on, "but Mamma hopes to be appointed regent, and if she gets her wish, it is Sir John who will actually rule England until you are eighteen—and long after that. He will try to control you the way he controls Mamma. Sir John is determined to have the power it will bring him. That's why he has so many rules for you—his so-called Kensington System—and why Mamma allows it."

Daisy muttered in her sleep. The book slid off her lap and fell to the floor with a thump. Fidi and I lay still as mice, hoping she had not awakened.

"I believe they're trying to break your will," Fidi said when it was safe to continue, "or at the very least to bend it so that you will always do exactly as they want. You must be strong, Victoria! Lehzen can't be of much help to you, for if she resists, Sir John will dismiss her with a snap of his fingers. It won't be easy for you, but you can depend on Uncle Leopold to do what he can to help you."

My head was whirling with questions, but before I could ask them, Fidi stroked my hair and kissed me tenderly. "I must leave, before Mamma comes up. Give me your solemn word that you will not tell Mamma or Lehzen or anyone else what I've told you. When they do tell you themselves, you must act very surprised. Do you promise?"

Solemnly, I crossed my heart and promised.

"Then tomorrow we shall be happy, shan't we? I'll pretend to be happy on my wedding day, and you must pretend to be happy for me. Know that I shall always hold you in my heart, and we will exchange letters often, and someday you will be free of these invisible bonds that now hold you so tightly."

Fidi crept out from beneath the coverlet and was feeling with her bare feet for her slippers when the door opened. *Mamma!* Daisy awakened with a start. It was too late for Fidi to make her escape.

"Feodore! What are you doing here?" Mamma demanded. She sounded startled, then angry.

"I came to give Vicky my blessing on my last night at Kensington," Fidi explained.

"I begged her to stay, Mamma. I shall miss dear Fidi so very, very much!" I added, beginning to weep. Fidi fled, leaving her slippers behind.

"We shall all miss her, Vickelchen, I know." Mamma's heart seemed to soften. She sank down on my bed. "But she will be content in her new life, once she gets used to it." She rubbed my toes through the thick, quilted satin. Her thoughts seemed far away. "I, too, once married a man I scarcely knew and moved far from everyone I loved." She smiled sadly. "But you are my reward, my dearest treasure."

The wedding was as lovely as one could ever wish. Sweet-smelling flowers filled the Cupola Room, where the ceremony took place. My sister was beautiful, of course, and when she made her marriage vows her voice was clear and strong. Sir John strutted among the guests, behaving as though he were Fidi's father, and his great, booming laugh drowned out all the other voices. My dress was made of the same delicate lace as my sister's wedding gown, and I had a little straw basket of favors to hand round to the guests. Fidi was as gay and charming as she used to be. Prince Ernst appeared to adore his new bride. I would have liked him much more if he were not about to take Fidi so far away.

Toasts were drunk to the health and happiness of the couple, and almost as much attention was paid to me as to the bride. At noon we sat down to a splendid wedding breakfast—stewed oysters, which I did not like, and a galantine of fowl, which I did. There were two cakes, a white one for the bride and a dark, fruity one for the groom. I ate some of both.

Uncle Leopold bent down to speak to me. "Ah, my little chick"—his pet name for me—"I see that you are enjoying your sister's wedding day!" Then he whispered close to my ear, "Remember, though, to eat slowly. Small bites! It will make you grow." It bothered my dear uncle that I was still quite small. Much as I wished to please him, my height did not change.

I tried to be happy, but as Fidi and her husband left in a borrowed carriage, I was unable to hold back the tears that had been threatening all morning. I waved and waved as they drove off on a cold, bright day, wrapped in furs with thick blankets over their knees, bound for Claremont. In a few days they would board a steamer that would carry them away to Germany.

"Good-bye, dearest Fidi!" I cried. "Good-bye, good-bye!"

Späth, 1829

A year passed, one uneventful day on the heels of the next. I waited impatiently for letters from my sister. They arrived less often than I'd hoped, but she always wrote that she was enjoying her new life. I wanted to believe her. Then came the news that she was expecting a child, and we were all very happy for her. I told everyone that I would become an aunt.

The two people at Kensington Palace of whom I was most fond were dearest Daisy and Baroness Späth. I loved them both. Of course I loved Mamma, too, but I spent most of my time with my governess and mother's oldest friend, and very little time with Mamma, who had much to occupy her.

Späth thought Daisy was too strict with me, and Daisy believed Späth was too lenient. Dear Daisy would not tolerate naughty outbursts, even the smallest amount of foot-stamping.

"A princess does not throw tantrums," my governess often had to remind me. "She controls her angry tongue."

Späth believed I was a perfect child in no need of correction.

There was another important difference: Daisy always kept her own counsel, while it was impossible for dear Späth to keep a secret. She had told Mamma of Fidi's love affair with Captain d'Este and spoiled it all. I learned from Späth's wagging tongue that nearly everyone in my papa's family was attached to some scandal or had been involved in some sinister affair.

"Perhaps I should not say this," Späth had a habit of beginning, and then went on to say it, whatever it was, anyway. "Perhaps I should not say this, but Sir John will do all he can to separate you from your papa's family. He has convinced your Mamma that King George means to steal you away and bring you up in court." When she saw my frightened look, Späth hastened to add, "Don't worry, child, such a thing will not be allowed."

Then one day I happened upon a scene that deeply affected my feelings toward my mother. For some reason I wished to speak to her and told Späth, who was with me that afternoon, "I'm going to find Mamma." Off I ran to the library, the cozy room with a lovely view of the gardens where Mamma had her desk for writing letters. The library also served as Sir John's office.

The door stood slightly ajar. Forgetting to knock, I pushed open the heavy door just enough to allow me to slip through. What I saw shocked me: my mother in Sir John's embrace. His mouth was firmly on hers. They were quite unaware that they had a witness. Mamma gasped and started to pull away from him, but then she seemed to change her mind and allowed herself to be pulled close. I stared at the pair, my mouth open, disbelieving what my eyes told me.

I backed slowly from the disturbing scene and rushed back to my room. "Darling girl!" Späth cried when I burst in. "What is it? What has happened?"

I shook my head. My lips were trembling so that I could scarcely speak. I could not explain it, and I did not understand it.

"Mamma," I stammered. "And Sir John. Together."

"Yes? What of it?" she asked. Then her demeanor changed. "Together? What were they doing, child?"

"They were very close," I ventured. "Embracing," I added. "Kissing, I think. But why were they doing that? Mamma is not his wife."

Späth gazed at me for a moment, her head tilted to one side. "Well!" she said, straightening and smiling brightly. "Because they are friends, of course! Now back to your studies, my love, and think no more of it! Let this be the end of it."

But it was not the end of it.

A fortnight later Späth broke the news to me that she was leaving. "I have been dismissed," she said. "And I shall return to Germany."

Dismissed? I gaped at her.

She tried to put up a brave front, but clearly she was deeply hurt.

"I shall speak plainly to you, my darling Victoria. Sir John Conroy has never been my friend, because I have openly criticized him and his methods. I do not like him, and I have never liked him. He was nothing, you know—just a captain in charge of your father's horses—until he became your mother's confidant and somehow persuaded King George to make him a knight. I reproached your Mamma, who is my oldest and dearest friend. I told her most forcefully that I believed she had become far too familiar with him. And him so common!"

She did not say it, but I guessed she was referring to the scene in the library that I had unwisely reported to her. "It is my fault," I cried, stricken, and threw myself, weeping, onto her lap. "But where shall you go in Germany?" I asked between sobs. "What shall you do?"

"You must not worry about me, my little love! Feodore is expecting her first child, and she has written to me that there's no one she thinks better suited to be the child's governess."

She kissed me, and two days later she was gone.

Späth's departure greatly distressed me, though dear Daisy tried to console me. "Späth will be with Feodore and Feodore's precious baby," she reminded me.

But I was deeply worried. Sir John had made Fidi leave, and now Späth. Soon it might be dearest Daisy! I thought again of the two I had glimpsed in the library, Mamma in Sir John's arms, and I realized that my mother would do whatever he wanted and I could do nothing at all to prevent it.

I hated him now more than I ever had. And I no longer thought well of Mamma.

EXAMINATIONS, 1830

Mamma was greatly concerned about my education.

"Before we leave on our spring holiday," she said, "you will undergo an examination. Two learned men, the bishops of London and Lincoln, will question you."

"Why must I do this, Mamma?" I asked. "My tutor thinks I'm doing well enough."

Mamma smiled stiffly. "I wish to have more than Mr. Davys's opinion. The purpose of the examination is to demonstrate that you are being educated in the best way possible and that you are learning all that is necessary to your future station." She did not say what my future station was, and I did not ask.

The Reverend George Davys had come to live at Kensington Palace when I was not yet four years old and had been stuffing knowledge into my resistant head ever since. I was not naturally a studious child. His first great challenge had been to teach me to read. Mamma's attempts had failed. Mr. Davys printed words on cards that he placed round my nursery and asked me to fetch them. "Cow," he would say, and I'd dash off to find the card with "C-O-W" printed on it. It seemed a game, and so I learned without realizing that I was being taught.

Since those earliest days, it had been Mr. Davys's charge to instruct me in history, geography, grammar (in which I was an indifferent student), and religion, and to read poetry aloud and understand it. He was my principal master; tutors came to cover other subjects: Mr. Steward in charge of writing and arithmetic and Monsieur Grandineau, French. I was fairly fluent in French, showed little facility for Latin, and spoke German easily and was often praised for my excellent pronunciation. I could read it well, too, but writing it was quite another matter.

My lessons began at ten o'clock, continued until noon, and resumed again late in the afternoon. On Saturday mornings Mr. Davys conducted a review of the week's work. Learning was no longer an amusing game but a tiresome burden. The lessons I enjoyed most were dancing and singing and drawing, but those weren't the subjects in which I would be questioned.

Mr. Davys reassured me. "All will go splendidly," he promised.

Still, I dreaded this odious examination. "I feel wobbly," I told Daisy.

"Who would not feel wobbly?" she asked. "I agree with Mr. Davys. All will go splendidly."

The bishops arrived, two elderly gentlemen, their shiny bald pates surrounded by fringes of wispy white hair. My hands were damp, and my stomach churned. The bishops settled in their chairs and popped their spectacles on and off their noses. They began by asking me questions about the Christian religion as set forth by the Church of England, and then moved on to the subject of geography.

"Name the five continents," said the bishop with a small, neat beard, and I did so handily.

"What is the longest river in the world?"

"What river flows from south to north?"

They required me to demonstrate my knowledge of the times tables. They asked me to conjugate the Latin verb *laudare*, "to praise," in several tenses and to decline the noun *agricola*, "farmer," in all its cases, which I did with some hesitation.

I was able to explain to their satisfaction the importance of the Norman invasion of the British Isles and the Battle of Hastings in 1066 and of Wellington's defeat of Napoleon at Waterloo just four years before I was born.

The bishops smiled and nodded, and I knew that I had done well. But this was still not enough to please Mamma.

"They have stated that they are perfectly satisfied," she said after they'd gone, "but I need still further approval. I shall ask the Archbishop of Canterbury to examine you. He is the head of the Church of England. There is no higher authority than he in such matters."

"*Again,* Mamma? But surely once was enough! I see no reason—"

Mamma frowned. "That will do, Victoria! You are being headstrong and impertinent. When I tell you that something is to be done, I do not expect you to contradict me! I shall ask Mr. Davys to arrange it. And you are excused."

A fortnight later the archbishop, a corpulent man with two trembling chins, focused on my understanding of the duties of a sovereign.

"Your grace, shall I assume that you are speaking of the duties of His Majesty King George?" I asked.

"Yes, my dear princess Victoria," replied the archbishop. "But not of His Majesty exclusively. My questions apply to any who might in future succeed him to the throne." He made a steeple of his fingers and pressed them to his fleshy lips.

I answered carefully. "It would seem to me, your grace, that a sovereign must first of all live for others and not solely for himself. Or herself," I added.

The archbishop nodded with a pleased smile. "Kindly express to me your opinion of King Henry the Eighth and his various wives."

"King Henry was a terrible tyrant. Catherine of Aragon, mother of Mary Tudor, was virtuous but much older than Henry and he did not much like her. Anne Boleyn, mother of Elizabeth, was certainly the most beautiful, though she was rather giddy and thoughtless."

I had not gotten to the rest of Henry's wives when the bishop interrupted. "And Elizabeth? Your thoughts on her queenship?"

"Elizabeth was a great queen but certainly not a very good woman and treated her cousin, Mary, Queen of Scots, most cruelly. Elizabeth surely inherited her harshness from her father and delighted in having her rival in her power."

"Well answered," rumbled the archbishop, and we continued in this manner. At last the great man pronounced himself satisfied, Mamma, too, was finally satisfied, and I was VERY relieved to have it finished.

Soon after the archbishop's visit, Daisy placed a history book on my writing table and pointed out the large, folded sheet inserted in the back of the book. "Your mother wishes you to look at this very carefully," she told me, hovering at my elbow. I thought she seemed rather nervous, unusual for her.

An elegantly drawn chart outlined the royal succession, hundreds of years of the past kings and queens of England. I traced my finger down through one generation after another until I reached the name of my grandfather, King George III. My finger moved across the page to note his several sons: Uncle King—George IV—followed by the duke of York with a black cross next to his name and the date on which he'd died; Uncle William, duke of Clarence; my father, Edward duke of Kent, also with the black cross and date; Uncle Cumberland, whom everyone feared and despised, perhaps because he was monstrously ugly; dear, eccentric old Uncle Sussex; and then Uncle Cambridge. Beneath my uncles' names were the names of their legitimate children—no *bâtards*. There were scarcely any. It was just as Fidi said.

I easily found my own name. The chart made it clear: After Uncle William, I was next in line. There was no one else. When King George died, Uncle William would become king. And after he died, I almost certainly would become queen. Not for a long time, perhaps, but someday. I was just two steps away from the throne.

If Mamma believed the secret had been kept from me until now, she was mistaken. It is not a secret when everyone knows it, even if no one actually speaks of it. And Fidi did speak of it. Baroness Späth had hinted at it. But now I saw with my own eyes the size and shape of my future. I considered this for a moment. Daisy was waiting for me to say something.

I did NOT say the first thing that came into my head: *When I am queen, I will send Sir John far, far away.*

I said the next thing I thought of. "I will be good," I told her.

I was not speaking of practicing the piano or attending to my studies, or even behaving faultlessly as was expected of a royal young lady. I was not sure precisely what I did mean, only that I wished to assure her that I understood the enormity of the challenge.

"Yes, I will be good."

"Of course you will, Victoria," Daisy replied, with tears shining in her eyes. She turned away and quietly folded the chart. Her shoulders were heaving.

Then I realized that nothing would ever be the same, and I too began to cry. I crawled onto her lap as though I were once again a little child. But I knew that I had said the proper thing.

Heir to the Throne, 1830

In June of 1830, King George IV died. Uncle William, duke of Clarence, was declared King William IV. I was eleven years old and just one step away from becoming queen.

The day after Uncle King's death, with the whole court in mourning, Mamma wrote to Parliament, asking that I be named heir to the throne with herself as regent. If King William should die before I turned eighteen, Mamma would govern in my place until I was of age. But I knew it was not Mamma who would have the real power. It would be Sir John. Mamma could barely conceal her satisfaction when Parliament approved, and Sir John strutted about with his usual arrogant air and his chest puffed out.

I truly loved Uncle William, as he wished me to call him, and not "Uncle King." He and his dear wife, Queen Adelaide, invited me to come to court quite often, and it was my greatest wish to spend time with them. But Mamma disliked my uncle and nearly always refused, if she could think of an excuse. Something unpleasant was brewing; I could sense it.

Mamma and Sir John had determined that the time had come for the English people to become acquainted with the girl who would someday be their queen. Sir John arranged a carriage trip, and in late summer we left Kensington to visit places he believed I would find informative, such as the manufactory where steam engines were made, and to meet interesting people, like the man who invented the gaslight.

Victoire Conroy was my traveling companion. It was not that I disliked her, but I did wish there were other girls with whom to spend my time. Someone not so tedious! My favorite game was battledore and shuttlecock, played with a racket and a little feathered cork batted back and forth across a net. Victoire complained that it made her perspire to chase the shuttlecock. Victoire did not like to perspire, but I minded not at all. She did seem to enjoy card games, but one could endure only so much of that!

Before returning to Kensington, we traveled by steamer from Brighton to visit the Isle of Wight. Every evening after dinner the ladies gathered in the parlor and played games. My favorite was The Hen and Her Chickens, in which I loved to play the role of the Fox, and Mamma or Daisy agreed to be the Hen. Fox sat down in the center of a circle, looking sly and hungry, and Hen and her Chickens gathered round. "What are you doing, Fox?" asked Hen, and I replied in a foxy voice, "I am making a fire."

"A fire?" Hen asked. "What for, Fox?"

And Fox replied, "To boil some water, Hen."

"Pray, what is the water for, Fox?"

Fox, in his slyest manner: "To cook a chicken."

Whereupon all the Chickens gasped, and Hen asked, "And where will you get a chicken, Fox?"

Fox cried, "Out of your flock, Hen!" and pounced on one of the hapless Chickens, creating a great deal of make-believe squawking and laughter.

The game went on until someone observed that Sir John and the other gentlemen would soon rejoin the ladies. This was the signal that my bedtime had come and I must say good night to the company. Sir John was perfectly suited to play the role of Fox without any need to pretend to be sly and hungry, and I felt like Chicken, unable to squawk or run away.

In February of 1831 I made my first public appearance at court. The occasion was the Queen's Drawing Room, Aunt Adelaide's reception for a very large number of people, held at St. James's. I loved my gown, English blonde lace over white satin, and Mamma allowed me to wear a pearl necklace and a diamond ornament in my hair. Mamma's gown had a pink velvet train trimmed with ermine and a headdress made of feathers and diamonds. Mamma and I rode in state in a carriage sent by the king; with us were the unavoidable Sir John and Lady Conroy and Miss Victoire Conroy, and my dearest Daisy. The gentlemen were all in black evening dress, and the ladies wore white satin gowns, all of British manufacture, with a profusion of feathered headdresses and glittering diamonds. Everyone said it was the most magnificent since the drawing-room presentation of Princess Charlotte when she married dear Uncle Leopold.

Dear Aunt Adelaide was seated on her throne, and it was

my duty to stand on her left. King William, on her right, spoke to me very kindly from time to time, but Mamma had advised me to remain quiet and dignified. We were present because we had to be. I knew that Mamma disliked the king because she felt he did not give her her due, and the king disliked Mamma for demanding more than her due. King William later complained that I had looked at him stonily, and I realized that my silence and my attempt to appear dignified had succeeded only in offending him.

Matters grew especially tense when Mamma decided that I was not to attend Uncle William's coronation in September. She forbade it, and for what I considered an utterly ridiculous reason: She had been informed that my other uncles—monstrously ugly Cumberland, eccentric Sussex, and harmless Cambridge—were to take precedence over me in the coronation procession through Westminster Abbey. They would walk ahead of me, signaling to everyone that they ranked higher than I did.

This angered Mamma. "Parliament has recognized that you are the heir apparent, Victoria, and you should walk *ahead* of the dukes, not *behind* them. I find this insulting, and I will not allow you to be insulted."

There was scarcely anything on which King William and Mamma agreed, and this was just one more sticking point. I blamed Sir John for much of it; he had convinced Mamma to stand firm when it would have been better to compromise. But there was one subject on which I did think Mamma was in the right: King William wished me to change my name. He did not like either of my names, Alexandrina or Victoria!

"Too foreign-sounding for an English princess," he informed Mamma. "The child would do much better to have a proper

English name. I propose that she take the name of Elizabeth. And if not Elizabeth, then certainly Charlotte."

Elizabeth! I did not like the name very much, and I did not wish to be named for a queen who treated her cousin, Mary, Queen of Scots, so cruelly. Further, I could not imagine now being called Charlotte.

"You have been given my name!" Mamma cried, outraged by the king's proposal. "Now King William wishes to change it to something *he* likes better! Well, I will not give in to that! You are Victoria, a very high-sounding name, and Victoria you shall remain."

Then there was the matter of my title. I was always to be referred to as "Her Royal Highness." When some person in the king's household mistakenly left off the "Royal" in writing to Mamma, my mother became extremely upset. It took only one word to upset her. It may have been because Mamma always made such a fuss about everything that King William decided not to give me precedence in his procession. Whatever the reason, it so infuriated Mamma that she decided I would not be in the procession at all. And I would not attend the coronation.

I was not consulted about any of this. I learned of it only after Mamma had sent word to the king. Surely, I thought, she would get over her temper and allow it. She must! I didn't mind if I walked behind my three uncles—I simply wanted to be part of the coronation.

"But *why*, dearest Mamma? How I should love to be there!" I pleaded. "I adore Aunt Adelaide and I love Uncle William, and I know they'll be disappointed if their dear niece does not attend. They are always *so very kind* to me!"

Mamma refused to listen. She was unmoved by my tears or my pleading.

"I really cannot afford the expense, Victoria," she told me. I could not argue with that, for I knew nothing of money matters. "Besides, my dear child, your health is much too delicate for such an undertaking. I have written to King William that your attendance is out of the question. Now, let us speak no more of it."

My health was not delicate! Mamma was simply inventing that as an excuse. I suspected the real reason, besides my being shunted to a place in the procession behind the dukes, was that Mamma did not approve of King William, because of *les bâtards*. All of his illegitimate FitzClarence children actually lived at Windsor Castle with him and Aunt Adelaide. I had visited Windsor only a very few times, though I loved going there and would have happily accepted every invitation. But if any of the young FitzClarences happened to enter the room where we were sitting, Mamma rose, seized my hand, and led me away, always making sure everyone saw her. It was most <u>horribly</u> embarrassing. *Les bâtards* were the cause of my rarely being allowed to visit Windsor. I couldn't imagine what harm could come to me if I happened to glimpse them accidentally, or even if one of them spoke to me.

"If Aunt Adelaide doesn't object to the king's children, why does Mamma object?" I asked dear Daisy. I did not dare ask Mamma.

"Your mother's moral standards are much higher than Queen Adelaide's," Daisy explained. "The duchess believes that if you are allowed to associate with children born to the king's shameful relationship with an actress, Mrs. Jordan, it will not be possible to teach you the difference between vice and virtue."

"But I do know the difference!" I protested.

"I am sure you do, Victoria."

I said nothing to Mamma, or she would have been "shocked" that I opposed her. Dear Daisy advised me to be patient.

King William did not go out of his way to pretend to care for Mamma, but he did not even try to conceal his complete disdain for Sir John. For his part, Sir John loathed the king. It was like the Battle of Hastings in 1066. I was somewhere in the middle, caught between opposing armies—King William and Queen Adelaide on one side, Mamma and Sir John on the other. I was always on pins and needles, and <u>I hated it</u>.

Behavior, Good and Bad, 1831

My mother had the distressing habit of writing me a letter whenever I somehow displeased her, and that seemed to happen VERY often. I wished everyone had not found it necessary to report to her <u>every little thing</u> I said or did, which then burdened Mamma with the duty of writing to chastise me, and me with the duty of writing an apology.

There was the episode of the piano shortly before my twelfth birthday. I disliked practicing my piano exercises. "Even a princess must practice," my teacher gently reminded me. But I felt I had done quite enough scales and arpeggios and little etudes by some young Polish composer—Chopin, I think.

"I do not wish to practice any more," I informed the teacher, and shut the lid over the keys quite firmly, perhaps a little <u>too</u> firmly.

This minor incident was reported to Mamma, who then

wrote a letter reprimanding me. As if I did not see her several times a day! It was not enough for me simply to say, "I am truly sorry," but now had to sit down and write her a letter in my most careful penmanship.

> *Dearest Mamma, I thank you for all your many kindnesses to me, and I hope to repay it by being your good and obedient child. I hope never any more to hear my dearest Mamma say "I am shocked" but rather, "I am pleased."*

I wrote many such letters, and there were times when I sincerely believed that my dearest Mamma should be writing such letters to me.

On the twenty-fourth of May at the dinner in honor of my birthday, my health was drunk and everyone assured me that this, my twelfth year, would be a year of great promise. I <u>very</u> much wanted to believe them, but only a month later I received news that was deeply distressing: Dearest Uncle Leopold had been elected king of the Belgians and would soon leave England. My uncle was like a father to me, always kind and affectionate, listening carefully to what I had to say and offering wise advice when I asked for it. I could not bear to have him go so far away!

Mamma and I traveled with Daisy to Claremont House, half a day's journey from Kensington, to spend time with my dear uncle before he left for Brussels. For once the Conroy family did not accompany us. Sir John did not trust Uncle Leopold, and I felt sure Uncle Leopold heartily disliked Sir John, perhaps even as much as I did. Though Uncle Leopold had been a great help to Mamma after my papa died, he often disagreed with her, which meant that he also disagreed with Sir John. Sir John was no doubt happy to see him go.

The visit at Claremont was a misery for me. Signs of my uncle's coming departure were everywhere. Portraits of poor Princess Charlotte had been packed for shipment, including my favorite, the two of them on their wedding day—Charlotte in her elegant gown of silver lamé embroidered with shells and flowers, and Uncle Leopold with all of his military decorations pinned in rows on his coat. Now, in just a fortnight, he would be on his way to Belgium by steamer. Claremont House already felt deserted.

Uncle Leopold and I walked for the last time through the gardens, then in full summer bloom. My uncle cut a red rose with a little silver knife, trimmed off the thorns, and knelt beside me, offering me the flower. "Look at me, Victoria," he said, lifting my chin. "You must promise to write to me very often. I expect I shall be very busy with my duties as king, but I promise that I shall write to you often as well."

"And will you come to visit, too, dear uncle?" I asked, trying not to sound overly demanding.

"Of course I shall!" he said, just as Fidi had promised when she married and went away to Germany. But Fidi had not come to Kensington, because she was either expecting a baby or had just had a baby and in any case could not travel. She did write to me, but not as often as I wished. I knew it would likely be the same with my beloved uncle Leopold.

After one last kiss, I struggled to hold back tears as our carriage drove away.

A few weeks later Mamma and I went on another visit, this one to the Conroys' home to celebrate Victoire's birthday. Visits to Campden Hill were somewhat enjoyable, because the Conroys had a paddock with several ponies and a kennel full of yelping, frolicking dogs. We presented Victoire with lovely gifts of jewelry, and I had made her a little box in which to keep her most important trinkets. After dinner, Jane Conroy, who was often ill and spent much time in bed, was feeling better. She played the harp, I played the piano, and everyone sang. Lady Conroy had a voice like a frog, but that did not inspire her to sing as softly as she ought. Then Mamma took a turn at the piano, and Jane and Victoire and their brother Edward and I danced a quadrille. Edward was a tiresome prig, but at least he danced well.

Mamma decided—or, more likely, Sir John decided for her—that I must now have a proper English governess, not a foreigner, especially not a German.

"I have invited Lady Charlotte Percy, duchess of Northumberland, to be your new governess," Mamma announced, as easily as if she were telling me that a new groom had been hired to look after my ponies. Was dear Daisy to be sent back to Germany, as Baroness Späth had been? I felt as though I had been struck by a thunderbolt and left entirely speechless. I stood before Mamma, my mouth opened and closed, but no words came out. My mother guessed what I was thinking. "No, Victoria, I would not dream of sending Baroness Lehzen away," Mamma assured me.

But I had reached an age when I often questioned my mother's sincerity. I never uttered my doubts aloud, of course—that would have been unthinkable—but the notion often entered my mind that I could not entirely believe her or accept her judgment without question. The doubts had begun the day I witnessed my mother in Sir John's embrace and had increased as I grew older. I felt sure that if Sir John decreed it, my dearest Daisy would be gone in a fortnight.

"Our Lehzen will stay with us as your lady-in-waiting," Mamma was saying. "She will continue to strive to improve your behavior," she said, adding pointedly, "and to curb your regrettable tendency to rebelliousness."

I lowered my eyes and murmured, "Yes, Mamma."

Mamma was not finished. "I must tell you that Lehzen's table manners are not of the very best, and you seem to have picked up some of her unfortunate habits."

I stared at Mamma. "What habits?" I asked, in what must have been a very surly tone that my mother chose at that moment to ignore.

"You have been observed eating your soup with your dessert spoon," she said. "Have you forgotten that fish must be eaten with the proper fish-knife and fish-fork? And I was appalled to notice just the other evening that you neglected to remove your gloves before you began to eat! That simply will not do, Victoria. I'm sure the duchess of Northumberland will be helpful in correcting these serious flaws."

"Yes, Mamma."

Indeed, Lady Charlotte was VERY helpful in straightening out my use of silverware. She was also kind and did everything possible to please me. I had no idea how she felt about Daisy, or how Daisy felt about being replaced. Both ladies acted with absolute correctness. But when the duchess invited Mamma and me to visit the ancestral Northumberland home in London, Daisy did not accompany us.

The duke of Northumberland grew rare and exotic plants, as well as vegetables and strawberries and even pineapples in a glass conservatory. In winter, blocks of ice were cut and hauled up from the large lake, packed in straw, and placed deep inside a brick icehouse built partly underground, so that the duke's guests could enjoy ice creams and sorbets all year round. The duchess made certain I had the delicious treat during my visit.

"And my dear princess," she told me, her smile showing pointy little teeth, "as soon the duke can arrange it, you shall have your very own little bedroom here, and your dear mamma will, too."

That pleased me very much indeed. At the age of twelve I was still not permitted my own bedroom at Kensington, but continued to sleep in Mamma's room. She would have it no other way.

The iced desserts, the strawberries, the promise of my own room in no way made up for one of the biggest disappointments of my young life. Mamma still refused to allow me to attend the king's coronation.

I felt utterly wretched. Nothing cheered me. I should have been in London at Westminster Abbey on Thursday the eighth of September, a major participant in all the glorious pomp and ceremony. Instead, I passed the day in Kensington, where it was just like any other Thursday. My lessons proceeded as though nothing of any importance were happening. Whenever I thought of what I was missing, I could scarcely keep from bursting into tears. I did not wish to see Mamma, afraid I would say something impertinent that would shock her, and then I would have to write another letter of apology. Dear Daisy tried to distract me, without success. I cried myself to sleep as Coronation Day ended.

Every aspect of my life was carefully watched and strictly controlled, always under the direction of Sir John. There was no room for error, no tolerance for failure.

As he promised, my dearest uncle Leopold wrote to me soon after he reached Belgium. I was VERY happy to receive a letter from him, though he did go on to lecture me in the kindest way possible, just as he had when he lived in England.

"If I were to give an opinion, I should say that a certain little princess eats a little too frequently, a little too much, and a little too fast."

He said nothing about my posture, leaving that to Mamma. To ensure that Fidi's back would be straight, my poor sister had been forced to wear a board strapped to her spine over her corset almost until the day she was married, but Mamma simply pinned a bunch of prickly holly under my chin as a reminder not to slump and to sit erect when I ate. If that had not succeeded, I knew, I too would be subjected to the board.

One morning I found on my writing table a small paperbound copybook, the title lettered on the cover: VICTORIA'S GOOD BEHAVIOR BOOK.

Mamma, and possibly Sir John, with dear Daisy's approval, had concluded that I must record every single instance of bad behavior in a Good Behavior Book. "This will help you," Daisy explained, "to become more aware of your failings and to correct them."

Must every child in the world struggle, just as I did, to conduct herself perfectly? Or are some people born always to do the right thing? It seemed so terribly difficult always to behave well, and I often yielded to tempers and impudence and foot-stamping.

For the next six months I wrote down every instance in which I was peevish, vulgar, or impertinent, or—worst of all—refused to obey immediately and without question or argument. I filled one whole book with notations of bad behavior and had to begin a new one. Daisy sat with me through my lessons, and if at any time my answers to one of my tutors seemed too sharp, or I displayed displeasure of any kind, I was reminded to make an entry in the Good Behavior Book. Each entry was dated, and the pages were ruled off in advance for Morning, Afternoon, and Evening. I also made notes on such things as my riding lessons and whether I was improving or not. (Usually I was. I loved to ride.)

"You must be scrupulously honest in your comments on your own behavior, Victoria," Daisy reminded me VERY often. "I see that you have written 'Good' and 'Very good' for your behavior this morning with Mr. Davys, but it seemed to me that you were rather pert when he corrected your Latin. And what about that little scene this afternoon when you were asked to wash your hands and you refused? That was quite disrespectful."

"I refused because my hands were not at all dirty. There was no need to wash them."

Daisy sighed and shook her head. "When you are told that you are to do something, then you must do it, at once and without dispute. Obedience, Victoria, is most important. And you were both disobedient and impertinent."

"That is your perception," I said stubbornly.

"And now you are being *very* impertinent and stubborn as

well. Please make a note of it in the Good Behavior Book."

I sighed. Was it impertinent to sigh? Even when the situation warranted? Daisy probably thought it was. Mamma surely did. My naughtiness nearly always had to be pointed out to me, for I obstinately refused to see it myself. Daisy opened the detestable copybook in front of my eyes and stood over me, watching as I made the required notation of my misbehavior. It was to be shown to Mamma at bedtime.

Mamma sent it back to me with these lines penned inside the front cover:

How pleasant it is, at the end of the day
No follies to have to repent;
But reflect on the past and be able to say,
That my time has been properly spent.

In my heart burned a fierce desire <u>not</u> to spend all my time properly! And <u>not</u> to repent! What would Mamma have said if she had known <u>that</u>?

Unbidden, the memory of my mother in Sir John's arms rose up and inflamed me. I wanted nothing more than to fling the Good Behavior Book, and all the naughty misdeeds recorded in it, across the room with a loud shout: *What about YOUR behavior, Mamma?*

But of course I did no such thing.

Chapter 7

TRAVELS, 1832

On the summer after my thirteenth birthday we set off on another journey. "It is important for you to learn about the country you will one day rule," Mamma explained. "It is equally important that your countrymen learn about *you*."

As we were leaving Kensington, Mamma gave me a small book of blank pages in which I was meant to make a record of my travels—events that occurred, people I met, and any detail that I found interesting. This was <u>not</u> the same as my Good Behavior Book, which could not be avoided even when traveling.

I took this new assignment VERY seriously. I had a small pendant watch on a chain, a gift from Queen Adelaide, and checked the time as our carriages rolled out of the palace grounds.

We left K.P. at 6 minutes past 7 and went through the Lower-field gate to the right. We went on, & turned to the left by the new road to Regent's Park. The road & scenery is beautiful, 20 minutes to 9. We have just changed horses at Barnet, a very pretty little town, 5 minutes past half past 9. We have just changed horses at St. Albans.

Throughout the day I dutifully noted in pencil every change of horses, every village through which we passed. When we arrived at our destination, Daisy read what I had written and suggested a few changes. Next Mamma asked to see it. "Well done, Victoria," she said approvingly. I flushed with pleasure. I wanted her approval, and so often I failed to receive it.

I did this every day.

Wherever we went, curious crowds turned out to have a look at me, and their greetings were always enthusiastic. Mamma insisted that I be dressed in white, which she believed made me look young and innocent. I found this notion tiresome—I was thirteen! I felt so very <u>old</u>, not at all like a child, old enough to wear the pearl earrings I had received as a birthday gift. But when I protested, Mamma said, "You are their princess, my dearest Vickelchen. The people want to see their future queen as a young, innocent girl, and we must give them what they want."

I got out my little wooden Fidi doll. Its dress made of scraps from Fidi's wedding gown was showing wear after five years of being stuffed in my pocket or hidden beneath my pillow.

Someday, I whispered to the miniature Fidi, *when I am grown, I shall dress however I wish, and furthermore I shall keep a journal that will be entirely private, and no one—least of all Mamma—will be permitted to read it and to know my secret thoughts. Someday, when I am queen, my thoughts will be my own.*

Meanwhile, though, I did exactly as Mamma said I must.

We passed through small towns where children welcomed me with flowers and song. I visited a cotton mill, a glove factory, and a slate quarry. We traveled north through country where coal was mined. I was quite shocked by the desolation everywhere—men, women, and children were blackened with coal dust, as were their houses. Burning heaps of coal, smoking and sometimes flaming up, were intermingled with wretched huts and broken carts and little ragged children. It was a heartbreaking sight.

"You may go over your entry now in ink," Mamma said when she'd read my travel entry that day. "Though I think you might have included more about the children's chorus and less about those wretchedly filthy urchins. It was so *very* unpleasant."

Our carriages plodded slowly through the rolling hills at the same tiresome rate. I wished we could go faster, but I seemed to be the only one who cared about speed.

The Conroy family, including Jane and Victoire, traveled with us. Our ponies, Isabel and Rosa, accompanied us, as did Lady Conroy's cunning little dog, Bijou. We required several carriages just to transport the trunks with our dresses and hats and shoes. My own small bed traveled with me and was set up for me at every stop.

One of the BEST days of the journey was a visit to Hardwick Hall in Derbyshire. We were treated to a magnificent fireworks display of rockets, wheels, and windmills, and my name spelled out in stars with a beautiful crown! Several weeks into our sojourn we crossed a suspension bridge to the Isle of Anglesey—more children strewing more flowers, more bands playing, more guns firing salutes, a number of formal speeches, and a men's choir singing "God Save the King."

> *God save our gracious King,*
> *Long live our noble King,*
> *God save the King!*
> *Send him victorious,*
> *Happy and glorious,*
> *Long to reign o'er us;*
> *God save the King!*

Everyone stood listening respectfully. I could not help thinking how, when I became queen after Uncle William's death, the words would have to be changed.

We arrived at Plâs Newydd, the home of Lord and Lady Anglesey and, at last, after so much traveling, settled down for a lengthy stay. What a dear, dear place it was, such a pleasant change from Kensington. When the weather was fine we boarded the royal yacht, *Emerald*, and were several times saluted by guns fired from the old castle as we sailed by.

I still attended to my lessons for a few hours every day— Scottish history, French grammar, arithmetic, religion, and writing—with dear Daisy acting as my master, but I found time to go out riding, even when the weather was foul. Dear little Rosa cantered beautifully and sometimes galloped like the wind. She literally <u>flew</u>! Finally, I could enjoy some speed!

On a fiercely hot day near the end of September, Victoire and I took Lady Conroy's little Bijou down to the water's edge. The strait was a channel of the Irish Sea and VERY cold. The dog rushed into the water, turned round and raced out again without stopping, and shook himself, splashing us. Victoire squealed and ran away, and I tried to coax the silly dog back into the water. Dear Daisy sat nearby on a bench with a parasol to keep her skin from darkening. If she had not been there, I might have removed my shoes and rolled down my stockings and waded into the water, no matter how cold. But that was not allowed. I blamed the restriction on Sir John, who maintained a long list of things I must not do, <u>owing to my station</u>. Perspiration dripped from under my bonnet.

The heat made me irritable, and I complained to poor Victoire, "If Sir John were not so *pertinacious,* we could go wading."

She gazed at me, blinking. "What does 'pertinacious' mean, Victoria?"

"Pigheaded," I explained spitefully.

Victoire's lip began to tremble. "You *do* say such dreadful things about my papa," she whimpered. "How can you be so cruel, when he does so much for you?"

I should not have said what I did, but I kept right on. "He does very little for me," I retorted, "and he himself behaves cruelly at times," I added, feeling entirely in the right, for he always did seem to take pleasure in teasing his daughters and me.

Victoire let out a wounded howl, scooped up wet and muddy Bijou, and ran up the grassy hill toward the mansion. I watched her retreating back without a morsel of regret.

Daisy was a witness to the scene. "Victoria," she said severely, "Miss Conroy is your friend. I am appalled."

Dear Lehzen closed her parasol with a snap and stepped aside, and I started up the hill, knowing she would follow close behind. We marched along in silence, the sun blazing hot on our backs. We did not exchange a single word until we reached the suite of rooms I shared with Mamma. The Good Behavior Book lay on the writing table. I opened it without being told and reached for my pen. Entries did not always have to be written first in pencil.

"24 September 1832. I was <u>VERY VERY VERY VERY HORRIBLY NAUGHTY!!!!</u>"

I underlined each word four times, the nib gouging a hole in the paper, blotted it more vigorously than was warranted, and clapped the book shut. *There!* It felt VERY, VERY good.

We had our last ride on Rosa and Isabel, and after a farewell breakfast we drove out amidst the shouts of the sailors. I waved farewell to the dear *Emerald* and her excellent crew, as we were on our way again. I felt quite sad to be leaving dear Plâs Newyyd.

In late afternoon we arrived at Eaton Hall, where we were well entertained for several days. Later, en route to Chatsworth House, we stopped in Chester where I opened the Victoria Bridge across the River Dee. All the while Victoire avoided me, turning her face away. I had written her a note of apology for saying that her father was <u>pertinacious</u>—I'd had a great deal of practice in writing letters of apology to Mamma, and this was not much different. I had not changed my mind about Sir

John—I never would—but I should not have spoken so harshly to Victoire. She did forgive me.

Then it was on to Alton Towers, where a foxhunt was arranged for the amusement of the gentlemen. The ladies followed in carriages behind the immense field of horsemen.

Victoire, sitting next to me, was among the first to sight the fox. "Look!" she shrieked, as a flash of rust-brown fur dashed past us. The sounding of the hunting horn and shouts of "Tally-ho!" from the hunters drowned out her cry. A great pack of baying hounds chased after the poor, terrified fox, pursued by dozens upon dozens of horses, their hoofs thundering on the damp ground.

Our carriage came to a stop in an open field at the edge of a thicket of small trees. Fox, hounds, horses, and hunters were far ahead of us. I stole a glance at Victoire. She looked pale and was unusually silent and kept her face averted.

I detected a change in the baying of the hounds, and soon the huntsman, the gentleman in charge of the hunt, rode out of the trees with the limp body of the fox. The huntsman made a ceremony of cutting off the fox's brush, affixing it to a stick, and presenting it to me. Then he cut off the ears and paws as trophies for the hunters and threw the mangled body to the dogs, which leapt forward and seized it, tearing it from side to side until there was nothing left.

Victoire, whose eyes had been shut throughout, opened them warily. "Thank goodness that's over," she said, her voice trembling.

"I found it quite interesting," I told her. "I was *very much* amused."

This was not precisely true, my stomach was churning, but

dear Daisy liked to remind me that I must learn never to show weakness. "A queen must not be weak," she repeated. "Queen Elizabeth may have been cruel, but she was never, ever weak."

Later, as we drove toward Wytham Abbey, the home of Lord and Lady Abingdon, Mamma commented on the woodlands surrounding the great manor house. Sir John, riding beside our carriage, said, "These woodlands are noted for having a large population of badgers." Then, glancing at Victoire slumped in the corner, he added loudly, "I understand that Lord Abingdon is planning a *badger hunt* in honor of our visit."

Poor Victoire, overhearing the remark just as Sir John intended, burst into tears. There was to be no badger hunt, but Victoire's wicked father enjoyed teasing <u>her</u> as much as he did <u>me</u>. I reached for her hand and squeezed it sympathetically.

After an absence of more than three months, we were back in our old rooms at Kensington. The journey had ended and with it the need to record the daily events, but both Mamma and dear Daisy urged me to continue the habit. And so I did.

LITTLE DASH, 1833

Christmas Eve was always celebrated in German style to please Mamma. After dinner, with the Conroy family in attendance, we gathered in the upstairs sitting room, the doors thrown open to reveal a beautiful evergreen tree decorated with little candles, sugared nuts, and sweetmeats. "Just as it was in my home as a child!" Mamma said happily.

Round the tree were several small tables on which our gifts had been arranged. I had a table for myself, on which I found several gifts from Mamma—an opal brooch and earrings, books, prints, a pink satin dress, and a cloak lined with fur. I received a pretty bag that Victoire had worked herself and a silver hairbrush from Sir John. Everyone else also got lovely gifts.

We sang Christmas carols, some in German, one or two in French, and several in English. Then Mamma led me to our bedroom, followed by all our ladies, everyone in a fine holiday mood. There I found my new toilet table, covered with pink and white muslin gathered in swags by pink ribbons. All my silver things—looking glass, comb, buttonhook, hair receiver, pin box—were arranged on it. I caught the look of pure envy on Victoire's face. I had glimpsed that look before, but it had never been so naked. I turned away, feeling I had witnessed something embarrassing.

"Oh, dearest Mamma!" I exclaimed. "How delightful! Thank you!" I embraced her as warmly as ever I had. I knew the toilet table was a recognition that I was growing up.

In the past months my feelings toward my mother had become increasingly strained. It was impossible to have a discussion with her. I had tried many times, approaching her in the most loving and reasonable way I knew how.

"Dearest Mamma, why must I still share a room with you? I should so like to have a room of my own," I had said only weeks earlier.

"Darling, it is beyond me that you should not want more than anything to sleep near the one who cares for you most deeply. And it's for the best, believe me."

Another time: "Mamma, why must I, at the age of thirteen, hold someone's hand when I go down a flight of stairs?"

"My dear Vickelchen, if you were to slip on the marble, or to stumble and injure yourself, I could never forgive myself! This rule is only for your safety!"

Rules, rules, rules. It was pointless to challenge them, for I never won a concession and often had to write yet another letter of apology.

My body was becoming that of a woman, but she still insisted that I wear childish dresses. I was allowed to see almost no other girls my age but the dull Victoire, and to read only books suitable for an eight-year-old. I often felt that she did not love me for who I was but for what I represented. It seemed more important for Mamma to be the mother of the future queen of England than of an English girl named Victoria. I owed everything to Mamma, as she reminded me often, but I withdrew from her, preferring to spend my time with Daisy. Did Mamma notice that my bond with my former governess was more intense than my bond with her? I didn't know. And I didn't care, for it was true.

There was one thing more that could not be dismissed: The memory of Mamma in Sir John's embrace still sprang unbidden to my mind. Perhaps there had been nothing to it. It may have meant nothing at all. But it did not escape my notice that Sir John made all the decisions. He ruled my life and my mother's too. I might forgive her that embrace, but I could not forgive her for allowing him to control us.

Early in the New Year Sir John brought Mamma a gift: the most beautiful and adorable little King Charles spaniel. He had long, floppy black ears, a white muzzle, brown spots on a white body, and large brown eyes that gazed at me with great intelligence. His name was Dash. He was very playful, yet always obedient and lay devotedly at Mamma's feet.

Little Dash was perfection. I soon began to earn his affection, and Mamma did not object—she was more adoring of her many birds. I dressed Dash in the scarlet jacket and blue trousers that Daisy ordered for him as a surprise for me. He didn't seem to mind being outfitted as a human and enjoyed the attention. It became clear that DEAR SWEET LITTLE DASH had declared himself to belong to me, and from then on he was with me constantly.

I was delighted to have him by my side during the long, tiresome hours I spent with the artist commissioned by Mamma to paint a full-length portrait of me. I had often sat for portraits, sometimes with Mamma, but none had ever been as wearisome—and as detailed—as this. I was dressed in palest pink, my hair done up in an elaborate braid arranged like a crown on my head. I wore gloves—or rather, one glove; the other had been stolen by my dear sweet little Dashy, shown frisking in the lower left corner of the painting. I was posed standing by a library table with a world globe nearby and Windsor Castle seen in the distance. Nearly every afternoon for seven weeks I had to stand motionless for two hours at a time, while the painter dabbed at his canvas. HOW TEDIOUS! But the finished portrait was to be a wedding gift for Uncle Leopold and his bride, Princess Louise of Orléans, whom he had recently married. It was also reproduced in black and white engravings intended to be widely distributed, so that my future subjects would have a likeness of their future queen.

During that busy winter and spring my evenings were often occupied with visits to the theater, the opera, and the ballet. In April we went to see Marie Taglioni, the dancer, make her London debut in Rossini's opera, *Cenerentola*—Cinderella. Madame Taglioni danced *sur la pointe*, on the tips of her toes, so lightly and gracefully. In May we saw her again; the ballet was <u>excessively</u> pretty. I took careful note of her costume, a sort of Swiss dress with a blue and white apron, and a little straw hat with her hair in plaits. She was not a beautiful woman—in fact I thought she was rather plain, though she danced beautifully.

I was <u>very much</u> amused, but I soon learned that Mamma was not.

"I do wish Madame Taglioni would not shorten her skirts *quite* so much," Mamma protested. "It's truly scandalous."

"They say she does it to show off her *pointe* work," explained Lady Charlotte, who often accompanied us to these events.

"One does not need to see her legs in order to admire her feet," Mamma sniffed disapprovingly.

I could not understand what was so improper about seeing the dancer's legs, but as Daisy once explained to me, Mamma's sense of moral propriety was much higher than most people's— maybe than anyone's.

In May I celebrated my fourteenth birthday. Among the many gifts were prints for my collection, books, embroidered handkerchiefs, little china figures, and a great many pieces of jewelry, including a lovely ferronière, a jewel on a chain worn on the forehead. I had wanted one ever since Mamma had her portrait done wearing a ferronière and looking so very pretty. I thought it made me appear grown up and elegant, though I did find it a bit difficult to get used to having something <u>dangling</u> there.

Throughout the day friends and guests stopped by. Sir John and the Conroy family came in the morning, and I must confess that my very favorite of all my gifts was given to me by Sir John: a life-size portrait of dear little Dashy! King William and Queen Adelaide arrived late in the afternoon and presented me with a pair of diamond earrings. Mamma and the king were barely speaking to each other, since she had refused to let me attend the coronation or even to visit them at Windsor. Dear Queen

Adelaide was always quite kind and pleasant to Mamma, possibly to make up for the king's ill humor.

My uncle Leopold sent me a very important and very serious letter in which he pointed out the need for regular self-examination to guard against the selfishness and vanity to which he said persons in high stations are known to be susceptible. "It is necessary that the character of such persons be formed so as not to become intoxicated by greatness or success, nor to be cast down by misfortune."

Dear Uncle Leopold! I thought, and placed it in the silver casket where I kept all his letters. *So kind, so wise! I could not have a better man advising me.*

The day being an unusually fine one, my guests and I went out into the garden and enjoyed bowls of sillabub—fresh cream whipped with sugar and wine—under the trees. That evening the king and queen gave a Juvenile Ball at St. James's in my honor. Mamma and I and the king and queen and a few others gathered in the Royal Closet, a large chamber next to the ballroom. When all was ready, servants in the king's livery opened the doors and a trumpet fanfare was played. I placed my left hand on King William's right wrist, and he led me into the ballroom. Victoire Conroy was present, as well as many other children.

I opened the dancing with my cousin, Prince George of Cambridge. This was followed by three more quadrilles before supper, at which I sat between the king and queen, and four more quadrilles after supper. I danced every one of them. Madame Bourdin, my dancing mistress, oversaw it with a critical eye, to make sure all was done properly. I enjoyed myself and was very much amused.

I am now fourteen! I thought contentedly as I drifted off to sleep in the hour past midnight, with dear little Dash asleep at my feet. *How very VERY old!*

Chapter 9

VISITORS FROM ABROAD, 1833

Nothing pleased me more than to receive visits from members of my family. I was delighted with the arrival that summer of two cousins, Alexander and Ernst Württemberg, the sons of Mamma's sister, Antoinette. Both were extremely tall. Alexander, twenty-nine, was excessively handsome; his younger brother, Ernst, wore a kind expression. These two young men were both very attentive to me. My brother, Charles, of the same age as Ernst, joined us, making it a very gay and happy party.

My cousins were perfect guests, always good humored, always completely satisfied with whatever was offered them. And such fine conversationalists! They spoke of such interesting things, such as their experiences growing up in Russia, where their father was a diplomat. Every day we went out driving and walking. In the evenings we attended the opera, and my cousins agreed with me that Madame Taglioni and her arch-rival, Fanny Elsler, both danced BEAUTIFULLY.

But there was one extremely unpleasant incident, and Mamma was to blame for it.

Dear Aunt Adelaide, who had always been so VERY kind to me and equally kind to Mamma, had arranged a ball at St. James's to honor my cousins. I was sitting on the dais beside the queen, chatting most agreeably, when Mamma abruptly rose and, though it was still quite early in the evening, signaled me that we were leaving—now! Her expression indicated that nothing could persuade her otherwise.

"Leaving?" Aunt Adelaide asked Mamma, puzzled. "But we are just about to go in to supper, my dear duchess. Can you not delay your departure a little?"

"I beg your pardon, your majesty," Mamma said in the sourest tone imaginable, "but my nephews have been at a review today, and they are quite fatigued."

"Fatigued? Those great young men are fatigued?" Aunt Adelaide smiled, raised an eyebrow, and shook her head in disbelief.

I stared at Mamma. My cousins were both over six feet tall and QUITE STOUT. It would surely take a great deal to tire them. *Why is Mamma behaving so ill?* I wondered. But I had no choice but to make my farewells to the king and queen—the queen looking surprised and hurt, and the king glowering FURIOUSLY.

My face was hot with embarrassment and shame as Mamma seized my hand, and with an imperious nod to my cousins, led us out of the ballroom. The ride from St. James's back to Kensington was accomplished in silence. My amiable cousins stared uncomfortably at the rain that drummed on the windows of the carriage. I sat miserably in the corner, certain that the ill will between Mamma and King William would only grow worse, and I did not understand why.

After a fortnight my cousins sailed back to the Continent. I missed them so VERY much, and I wished they were still with us. The days were wretched, with pouring rain, and the trees were bare. Kensington seemed <u>dull and stupid</u> and gloomier than ever.

Daisy was no longer my governess—Lady Charlotte held that title—but she was surely my most devoted and affectionate friend. I trusted her more than anyone, including Mamma. <u>Especially Mamma!</u> As Daisy and I walked in the garden on one of those foggy, drizzling days soon after the king's ball, I put my questions to her. "Why did Mamma insist upon leaving so rudely? Why does she dislike him so much? Has it anything to do with me?"

"No, my dear Victoria," she said, "it has nothing whatever to do with you, and you must not trouble yourself with matters that concern only King William and your mother. It's true that they do indeed have their differences," she added.

I stopped to pick a few late summer flowers, causing my friend to stop as well. "Dearest Daisy," I said, planting myself firmly in front of her, "please speak to me frankly. It is important to me to understand *why* things are as they are. Even if it has nothing whatever to do with me."

Daisy sighed. "You're right, of course. I shall try to explain matters to you as I see them."

"Without glossing over the truth, however unpleasant," I prompted.

"Without glossing over the truth," she promised, and we walked on together while I continued to gather a soggy, dripping bouquet.

At the root of the problem, according to Lehzen, was Mamma's refusal to recognize the king's illegitimate sons and daughters. "The duchess has always behaved uncivilly to *les bâtards*, even when she was a guest at Windsor Castle, the king's own house, and he resents it."

"But they weren't even present at the ball! It was horribly embarrassing!"

"I don't know, but I suspect that something must have been said to upset her. The king is much perturbed by what he calls the Royal Progresses arranged by Sir John, traveling round the countryside and being greeted as though you are already the queen and he no longer exists. King William has sent word that whenever you and your mother are sailing on one of his majesty's ships, you are not to receive the naval salute—the 'pop-pop,' as he calls it."

I nodded, remembering that guns were always fired as a greeting when the dear *Emerald* arrived in a harbor. I thought it was how everyone with a royal title was greeted.

"When the king's message was delivered to your mother, she immediately called on Sir John. He told her as her confidential advisor that he could not possibly recommend that she yield on this issue. The duchess took Sir John's advice and informed the king's Privy Council that she would expect to continue to receive the naval salutes. She believes she's entitled. The king then convinced the Privy Council to issue an order stating that only the ships with the king and queen on board are to be given a naval salute. And that further infuriated your mother."

Everything the king did made Mamma furious.

"Even without a naval salute, you are always the cause of much excitement among the crowds that turn out to see you," Daisy continued.

"That can't be helped, can it?" I asked.

"No, my dear Victoria, it cannot. There is nothing you can do to change the situation, and I'm afraid it will not improve." Then she added, "Let us speak no more of it."

I flung aside the sodden bouquet. All of this saddened me VERY much, and I wished that I could write it all down in my journal. But that was out of the question, for Mamma read every word I wrote. Dearest Daisy did not wish to discuss it further, and my tattered Fidi doll could give me no advice.

What if I kept a secret diary for my eyes alone? I thought. *Then I could write whatever I please!* But I quickly dismissed that notion. I couldn't risk being found out. I would simply have to endure.

Chapter 10

MORE VISITORS, 1834

For much of that winter I felt poorly, and in the early spring I suffered from a succession of indispositions: headaches, backaches, sore throats, stuffy noses, and a persistent cough. Mamma worried and fretted and often visited my bedside, but it was dearest Lehzen who sat quietly nearby hour after hour, reading to me and coaxing me to swallow ill-tasting potions.

In mid-April I at last felt well enough to go out. We attended an opera, *Anna Bolena*, the story of that unhappy wife of Henry VIII, Anne Boleyn. It was made VERY enjoyable by the singing of Giulia Grisi, an excessively pretty young woman who acted and sang most sweetly and beautifully. I was VERY MUCH AMUSED and honored Madame Grisi's performance with a watercolor in my sketchbook.

In May the arrival of more visitors pleased us all. One was Mamma's brother Ferdinand, whom she had not seen since before I was born; the second was my brother Charles. But the best was yet to come: on the fifth of June my DEAREST sister Fidi and her husband and two older children arrived from Germany. The younger ones had been left at home under the care of our dear Späth. The family planned to stay with us for nearly two months.

My heart was full to bursting at the first sight of Fidi. More than six years had passed since I last saw her, a nervous young bride. Now the PERFECT MOTHER to four children, she had grown stout but looked very well. Prince Ernst beamed with pride as he escorted his family. Little Carl, four and half, was very tall with light blue eyes and fair hair, a nice-looking boy though not handsome (neither, of course, was his father, whom he favored), and a good-tempered little fellow. His sister Elise, a year younger, was a perfect beauty, with light brown hair and immense brown eyes just like her mamma's. She was clever and amusing and spoke German and French very nicely. The children were the dearest little loves, not at all shy, and so VERY good!

The first days of the visit were delightful, but I longed for time alone with Fidi and the chance to talk to her about SO MANY things. This proved difficult. Mamma naturally wanted to spend as much time as possible with my sister and had arranged dinners and entertainments nearly every day and evening for the adult visitors. To my extreme displeasure, and Fidi's, too, Sir John and the rest of the Conroys were always included. Fearing that Feodore could exert undue influence over me, Sir John and Mamma no doubt conspired to ensure that I would not be alone with my sister as much as I wished.

Only a fortnight earlier, just after my birthday, Mamma

had appointed a new lady of the bedchamber, Lady Flora Hastings, and informed me that Lady Flora was to serve as my chaperone. I had not been consulted, I had not chosen her, and I was given nothing to say about it. I was fifteen years old, I would someday be queen, and still I was not allowed to choose my own ladies!

I disliked Lady Flora from the start. Now at every moment she hovered somewhere close by, so that it was nearly impossible to be entirely alone with Fidi.

"Who is this Lady Flora?" Fidi asked when at last we managed to escape. We were riding at an easy canter by the Serpentine in Kensington Gardens.

"Perhaps you should ask Mamma," I replied tartly. "All I know is that she is a great friend of the Conroys. That explains it all, doesn't it?"

"She is very attractive," Fidi said thoughtfully. "And in the brief conversation I had with her, she struck me as intelligent, even witty. What is it that you so dislike about her?"

"She adores Sir John excessively and looks up to him," I explained. "I'm certain it was his idea entirely to assign her as my chaperone. Mamma goes along with whatever he says."

"So that has not changed," Fidi said. "Not that I expected it would."

"I think she's a spy," I added darkly.

Fidi laughed. "But what is there to spy upon?"

"Oh, Fidi! Mamma and Sir John want to get rid of dearest Daisy, and they insist on finding fault with her! The duchess of Northumberland replaced her as my governess because Sir John insisted that I need someone who is English to make sure I always use the correct fork. I don't dislike Lady

Charlotte. She's very kind and pleasant and honest and always takes dearest Daisy's part. But it's a different matter with Lady Flora, who makes clear her disdain for Lehzen. 'Why is it you are so fond of caraway seeds, my dear baroness?' Lady Flora asked haughtily last week at lunch. 'You sprinkle them on your meat, your vegetables, your bread and butter. I should not be surprised if you put them on gooseberry fool.'"

"Poor Daisy!" Fidi exclaimed. "What did she say?"

"She answered very mildly, 'They are an aid to digestion. Perhaps you would also find them helpful.' One can see that she distrusts Lady Flora, and for good reason. I'm sure they'll send her away, just as they did Späth. I worry every night that I'll awaken the next morning and find our dear Daisy packing her bags for Germany."

"I must confess that it has been to my great benefit, and surely my children's, that Späth was dismissed," Fidi said. "She came to me straightaway, and I don't know what I would do without her! My children adore her. But for your sake, we must do everything we can to keep Lehzen with you."

"But what can be done?" I asked anxiously.

"I don't know," she admitted. "But I'll try to think of something." Just then Fidi happened to glance over her shoulder and observed Lady Flora and another lady trotting behind us in an open carriage and closing the gap. "Speak of the devil," she said, "and she doth appear."

Fidi urged her horse into a gallop, and I followed, laughing immoderately.

Soon after the arrival of my sister and her family, we all set out for Windsor to attend the Ascot races. King William and

Queen Adelaide were warmly attentive to me and to Feodore. "I've been hearing about your precious little ones," said dear Aunt Adelaide to Fidi. "I do so look forward to meeting them."

Fidi assured the poor queen, whose own babies had died in the cradle, that she would bring little Carl and darling Elise to visit her. The loss of a child happened so very often, and it always brought heartbreak. Just two months earlier we had mourned the loss of the first-born of my uncle Leopold and his wife, Queen Louise. Little Louis-Philippe—his parents called him Babychou—had died in May before reaching his first birthday.

Queen Adelaide behaved graciously to Mamma, despite Mamma's rude conduct during my cousins' visit the previous summer. Uncle William ignored her. None of *les bâtards* were in evidence, and so Mamma was not encouraged to make one of her embarrassing exits.

In a caravan of nine open carriages we drove to Ascot and down the racecourse to the royal box, waving greetings to all those who craned for a look at us. King William later offered to make what he called "a friendly little wager" with me on the winner of the Gold Cup, the most important of the races. The stakes were high—one of my ponies for one of his. I had no idea which horse to bet on, but I did like the look of a stallion named Glencoe and placed my bet on him. When Glencoe took the cup, I discovered that I had won the king's beautiful little chestnut mare, named Taglioni for the dancer. I was VERY MUCH AMUSED!

We returned to Kensington. I contrived to spend every possible moment with Fidi. She and Lehzen and I often went out riding together, and it was so much like the old days when Fidi was living here that I often felt VERY sad, missing what I no longer had.

"It's a mistake to yearn for what is past," Fidi warned me.

I felt my eyes filling with tears. "Is that what you did?"

"Yes, for a short time. Then I started to realize that I was married to a man who cares deeply for me. And when the children began to arrive, I realized that I care deeply for Ernst as well. And I regret nothing." She hesitated, gazing at me thoughtfully. "Have they begun speaking about a future husband for you?" she asked. I shook my head. "No? Well, they're certainly thinking about it, I promise you. Rumors have been flying since the day you were born. It's a favorite topic of newspaper writers."

"I'm not allowed to see any newspapers."

"I know. And you're just fifteen, so there's still time. Of course, it's better if you make the choice yourself, rather than having it made for you. I worry about that, for Sir John seems determined to make every decision for you. In three years you'll be of age, and you won't require a regent to govern for you. So now Sir John asserts that he intends be your private secretary."

I was stunned. "Private secretary!" I cried. "That's impossible!"

"Vicky, I learned long ago that with Sir John Conroy, nearly anything is possible, once he is determined to have his way."

"I know," I agreed sadly. "Sir John has everyone fooled. Only dearest Daisy sees through him, but I'm afraid he will convince Mamma to send her away. Once you're gone, Daisy is the only person in whom I can confide!" I thought of the little wooden doll, her painted features all but worn away and her costume in rags, that I kept well hidden. "And of course, my dear sweet little Fidi doll! She has no advice for me, but she does keep a secret."

The rain that had blotted out the sky for several days gave way to puffy white clouds eagerly identified by little Carl as tigers and elephants. Having exhausted himself with running about all day, he was already fast asleep. Now I watched with delight as Feodore bathed DEAR little Elise.

"I prefer to do it myself," Fidi said, "rather than to delegate the task to our French nursemaid. That shocks Mamma." She cooed at her little daughter. "And I didn't hire wet nurses when my children were born, but don't tell Mamma I nursed them myself! She'd be horrified."

Together we listened to Elise recite her bedtime prayers that included blessings asked for everyone in her family and even for dear little Dashy—VERY amusing—and then we tiptoed away to a quiet alcove. Soon we would have to dress for dinner. It was a peaceful moment, but the time was slipping away, the days passing far too quickly, and I had already begun to despair of my sister's departure. There were so many things we had not yet spoken of.

"Mamma still treats me like a child!" I burst out as soon as we had sat down. "I can't even choose what to wear, because Mamma insists on dressing me like a little girl. I may be small, but I'm not a child! I have no friends of my own choosing. Sir John wants his daughter Victoire to be my bosom friend, but she is not. I can't talk to her about anything of even the slightest importance, because she will immediately report every word to Sir John. With Victoire there is no such thing as a confidence." Once I'd begun to pour my heart out to my sister, I could not seem to stop. "It's terrible, Fidi! Would you speak to Mamma? She might listen to you."

"She won't listen to me, I promise you. But I shall write to Uncle Leopold. Perhaps he can help."

"It does no good to complain to Uncle Leopold! Mamma doesn't listen to him either. She listens only to Sir John and reminds me that I must be grateful for all he does for us."

Fidi tutted. "Unfortunately, Mamma is completely under Sir John's domination. I had hoped, for your sake, that the situation might have changed, but obviously it has not." My sister jumped up, seized my hands in hers, and pulled me to my feet. "I have an idea, Vicky! Let's go for a walk in the garden."

I hung back. "We're expected at dinner soon—another dull one. Daisy will be looking for me when it's time to go down."

"Does Lehzen still hold your hand whenever you go down the stairs?"

I had been fighting back tears, but now they flowed freely. "Yes, she does! Mamma's orders! And if not Daisy, then Lady Flora performs that duty."

"Then I shall perform in their stead. Come, dearest Victoria! The *bonne* will watch over the children. Dry your tears and come with me!"

Fidi led the way to the servants' stairs, which I was always forbidden to use. For the first time in my life I went down a staircase <u>without having my hand held</u>—a taste of freedom! We escaped through a small, nondescript door opening to a kitchen garden. Beds of tender young vegetables were surrounded by potting sheds and a small glasshouse. It was close to Midsummer Night, and the sky was still as bright as midday, a glorious change from the suffocating palace.

"It's altogether charming!" I exclaimed as we strolled among rows of lettuces, leeks, and radishes, peas and beans climbing wooden stakes, pots of herbs arranged in tiers, and trees laden with ripening fruit. The air smelled of damp earth. "I never even knew it existed!"

Fidi laughed. "Mark it well, dearest sister," she advised. "This is where I used to have my secret trysts with Captain d'Este."

I gaped at her, rather shocked. "Here?"

"Here, among the strawberries." She bent down and plucked a few fat red berries that peeped from among the dense green leaves.

We sat on a rough wooden bench and shared the succulent berries. I had never eaten them directly from the garden, still warm from the sun. "Delicious," I remarked. "I have only had them sliced in a trifle, or served with cream."

"They're best this way, I think," said Fidi. "It's one of the pure joys of not having to be a perfect princess."

"Fidi, what am I to do?" I asked, sighing. "Do you know that Mamma still insists I sleep in her room?"

"High time that you have a room of your own!" We were quiet for a while, enjoying the companionship and nibbling the strawberries. "I know you disagree, Victoria, but I do believe Uncle Leopold is the one most likely to help you," Fidi said. "I correspond with him rather often, and he's aware of problems here at Kensington. But he's far away, and his duties in Belgium take all his attention. Mamma ignores his letters, but perhaps when he comes here to visit he can convince her to pay attention." She rose and brushed off her skirt. "Now I suppose we should sneak back inside the same way we came."

We climbed the dimly lit stairs, startling a servant on her

way down. "You must not give up, Victoria," Fidi whispered. "Someday these difficult times will end and your life will be your own. You'll see."

As the final days of Fidi's visit ticked by, I became deeply despondent. I hoped that by some miracle her visit might be extended, but it could not—two tiny children waited at home for their mamma and papa. The time inevitably came for dearest Fidi and her kind husband and ADORABLE little children to leave.

On our last day together, my sister suggested that we exchange the morning caps we always wore before we dressed each day to appear in public. I clutched Fidi's little lace-edged cap that smelled so sweetly of her hairdressing. "I shall always treasure this reminder of you!" I promised.

I clasped her in my arms and kissed her and cried as if my heart would break. And so did she, my DEAREST SISTER. We were forced to tear ourselves from each other in the DEEPEST SORROW.

Then she was gone.

KENSINGTON, 1834

I grieved for days after my sister left. Dearest Daisy understood my heartache; she missed Fidi nearly as much as I did. But Mamma paid little attention—she was busy making plans for our summer holiday in Royal Tunbridge Wells. Sir John and his family would accompany us, and Lady Flora too. The servants were ordered to begin packing.

Bessie, my maid since I was quite young, helping me dress and undress several times a day as the situation required, had left my service to care for her aged father. Her younger sister, Maggie, had taken Bessie's place. I became quite fond of Maggie, only a year or two older than I and very clever in doing my hair. Though we were forbidden to converse on any subject other than my clothes for the day and my coiffure, Maggie and I did sometimes exchange a few whispered words. One day before we were to leave for Tunbridge Wells, we found ourselves alone when dear Daisy was indisposed and Lady Flora had not yet arrived in her place. Maggie, against all the rules, suddenly confided that she had fallen in love. Her plain round face glowed when she described the boy she loved—his fair hair, his sweet smile missing a tooth that made it all the sweeter.

"I'll miss my Simon like anything when we go to Tunbridge Wells and he must stay behind," she admitted, drawing a comb through my hair and parting it in the center.

"Maggie," I begged, "tell me what it's like to be in love! I truly have no idea of it."

"Oh, mistress, 'tis the most wonderful feeling! When my Simon holds me in his arms and kisses me, I think I'm going to melt—just like butter," she said rapturously, the comb in one hand, a lock of my hair in the other.

"He kisses you?" I asked. "And you're not yet married?"

"We hope to marry someday, your highness," she said, her cheeks growing rosy. "Once we've put aside a little money for our wedding."

I was eager to hear more about her plans for the future, her feeling like melting butter. My hair was finished doing, and we were deep in conversation when Lady Flora came upon us. Her disapproving look was enough. Maggie fled. I knew that my chaperone would report the incident to Sir John, and I was correct. The next day Maggie was gone, replaced by Agnes, a doughy woman with thick, clumsy fingers.

I flew at Conroy in a tearful rage. "How could you do this? Maggie did nothing wrong!"

"You are not to speak personally to any servant, Victoria. I felt sure you understood that, but apparently you do not. It was your chaperone's duty to report it to me."

"I won't do it again! Let Maggie come back!" I pleaded.

"You're being childish," Sir John said coldly. "As usual."

We left for Tunbridge Wells without her. *At least now she will not miss Simon*, I thought glumly.

We stayed for three months, drinking several goblets of water each day from the mineral spring. It was said to be good for one's health, but I felt neither better nor worse for drinking it. At the beginning of November we moved on to St. Leonard's-on-Sea.

Sir John strutted about in his usual offensive manner, breathing deeply, his nostrils flared, arms thrown wide. "Nothing like it," he declared in a loud voice. "Nothing like the sea life!"

I pretended to ignore him.

The hostility increased daily between the two women with whom I spent my time: my dearest Daisy and the sharp-tongued Lady Flora Hastings. I felt caught between them, pulled first one way and then another. The tension made me ill, and I slept poorly and ate little. I composed a letter to my dear, good uncle, but I knew it would be read by Mamma before it was sent and I could not tell him what was troubling me—my growing hatred of Sir John, my dislike and suspicion of Lady Flora, my fears that Daisy would be sent away, my aching loneliness. And so I wrote to him about things that didn't matter at all. My journal was the same, because Mamma read every word in that as well. For her benefit I wrote that my misery was caused by the incessant roaring of the sea—a lie.

When we returned to Kensington at the end of January 1835, a surprise awaited me. My sitting room had been freshly papered and newly furnished, even down to the carpets. Mamma's room, too, had been redecorated. My bed was placed opposite hers.

I hid my disappointment and did not say what I was thinking: *Am I not yet old enough to have a bedroom of my own? I will soon be sixteen!*

It would have been futile. I knew exactly what she would say: *It is for your own protection, Victoria. Your welfare is my chief concern. I am responsible, not only to you, but to the people of England. And to the memory of your dear father!*

Suddenly I was VERY angry. If I voiced my real feelings, I would have been required to write a letter of apology. Of late my mother had begun to add a new burden. *Someday, my dear Victoria, my time on this earth shall come to an end, and you will no longer have your fond mother to look out for you. But I shall die knowing I have done all that I can for you, no matter what the sacrifice of my own desires.*

My mother knew well how to use guilt to control me.

"You are pleased with our rooms, are you not, Victoria?" Mamma asked.

"Oh, yes, Mamma, very pleased," I said, forcing a smile. "It looks very nice indeed—so fresh and clean."

I went looking for Daisy, and my anger, held back for a long time, now spilled out.

"I suppose my room is very pretty," I said. "But could I not have been consulted? I am not fond of yellow and I do not care much for green. Everyone knows that blue is my favorite and purple is my second favorite. Yet there is nothing but green and yellow, yellow and green, on walls and floor and furniture! But the worst is that my bed is *still* in my mother's bedroom. What does Mamma think could possibly happen to me if I were to sleep in a room of my own?"

I began to sob. Dearest Daisy reached for my hand. "You know that I have no influence here. Perhaps the time has come to speak of this honestly. Sir John despises me and always has, because he knows that I'm not taken in by his charming ways. Now he has brought Lady Flora into the household, and like your dear mamma she believes that he can do no wrong."

"I hate him!" I cried, pulling away. "I shall always hate him!"

Daisy rose and put her arms round me, stroking my hair. "Lady Flora and your mamma are of one mind: They trust him completely. His every opinion is taken as gospel. I believe they're deceived, as are so many others. I see him as he really is—a man of unfettered ambition—and I don't trust him. He knows this, and he wishes to see the last of me. Lady Flora agrees with him."

The issue of the new color scheme shrank in importance. "Surely he won't send you away—he couldn't be so cruel! He knows how much I care for you and how much I depend on you!"

"Precisely why he wants me gone." She kissed my forehead. "Whether I go or stay, the day is coming when you will have as much blue and purple as you wish. Now, my dearest Victoria, I advise you to write to your uncle Leopold and keep him informed of what is happening here."

"But Daisy, Mamma reads all my letters! I dare not criticize Sir John—Mamma will not allow it." Then I had an idea. "But if I wrote it, perhaps you could post it for me. We would not tell Mamma." Never before had I proposed going behind Mamma's back. But never before had I felt my situation at Kensington had reached such a wretchedly unhappy state. I held my breath, waiting for Lehzen's reply.

Daisy smoothed back a lock of my hair that had worked

loose from its pins. "If I did such a thing, I would be very disloyal to your dear mamma, whom I have known for a very long time," she said. "I can't bring myself to do that. We will have to think of something else."

Lady Flora and Sir John continued to beleaguer dear Daisy, making sarcastic comments, loud enough for her to hear, about her unfashionable clothes, mocking the way she spoke, laughing at her habit of chewing caraway seeds. Mamma no longer invited Baroness Lehzen to attend her many dinners. Now it was Lady Flora Hastings who held my hand as we descended the stairs, Lady Flora who sat near me at the table while my dearest friend ate alone in her room. It was Lady Flora who appeared, unasked, while I was dressing or my hair was doing, times when Daisy used to read to me and now had to quietly excuse herself and leave.

Sir John ordered Lehzen moved from her cozy bedroom near my sitting room to a gloomy space in another part of the palace. He pompously informed her that her small stipend was too generous and must be reduced, explaining, "Economies are necessary."

I agonized about what to do. As it happened, I did not need to go behind my mother's back and write to Uncle Leopold. The duchess of Northumberland was a witness to the indignities being heaped upon the person I loved best. Lady Charlotte wrote to my sister, asking her to contact Leopold and implore him to help my poor dear Daisy.

If Daisy was aware of Lady Charlotte's efforts, she did not tell me. Fidi had already promised to write to our uncle, and I hoped she had. But it surely did not hurt to have Lady Charlotte adding her voice to my pleas for help. Everyone, it seemed, conspired to keep me isolated and in ignorance, and I didn't learn of the duchess's letter until later. If Sir John and Mamma discovered that she had written to Fidi, it would be only a matter of weeks—even days—until Lady Charlotte and Daisy were gone, and I would have NO ONE.

Chapter 12

ANTAGONISTS, 1835

My sixteenth birthday arrived, a VERY important milestone: In just two years I would come of age. I filled the entry in my journal that day with lofty promises to make the best possible progress in my lessons in preparation for what lay ahead. That was for Mamma's eyes. Secretly I vowed that, when that day finally came and I was at last of age, I would then answer chiefly TO MYSELF.

Mamma, who often seemed to have <u>no</u> understanding of what I truly valued, gave me a VERY exciting gift, a private concert to be performed at Kensington Palace. A program of arias from my favorite operas were sung by a quartet of my favorite singers: Luigi Lablache, the finest bass in England; Giulia Grisi, whose performance I had so greatly admired in *Anna Bolena*; Antonio Tamburini, the famous baritone; and Maria Malibran, the magnificent mezzo-soprano. It was <u>utterly delicious</u>! I stayed up until after one o'clock, still too excited to close my eyes. From that night on, my fondest wish was to study singing with Signor Lablache, and Mamma agreed that it might some-day be possible.

A few days later I traveled to Windsor with dearest Daisy and Lady Flora. After two and a half tedious hours shut up in a carriage with two ladies who were being excessively polite to each other, I was able to enjoy a delightful visit with my uncle and aunt. As a relief from the oppressive heat, we boarded the royal barge and sat under the green silk canopy while six oars-men rowed us round the pretty lake. It was all VERY pleasant, but back at Kensington a barely concealed antagonism seemed to lurk round every corner and behind every door. I ignored it as well as I could.

It was Mamma's ardent wish, as well as mine, that I be confirmed in the Church of England by the Archbishop of Canterbury. But everything possible went awry in making the arrangements, one more distressing example of the ill feelings that existed between Mamma and King William.

Lady Charlotte, as my official governess, conveyed to Mamma the king's wishes concerning the date and time of the service. But Mamma resented Lady Charlotte and no longer trusted her, no doubt sensing her disapproval of Sir John. Instead of replying to the king through the duchess of Northumberland, as etiquette required, Mamma went around both of them and wrote directly to the archbishop.

According to Daisy, when Mamma treated Lady Charlotte rudely by ignoring her, King William sent a stern message reminding Mamma that she must use proper channels and was on no account to contact the archbishop herself. But Mamma refused to obey the king's order.

"This was an insult to Lady Charlotte," Daisy told me. "I believe your mamma and Sir John want to terminate her duties as your governess, but they're going about it in a way that is sure to infuriate the king. The duchess of Northumberland is one of the greatest ladies in England. She enjoys the friendship of both their majesties. Your mother is making a grave error."

"Mamma refused to do as the king asked?" I asked. "How *could* she?"

"Your mother can be very stubborn," Daisy reminded me. "Sometimes her stubbornness stands her in good stead, but this time it served only to make the king even angrier. I am told that he stomped through St. James's Palace roaring, 'My niece the princess will not be confirmed in any of the royal chapels, and I shall so order the archbishop!' And that is what he did."

I was aghast. *What has Mamma done?* "Have you spoken to my mother about this?" I asked, burying my head in my hands. "Is there to be no confirmation then?"

"I am no longer a person from whom your mother either seeks or accepts advice," Daisy said, "but the archbishop himself intervened, and your mother has reversed herself. Your confirmation will be held at St. James's on the thirtieth of July. I'm certain it will be a lovely day."

This was to be one of the most solemn and important events of my life, but I felt as though I were standing undefended in the middle of a field of battle with the advantage shifting almost hourly from one army to the other. Still, I attended to my duties: I studied the Book of Common Prayer and had intense conversations with Mr. Davys. My morning and evening prayers grew longer and more impassioned. I was determined to become a true Christian, to do all I could to comfort my dear Mamma in all her grief, her trials and anxieties, and to become a dutiful and affectionate daughter to her. I wrote this in my journal— not just for Mamma's eyes, but because I truly meant it.

Perhaps it was my fault that Mamma seemed driven to such extremes in her dealings with King William and Queen Adelaide. She behaved this way not only with their majesties, but also with others whom I liked and admired—Lady Charlotte, for example, and dearest Daisy. The only one who remained in Mamma's full favor was Lady Flora Hastings, and the higher Lady Flora's star rose at Kensington, the more I turned away from her.

On the day of my confirmation, wearing a white lace dress and a white bonnet with a wreath of white roses, I drove to St. James's with Mamma and Daisy and Lady Flora. I tried to keep my thoughts on the religious significance of the day and shut out all else. But I could not avoid noticing that each time Lady Flora spoke to Daisy it was to disagree with her, and my thoughts turned angry again.

"Unusually warm today, is it not?" asked Daisy of no one in particular, fanning herself with a handkerchief.

"I find it quite pleasant, actually," replied Lady Flora airily. "Perhaps you are overdressed, dear baroness. Or have applied an excessive amount of rouge," she added.

"And I find it altogether stifling!" I exclaimed. Mamma frowned but said nothing.

I was unaccountably nervous when at last we arrived at St. James's, and tried to convince myself that nothing could possibly go wrong.

King William signaled that it was time to begin, offering me his arm and leading me into the chapel. We were followed by dear Queen Adelaide and Mamma, who barely nodded to each other and did not speak. The pews were filled with members of the royal family, my uncles and aunts, and a few close friends—including, of course, Sir John. The king stopped suddenly, gazing at the assembled guests. "It is much too crowded in here!" he announced loudly, glowering at Sir John Conroy. "Only members of royalty are invited to attend. We shall ask any who are not royalty to leave us at once."

Mamma gasped and let out a little cry. Apparently, the only one present without a noble title was Sir John. His jaw dropped and he looked stunned, but he stepped out of the pew, bowed to the king, and stalked out.

Trembling, my lips quivering, I took my place in the royal pew. Mamma was sobbing. The service commenced. No windows were open, and the chapel grew unbearably warm. I knelt before the archbishop and made my vows and received his benediction. I wept all the way through his long and very sobering homily. What was supposed to be one of the most significant days of my life had turned into one of the most wretched. I nearly drowned in tears.

That night as I was preparing for bed, a servant brought a letter from Mamma. My mother claimed that she could best express herself to me in writing, rather than speaking of important matters face-to-face. That meant our communication was entirely one-sided, a lecture, an effort to bend me to her will. I dreaded these letters.

I broke the wax seal and unfolded the cream-colored sheet closely covered with Mamma's cramped handwriting.

*You have now reached a new stage of life with your
sixteenth birthday and your confirmation, and your
life will take a different direction. Your relationship
to Baroness Lehzen must now undergo a necessary
change. From this day forward, you are to treat your
old friend with dignity, but at the same time you
must place a certain distance between yourself and
her. Your friendship may continue, but on a different
level of intimacy.*

I began to weep—not from sorrow, but from anger. I forced
myself to read on.

*You must always confide first in me, your devoted
mother. The sacrifices I have made on your behalf
have been great and will continue to be so, and you
will continue to live and to thrive under my guidance
until you reach the age of either eighteen or twenty-
one years, and I shall be the determinant of that.*

There was more, ending with her usual protestations of love
and devotion.

I read the letter a second time, grappling with what my
mother had said and growing more and more upset. What
was this "different level of intimacy" I was to have with dearest Daisy? Did Mamma really expect me to confide in her and
not in Daisy? I would confide nothing! And what of this: "Until
you reach the age of either eighteen or twenty-one years, and
I shall be the determinant of that." Royalty always came of age
at eighteen—I <u>knew</u> that! Why was Mamma suggesting that I

might have to wait another three years, if she said so? Was she trying to prove that I would not be capable of ruling without her—and without Sir John?

I crumpled the letter and flung it to the floor. For good measure, I stamped on it.

"Victoria," said Daisy softly. That was all: "Victoria," as though she knew.

Silently I bent and picked up the ball of paper, smoothed it out, and offered it to her. I watched her face as she read it. Her expression scarcely changed. Perhaps she had been expecting something like this. "Oh, my dearest Victoria!" Daisy sighed and placed the abused paper on my writing table, shaking her head sadly. "Someday it will be all right," she said. "You must have patience."

"But I have no more patience!" I cried, pounding the table. "She is my mother, and I hate her! *I hate her!*"

Three days later, Mamma and I returned to the royal chapel and took communion together. I could scarcely bear to look at her, my own mother. As we knelt side by side before the altar, I pretended that a certain letter had never been written and never read. I struggled to repent of the harsh feelings I held for my mother and earnestly prayed that I could be her loving and obedient daughter. Yet even as I sent the words "obedient daughter" drifting up toward heaven, I tried to snatch them back, like a hat blowing away on a wind-swept beach. Obedience was SO difficult!

ANOTHER TOUR, 1835

After a summer holiday in Tunbridge Wells, we returned to Kensington. I felt stronger, less fatigued. But my things had scarcely been unpacked when Mamma sent a note informing me that she and Sir John had decided the time was ripe for another tour. We would leave in a few days to visit the northern counties.

Travels that had been an amusing distraction when I was younger were now a wearying chore. King William hated my "progresses," as he called them. Going on another one surely meant yet another battle. I dreaded the battle, the tour, the speeches, the dinners, all of it.

"I do *not* want to do this!" I raged, and I rushed to the library.

Mamma was alone at her desk, writing a letter. "Yes, Victoria?"

"Please, Mamma," I begged, "I feel so *very* tired, and I sleep poorly, and I can scarcely eat. Must we go on this tour?"

She laid aside her pen. "It is your duty," she declared. "Your position demands that you travel and show yourself to your future subjects. Are you really unaware of that, Victoria? For once you must stop thinking only of yourself and the easy life you may think is owed you. This is only the beginning of the many claims that will be put on you in the future." Mamma glared at me, picking up her pen. "Do your duty, Victoria," she said sharply, and turned back to her letter.

I refused to be dismissed. Mamma had to listen to me!

"The king does not wish me to go on these progresses," I said. My hands were balled into tight fists. I unclenched them and tried to keep my voice calm and reasonable. "He disapproves quite strongly of you and Sir John racing about the country with me. And if it displeases the king, then I *must* not go! It would be in plain defiance of the king's wishes. Surely you don't want to offend him."

Mamma's eyebrows descended into a deep frown. "I don't know how you have come to be so certain of the king's disapproval. I do have my suspicions, however, for there are those around you who have loose tongues and speak to you of matters that should not concern you."

"This *does* concern me, Mamma," I argued. "How can you claim otherwise?"

My mother stared at me with a shocked expression. "You speak to me disrespectfully, Victoria. It is unbecoming. Since you appear to know so much, let me tell me what you appear *not* to know. I have spoken to the prime minister, Lord Melbourne, and asked him on what grounds I can be prevented from taking you on visits to various parts of the kingdom you will one day rule. He assures me that I am entirely within my rights to travel with the heir apparent wherever and whenever I wish, and that it is entirely advisable to do so. And the king can do nothing to prevent it!" she concluded triumphantly.

"I don't care what Lord Melbourne says! The king does not wish it. He is so *very* kind to me, and I do not want to displease him." I took a deep breath. "I shall not go," I declared.

I had never spoken to my mother like this. Mamma appeared stunned, but she quickly recovered. "Don't be foolish, Victoria," she snapped. "The king is simply jealous—of your youth, of the love the people have for you, of the enthusiastic receptions you are given wherever you go. If the king really loved you, as you are so certain he does, then he wouldn't try to stop you but would approve of the journey! It's your obligation to go, Victoria. You should be seen, you should know your country and be acquainted with people of all classes and all walks of life. This is of the greatest consequence, yet you choose not to recognize it."

"Perhaps later, Mamma," I pleaded. I was near tears, but my mother had never been moved by my weeping. I tried another approach. "I so often feel tired, and we cannot travel like other people—"

"My dearest love," Mamma interrupted, using the sweet tone that sounded so false. "Listen well. If it were to be known that you are too lacking in will to undertake a journey that I and my advisors"—she meant Sir John—"feel is absolutely necessary, and that you fail to grasp the benefits to your people, then you are bound to fall in their esteem. And such esteem would be very hard to restore, I assure you!"

It was useless to argue further. Servants bustled round, packing and preparing, and it would not do for them to hear us quarrel. My will collapsed. "Very well, Mamma," I said, surren-dering. "I will be ready to leave in the morning."

I turned and fled. It had been a terrible scene. My head throbbed, my stomach felt very unwell, and I knew that sleep would not come easily that night.

For the next twenty-five days I endured the most grueling journey yet. I experienced it as long, slow torture, but Mamma pronounced it a triumph. The days were unbearably long and arduous. By the end it was a blur, one town after another decked in flags and flowers and triumphal arches with children's cho-ruses and pealing bells. Cheering crowds stared and jostled and sometimes blocked the road so that our poor horses could make scarcely any headway.

We visited one stately mansion after another, dined at one lavish banquet after another, though my appetite had disap-peared, and attended ball after ball. After one such, my head throbbed and my back ached so badly I could not continue after the first dance. Everyone was very cordial, but I could only pray for the day to end and a chance to lie down with a cold cloth on my forehead.

Never had I been so happy to see Kensington as I was on the day our carriage again rolled through the palace gates. I devoutly wished it would be a VERY long time before I had to spend another day like the previous twenty-five.

UNCLE LEOPOLD, 1835

At the end of September we did travel again, but this time for the happiest of reasons: My dearest uncle Leopold came from Belgium by steamer, and we met him and Queen Louise in Ramsgate. What a joy to throw myself into the arms of my uncle, who had always been like a father to me! I had not seen him for four years and two months. This was the first time I had met my aunt, and I loved her at once. Such a perfection! She had a very pretty, slight figure, hair of a lovely fair color, light blue eyes, and a charming expression. She was dressed simply in light brown silk with a sky-blue bonnet. She was only seven years older than I, and in a very short time we became like sisters.

Uncle Leopold came to my room only an hour after their arrival. "I will be here for just one week," he said, sitting down by my side, "and we must make the most of our time, for there are serious matters to be dealt with."

Dear Daisy quietly slipped away, leaving us alone. "The most serious matter is John Conroy," I told him bluntly.

"I've heard this from more than one source, and I'm not surprised," replied my uncle. "I once thought highly of Sir John, but he seems now to be suffering from a form of madness. He desperately wants authority as a means to raise himself and his family to the level he believes he deserves. The way to that is obviously through you. Tell me what he does that offends you."

At last, I could speak to someone who understood and could help me! "He treats me like a foolish child," I said, "one who must be guided in her every word and act by a strong, intelligent person like himself. He boasts about his dreadful Kensington System with a strict rule for everything I do, and he isolates me from the king and queen and nearly everyone else. The second serious matter is Mamma. I'm still not permitted to descend the stairs without holding someone's hand! I'm still not permitted to have my own bedroom! Mamma allows Sir John to speak to everyone of my youth and inexperience and to use that as an excuse for exercising authority if dear King William should die before I come of age."

Once started, I could hardly stop.

Uncle Leopold strode to the window and stared out toward the sea, frills of whitecaps now under heavy gray clouds. "We are aware that the king is in failing health. We pray for his strength to endure until you are of age—and well beyond, if it be God's will. In the event that he dies before your eighteenth birthday, your mother will rule in your stead as regent, but it is Sir John who will pull the levers. Even after you're of age, he'll look for ways to control you."

"Mamma says I may not come of age until I am twenty-one."

"She said that?" Uncle Leopold let out a bark of laughter. "It is not your mamma's place to decide!" he exclaimed and continued his restless pacing. "I shall have a frank talk with my sister. And with Sir John Conroy as well."

I nearly wept with gratitude. I hoped Mamma would see that I was becoming more capable every day and took my duties VERY seriously, that I was not a silly, foolish child but a young woman with my eyes fixed on my future responsibilities. I did not need her lectures, and I most certainly did not need Sir John's.

I was still exhausted from our tour and had felt poorly for several days. My throat was sore and my head ached. Daisy had given me a dose of tincture of rhubarb—nasty stuff—that was her usual treatment when I complained of being unwell, but it did little to improve me. Worried, Daisy had suggested that my physician, Dr. Clark, should be called down from London to examine me. Mamma and Sir John had disagreed, and I was determined not to allow my fatigue or my illness to interfere with my time with my DEAR uncle and aunt. But now, in the midst of this VERY important conversation with my uncle, the room began to spin.

"Victoria? Can you hear me, dear niece?"

Uncle's voice seemed to be coming from a great distance. Somewhere a bell rang, and another voice called out, "Send for Dr. Clark!" Uncle Leopold murmured close to my ear. "I will not allow him to be turned away without examining you."

I slept, and time passed. The physician came and sat by my bedside, peering down at me. Mamma was with him. He asked me how I felt.

"I feel so very tired," I began.

"The princess is given to whims," Mamma quickly interrupted. "And her companion Baroness Lehzen has a vivid imagination."

I closed my eyes. *How can she say that*? But I felt too ill, too dispirited, to argue.

"Allow me, your highness," said Dr. Clark, and placed his ear against my chest. "Nothing to be concerned about," he concluded after listening for a moment. "A dose or two of rhubarb tincture and she will be right as rain."

He went away, even when Daisy told him she had already tried that remedy.

Mamma still insisted there was nothing wrong with me.

In a day or two I began to feel somewhat recovered; no doubt it was the relief of having Uncle Leopold and his delightful wife there with me. Aunt Louise had completely won my heart during their short visit. One afternoon she brought her French hairdresser to try arranging my hair in several different ways, "in the style of the Continent," she said. A maid followed with her arms full of dresses from Aunt Louise's own wardrobe.

"That is the perfect color for you," Aunt Louise announced when I held up a rich ruby velvet. "It goes beautifully with your fair skin."

"Mamma favors very pale colors, and she prefers white above all," I told her. "To emphasize my youth and innocence."

"You are sixteen, are you not? Perhaps it is time to emphasize your maturity and elegance, as the French would," said Aunt Louise. "No doubt your mother will dislike this purple gown as well." She spread out the rustling taffeta skirt.

I laughed. "She'll hate it!"

"Why not try it on?"

I did not need to be coaxed. The dress was too long and the sleeves hung over my fingers, but Aunt Louise used pins to make a few tucks here and there until it fit perfectly. I gazed at my image in the looking glass.

"Very sophisticated," she said approvingly. "Allow me to make you a gift of it, if you'd like to have it. Your seamstress can make the adjustments."

"Oh, yes!" But then I said, sighing, "Mamma will not permit me to wear a dress that is, as you say, so sophisticated." Reluctantly I began to remove the elegant dress.

"I am sure you find it hard to imagine," Aunt Louise said as helped me out of it, "but one day soon you will be free to decide what you wish to wear. You will no longer have to dress for a role that Sir John or anyone else has chosen for you."

On the day they were to leave, Aunt Louise selected four lovely dresses to leave with me, among them the beautiful purple one that I loved most of all. "Soon you will be wearing it," she said gaily. "And I shall send you several more," she promised. "Hats, too."

We traveled from Ramsgate to Dover by carriage to see them off. Uncle Leopold insisted that I be allowed to ride with him for one last conversation before they boarded the steamer bound for Belgium. Mamma and Sir John no doubt disapproved of this arrangement, but they could not forbid it.

"I have spoken sternly to Conroy and to your mother," Uncle Leopold assured me. "They do not dare get rid of Baroness Lehzen, and you know that you can rely on her support. But you must be on guard: Conroy is determined to have himself installed as your private secretary even *before* you come of age. Then, when you become queen, Sir John will be precisely where he intends." Uncle lifted my chin with his finger and gazed at me earnestly. "Do not allow him the slightest opportunity to point out your youth and inexperience. Discipline, my dear, is the key."

"I will not disappoint you, dearest uncle," I promised.

"Of course you won't, Victoria," he said, patting my hand.

As the steamer moved slowly away from the Dover pier, I stood with Mamma and the Conroys and Lady Flora. Uncle Leopold waved his hat, and Aunt Louise fluttered a white hand-kerchief until the ship was swallowed up in the mist.

Chapter 15

VILLAIN, 1835

I would not allow anyone, especially Sir John, to see how wretched I felt after Uncle Leopold and Aunt Louise had gone. But I could not keep up appearances for long, and a few days later I gave in to my illness. I was feverish and barely able to swallow. Daisy, truly frightened, asked Mamma to summon Dr. Clark again. But Mamma dismissed Daisy's worries as needless.

"Your mother persists in her belief that it is all our imagination, that you only *think* you are ill," Daisy reported, her lips pressed in an angry line.

"Mamma, please," I begged when my mother came to see me. Speaking seemed SUCH an effort. "I am so very, very ill."

"Dr. Clark is in London," she told Daisy, loud enough for me to hear. "It is unthinkable to summon him all the way to Ramsgate."

"Then we must call in a doctor from the village!" Daisy insisted. "The princess is seriously ill."

I lay quite still, my eyes closed. Sir John entered the conversation. "That would be a foolish thing to do," I heard him say. "If word were to get out that the princess is ill, the whole town would be gossiping. It would be damaging to our reputation."

"You would gamble with the princess's life for political reasons?" Daisy demanded, raising her voice.

"The local press has already begun to ask embarrassing questions," Sir John said sternly. "They claim to be making special inquiry into the rumor that their future queen is dangerously ill—'hovering at death's door,' is how they have stated it."

"And what exactly have you told them?" Daisy challenged.

"That one of the servants has fallen ill, and the princess suffers with a very slight indisposition. And that is what you must say, baroness, should anyone ask you."

You lied to them, I thought, my head throbbing. *Just as you lie to me, to Mamma, to everyone.*

"We must let the princess rest," Daisy said, her voice trembling with anger. "But I insist that she needs medical attention, and she needs it immediately."

All three left the room, the door closed, and I fell into a feverish sleep. When I awoke, a new doctor hovered by my bedside. He produced a pocket mirror to reflect light into my throat and peered at it. "Dr. Clark will come down from London tomorrow," he said kindly, and then he went away.

Dear Daisy wrung out a cloth in cool water and placed it on my forehead. "The town doctor did not wish to prescribe any treatment before your usual physician has seen you. A mistake, in my view."

"My usual physician has been convinced by Mamma and Sir John that nothing is wrong with me," I whispered. My throat was so swollen that I could not speak aloud. I drifted off to sleep again.

Dr. Clark did come the next day. He placed one end of a wooden tube against my chest and held the other end to his ear. He, too, looked into my throat. At the conclusion of his examination he told Mamma, "The princess suffers from a bilious fever. I recommend that she receive complete rest to allow her to recover. Under no account may she be taken back to Kensington until her fever has dissipated."

This time Mamma did not protest that I was subject to whims or dear Daisy to flights of fancy.

For the next month I remained in the care of dear good Daisy. Mamma visited me every day and seemed much concerned about me, but Daisy rarely left my side. While I was ill, so weak that I had to be carried up and down stairs, Sir John always accompanied Mamma on her visits and told Lehzen to leave.

I dreaded these visits. The subject turned again and again to my future, and I was much relieved when one morning Mamma came alone. Daisy gave me a long look and left us.

Mamma drew a chair close to my bedside. "You must understand, dear Victoria, that it is very unlikely you will be fit to reign on your own, should you come to the throne even once you are eighteen," Mamma explained in a syrupy voice. "This unfortunate illness proves that you will need a great deal of assistance in performing even the least demanding of a queen's duties. Fortunately"—she smiled insincerely—"we have the ablest of persons here to be of service, to you and to the country."

"I suppose by 'ablest of persons' you mean Sir John," I muttered.

"Yes, I do refer to Sir John Conroy!" Mamma replied brightly. "Until you are eighteen I will be your regent, of course. But once you are eighteen, or more likely twenty-one, then a private secretary can be of the utmost help. And therefore, my darling Victoria, I have here a little paper for you to sign—a contract, we shall call it—in which you name Sir John to that position."

"I do not wish to do this, Mamma," I said as firmly as possible.

"It is wrong of you to refuse, when Sir John has done so much for you," Mamma said in a tone intended to make me feel guilty.

"I will not sign."

Cajoling and coaxing, Mamma tried every way to persuade me. I refused. When that failed, she tried to convince me that I was spoiled and ungrateful to refuse. Still I remained unmoved, until finally Mamma flounced angrily out of the room.

Daisy had not yet returned when Sir John appeared, smiling broadly, joking as usual. "You're looking very well, Victoria! Ready to get up and dance a quadrille, I should say!" He asked what I had eaten that day.

"A dose of quinine and a little veal broth," I answered.

"Good, good! And if in fact you're not ready to dance, perhaps you'd enjoy a promenade in the garden?"

I shook my head.

"Ah, but look how the sun is shining! It will do you a great deal of good! I will carry you down. Just for a few minutes."

"No," I said.

"Very well," said Sir John less agreeably. He sat down and leaned toward me, his face only inches from mine. "Now I want to have a serious talk with you, my dear princess." He went over the same arguments that Mamma had advanced—how I would need help, how he was the one person in the world to provide that help, how I must now sign the paper making it so.

"You waste your time, Sir John. I will not sign," I repeated wearily. "Now please leave me to rest."

I turned my head away and closed my eyes. I felt him bending over me, his breath on my face. "Stubborn, insufferable termagant!" he hissed in my ear.

My eyes flew open. *I, a termagant? A quarrelsome scold?* He had never spoken to me so harshly. I gathered my strength and sat up. "Get out of my sight, Captain Conroy," I said, spitting out the words. "Do not come here again and attempt to coerce me. I will not sign your paper."

We glared at each other. Sir John moved away, and I fell back on my pillow. He paused at the door and turned to utter one last threat. "Your rebellious behavior is very painful to your dear mother. It could bring great harm to her health."

"I am very sorry that she finds it so," I said, staring him down. "But I will not change my mind, and I will not sign."

The door slammed behind him. I lay in my bed, trembling, for what seemed an interminable length of time until dear Daisy burst in, breathless. "I would have returned much sooner," she explained, "but your mother wished to speak to me on several matters and kept me for much longer than I wished. I could not seem to get away."

"It's all right, Daisy. I know why she detained you," I said, and described my visit from Sir John.

"That villain!" she cried. "He's clearly becoming desperate. Is there nothing I can do to keep him away from you?"

"Dearest Daisy," I said, "I'm more concerned about keeping

him away from *you*. My greatest fear is that while I'm ill, Mamma and Sir John will find a way to dismiss you, and I won't be able to prevent it."

"You may not be able to do much, Victoria, but there are others who can," she reassured me. "The duchess of Northumberland is aware of the situation and has written to your sister. Fidi advised the duchess to go to King William himself. Lady Charlotte has great influence with the king, and if his majesty directs that I must stay, then I stay. I believe that at least for now my position is secure."

Her words were reassuring. There were only four people in the world in whom I could put my whole trust: dearest Daisy and Fidi, and my uncle Leopold and aunt Louise. Excluded from the list was Mamma, whom I had come to despise. So long as she remained in the thrall of the man I hated, I would never trust her. It was dearest Daisy who would forever be my true mother.

As the days and weeks crawled by, Daisy watched over me tirelessly and cared for me tenderly. She massaged my feet whenever I asked and read to me to make the hours pass more pleasantly. Mamma's visits were brief. More often, she sent gifts. Once it was a print showing the harbor at Ramsgate. Another time, it was a china figurine, a shepherdess carrying a small sheep, with a note attached: "You are my dearest lamb."

Sir John made no further attempts to bully me. I did wonder if he had given up, or if he was planning some other devious way to get the power he craved.

Recovery, 1836

During my illness that autumn I did not make any entries in my journal, but as my health improved I resumed the habit. I began to draw again and attempted a self-portrait by sketching my image in the glass—a good likeness, though the mouth was too small. I wrote to Uncle Leopold, who never failed to send me his weekly letter, and assured him that I was feeling much better.

In January, Dr. Clark pronounced me well enough to leave Ramsgate and issued explicit instructions for improving my health. "Regular walks every day without fail, indoors if the weather is intolerable. Take care not to sit too long at your lessons but get up frequently and move about. A standing desk would be advisable."

I nodded.

"A warm bath twice a week," he continued. "Windows open

as much as possible, especially at night, to avoid the weakening effects of the air at Kensington."

At the end of the consultation Dr. Clark produced a pair of curious wooden clubs, explaining that they had been brought to England by British soldiers returning from India, where they were part of exercise routines. "I recommend that you use these Indian clubs for a certain period of time each day to strengthen your arms."

He summoned one of the royal guards familiar with their use. "Sergeant Owen has been exercising with them regularly and has achieved an admirable musculature. I have arranged with your mother for him to spend half an hour with you three times a week."

The sergeant demonstrated a series of movements, beginning slowly, then faster and faster, finally manipulating the clubs so rapidly that they became a blur. He handed me a pair of smaller clubs and guided me through a series of simple exercises that I performed rather clumsily. The sergeant saluted smartly and marched away, and the physician moved on to his next admonition.

"Eat slowly, take small bites, and chew each mouthful thirty times. That's the way to good health," he said. "Avoid singing or reading aloud after meals, as this can cause an intake of air, which interferes with proper digestion."

Later, at dinner, I attempted to follow Dr. Clark's prescription with a small portion of boiled beef: *one, two, three, four, five, six*—I was still chewing when someone addressed a question to me. I swallowed, made a reply, started on the next bite, got bored before I had reached nine, swallowed—how extremely tedious! Especially if one were the least bit hungry!

I did find the wooden clubs VERY AMUSING and looked forward to my next training session with Sergeant Owen. The sergeant indeed had admirable musculature and a determinedly sober mien, and though I tried hard, nothing I said or did would induce him to smile.

On a bitterly cold day in mid-January we returned to Kensington and discovered that we now occupied entirely new quarters.

Mamma had long wished to move from the dark, cramped rooms on the ground floor and first floor of the palace to far brighter and more spacious sitting and sleeping apartments on the second floor—seventeen rooms in all—and she had gone ahead with her plan. I did not know until we arrived that she had arranged for the apartments to be redone and made ready for us, once again without consulting me.

I was still to share a bedroom with Mamma—a VERY DEEP disappointment, for I yearned more than ever for a bedroom of my own. With such a large suite it was surely not a question of space. Our bedroom was very large and lofty and prettily furnished, though still no blue or purple was to be seen. Next to it were a little room for the maid and a dressing room for Mamma. A former gallery had been partitioned into three fine, cheerful rooms; one of them was my sitting room, next to it the study where I would do my lessons, and the third an anteroom. Dear Lehzen would take my former sitting room on the first floor—too far away, in my opinion.

I spent several days arranging my books and deciding where my pictures should be hung and my growing collection of china figures displayed. By the end of the month everything was in place, and I had resumed my studies with Mr. Davys, who increased emphasis on geography and literature. Daisy and I read Madame de Sévigné's memoirs together in French, and to gain fluency, I composed weekly letters to dear Aunt Louise.

Sergeant Owen appeared according to schedule to lead me through a complicated routine that left my arms as weak as water. Dear Lehzen favored long, health-giving walks; the foulest weather was never a deterrent. Sweet little Dash went out with us and was VERY amusing.

So it went through the remainder of the winter that I thought would NEVER end. With little gaiety or merriment, it was a very DULL and TEDIOUS sort of life. At last spring came, bringing with it some pleasure: opera season.

We had a visit from Mamma's brother, my uncle Ferdinand, accompanied by his two sons, Ferdinand and Augustus. In January my cousin Ferdinand had married Queen Maria da Gloria of Portugal by proxy, and he was on his way to Lisbon to join her. I did wonder how they felt at the prospect of meeting for the very first time the spouse to whom they were already married!

"Our uncle Leopold arranged it all," Ferdinand told me. "He has many ideas for how I should reorganize Portugal, and he has written everything out for me in a book." As consort, Ferdinand explained, he would be the one to govern, though Dona Maria was the queen.

That interested me very much. At some time in the future I would no doubt marry. Did Uncle Leopold intend that my husband, as consort, would be the one to govern, and I would have only the appearance of ruling? That idea would certainly require some discussion!

Ferdinand was just nineteen and very good looking, with

beautiful, dark eyes, though he did have a high-pitched voice and spoke through his nose in a peculiar way. His brother, Augustus, was also tall and handsome but had scarcely a word to say and seemed VERY DEEP. I liked these cousins much more than my other cousins, Alexander and Ernst Württemburg, who had visited a few years earlier and of whom I had been very fond until they left after Mamma's humiliating performance.

King William and Aunt Adelaide hosted a huge dinner and ball at Windsor to honor Ferdinand and celebrate his marriage to the Portuguese queen. No *bâtards* appeared, Mamma did nothing to antagonize the king, who appeared to be in good health, and we returned to Kensington. Mamma arranged two grand balls, one in fancy dress to which we all wore costumes and masks. I chose to go as a shepherdess in a flowered skirt and white apron. Had I been able to dress dear Dashy as a sheep, I would have, but instead I carried a toy lamb. It was a splendid ball, and I danced seven quadrilles before supper and was not in the least bit tired.

My excellent cousin Ferdinand left for Portugal after only ten days, and I felt so very sad to see him go! His brother, Augustus, stayed on, silently reading a newspaper in my sitting room or helping me seal letters. We had a great deal in common, for he wrote in a journal every day, just as I did. I wept when Augustus, too, had to leave and for days felt very lonely without their company.

In April I began singing lessons with Signor Luigi Lablache, just as I had dreamed of. Signor Lablache was a large man with a profusion of gray hair mingled with some black locks and comical eyebrows that gave him a clever expression. Nevertheless, I was so nervous that when he sat down at the piano and asked me to sing a few notes of a scale with him, I could not produce a single sound. Not even a squeak!

"Ah, my dear princess," he said kindly, "no one has ever been afraid of me. Please do not be the first!"

Soon he had me singing Italian arias, sometimes solos and sometimes duets with Mamma, who had a very nice voice, and sometimes with Signor Lablache himself. Imagine, singing with the finest bass in all of England!

We often discussed music, and often disagreed. He considered Mozart the greatest composer who ever lived. I respectfully took an opposing view. "I am a terribly modern person," I told him, "and I prefer the Italians, Bellini and Rossini, for example, to any other."

Signor Lablache smiled and shook his head and waggled his eyebrows. "Mozart is the father of them all," he insisted.

Those lessons were the high point of my week; I wished I had a singing lesson EVERY DAY. We attended concerts in addition to the opera, and there were excursions to the zoological gardens. My mother frequently entertained distinguished guests to whom I was introduced, and we were invited to the homes of important people. All of this was with an eye to my future.

I should have been contented with my life, but I was not. I needed mirth; I craved merriment. Instead, I endured the unending stresses and tensions of life at Kensington. I could not bear to be around the Conroy daughters, dull Victoire and insipid Jane, and avoided contact with them, which was not easily done. I had become fond of Lady Charlotte, duchess of Northumberland, but she fell out of favor when it was learned that she had asked King William for help in protecting Daisy from Sir John's determination to be rid of her.

Lady Flora Hastings, always a <u>great friend</u> of Sir John and Lady Conroy, and of Mamma too, was excessively sharp-tongued and much too critical of dearest Daisy ever to be a friend of mine. Mamma avoided Aunt Adelaide, and she despised my dear old uncle, King William, who returned her sentiments. Trouble flared again and again between them. Sometimes the king was at fault; sometimes it was Mamma. When my brother, Charles, brought his wife, Mary, for a visit, the king refused to receive her, claiming that she was not of royal blood and therefore by tradition could not be admitted to the Royal Closet at St. James's.

Mamma was enraged. "I will not have my daughter-in-law insulted!" she fumed, and I could not blame her, for Mary was very sweet.

My daily life had become a chess game. The challenge was to elude the knight—Sir John—and the trouble he created everywhere I turned. Even a dinner or a ball or a visit to the opera offered little relief and could spark an incident that escalated quickly into a battle. War at Kensington seemed inevitable.

But then I learned that several VERY intriguing guests were expected to arrive for the celebration of my seventeenth birthday: my cousins Ernest and Albert and their father, the duke of Saxe-Coburg-Gotha, who was Mamma's oldest brother. This was exciting news, because it was JUST POSSIBLE that one of these cousins would be my <u>future husband</u>.

THE COBURGS, 1836

The subject of my future husband had been under discussion for a long time. Now I was approaching my seventeenth year, an age at which other princesses had already been betrothed, if not actually married. I was never included in any of the discussions. If I could not be consulted on the color of my sitting room walls, I would certainly not be consulted on a future husband.

Though she was out of favor with Mamma and Sir John, Lady Charlotte was a fine source of gossip on this important subject. A number of candidates representing nearly all parts of the continent had been suggested at one time or another. Certain members of the royal family hoped I would marry one of their own sons. I was rather fond of George of Cumberland, who had lost the sight in both eyes, but his father, the duke of Cumberland, was so ugly that everyone shuddered at the mention of him. I had no fondness at all for George of Cambridge, put forward as a possibility by his father, nor had he any affection for me.

"The newspapers speculate that, if not an English cousin, then an Englishman of noble birth would make you a satisfactory consort," Lady Charlotte reported. "If I were to offer an opinion, I would favor your Coburg cousins."

Fidi also offered an opinion. "I am very fond of them both," she wrote. "Ernest is my favorite, so honest and good-natured, but Albert is much handsomer, and cleverer too. I shall be very curious to hear your opinion when you meet them."

Uncle Leopold, too, wrote to me about his Coburg nephews. I knew that my uncle was a great champion of Albert, the younger of the two; his seventeenth birthday was in August, three months after mine. "I think Albert would suit you very well, Victoria. I have given this a great deal of consideration, and I believe it would be a fine match. But you will soon judge that for yourself."

Ernest, a year older, would not do, my uncle explained, because he was heir to his father's lands and titles.

Unfortunately, as Mamma and Uncle Leopold were arranging for the visit of my Coburg cousins, King William had some definite ideas of his own. He had invited another King William—this one king of the Netherlands—to come from Holland with his two sons, Prince William and Prince Alexander of the house of Orange. My uncle the king made no secret that he favored such a match, and that made Uncle Leopold furious.

"I am astonished at the conduct of the old king!" he wrote. "He has informed me that it would be highly desirable to put off the visit of your mother's relatives for another year!"

My Coburg relatives were already on their way, Mamma informed the king. It was too late to stop them.

The Oranges arrived. King William and Queen Adelaide put on great entertainments for them, and there was a grand fête at St. James's, which I, of course, attended. It was clear to me, as it must have been to everyone, that the two boys from Holland were not at all prepossessing. Both were VERY plain and looked heavy, dull, and frightened. I dismissed the idea of any sort of match almost as soon as I met them.

"So much for the Oranges, dear uncle," I wrote to Uncle Leopold, who must have been relieved. He made it clear that he set a very high store by his two nephews, and because I valued his advice above all others, I took this visit seriously.

The Oranges had departed, and now the Coburgs arrived. I put on one of the dresses dear Aunt Louise had given me, a pale blue silk trimmed with blonde lace, with very full sleeves puffed up with plumpers, as was the fashion. While my hair was doing, Daisy read to me—a good thing, because I was excited and even a little nervous. Then, at a quarter of two in the afternoon, a servant came to my apartments and announced, "The gentlemen are in the Great Hall, madam."

Daisy smiled encouragingly as she held my hand and we descended two long flights of stairs. Uncle Ernest and his sons were waiting to be presented. I immediately liked what I saw.

Both boys were very tall. Ernest had dark hair and fine, dark eyes and eyebrows, a most kind, honest, and intelligent expression, and a very good figure, but I saw at once that his nose and mouth were NOT good. Albert was just as tall, somewhat stouter, but EXTREMELY handsome. I found myself staring at him—he was that good looking! His hair was about the same color as mine, his eyes were large and blue (like mine!), and he had a beautiful nose and a very sweet mouth and fine teeth. I could not stop smiling at him and wondered if he might think my teeth were too small or too much of my gums were showing.

After the formal greetings were complete, I returned to my apartments and sent word to our guests that I would receive them in my sitting room at four o'clock. Then I looked for ways to amuse myself, anything to occupy my mind until the appointed hour. I played the piano and practiced some of the singing exercises that Signor Lablache had assigned. I leafed through my sketchbook and examined some of the drawings I had made of my favorite singers. I stared out the window at the rain-swept garden. I checked the time.

"Is my hair all right?" I asked Daisy, who was hovering nearby.

"You look lovely, Victoria," she replied calmly. "Very lovely indeed."

Soon the three of them, father and sons, arrived. We sat side by side like birds on a fence, leafing through my collection of drawings and speaking of them in a most educated way. It was obvious that these cousins were much more men of the world than any of my other cousins. Ernest and Albert spoke English very well, and I continually stole glances at Albert, seated next to me. The charm of his countenance was his delightful expression, full of goodness and very clever and intelligent. Oh, I would enjoy this visit VERY much!

The next few days passed TOO quickly. My cousins and I went on walks together—Albert was particularly fond of the natural world—with Daisy and Lady Flora trailing along behind us. Albert and Ernest were both excessively fond of music and took turns playing the piano. They both drew very well, particularly Albert. At dinner I sat between them, and there was seldom a pause in the conversation except when I was chewing and chewing and chewing, as per doctor's orders, which I confess I did not always follow. The more I saw these two brothers, the more I was charmed by them, and the more I loved them.

But one thing I discovered about Albert that I considered very strange: He retired every night at an excessively early hour, as though he were scarcely out of the nursery. Mamma had prepared a vast number of entertainments that seemed to tire Albert before the evening had scarcely begun. When concerts went on until one or two in the morning, which was certainly not unusual, he looked truly miserable. On the night before my birthday, Mamma gave a grand dinner party at Kensington. Albert approached me as I was talking to an important gentleman, Lord Melbourne, the prime minister, and said in a trembling voice, "Your highness, I beg your kind indulgence, but I must excuse myself."

He did not explain why, as that would not have been required or even proper. I learned later that he was simply fatigued and had gone to bed. It was only half past nine!

The next night my birthday ball was held at St. James's. Everyone was there—and by "everyone" I mean three thousand people. The dancing began. But after dancing only two quadrilles, Albert turned as white as ashes, looking as though he might faint.

Albert left the ball with his valet and was taken back to Kensington by carriage. Two days later he suffered a bilious attack that kept him a prisoner in his room. Soon he recovered and was out among us again, but he appeared pale and delicate. I did wonder at his apparent lack of vigor.

The week after my birthday Mamma gave another large ball, this one at Kensington, and Albert and I danced together for the first time. He was quite graceful, and he seemed to enjoy some of the more spirited dances. But when I led off an English country dance at the conclusion of the ball at nearly four o'clock in the morning, Prince Albert was nowhere to be seen.

The last week of my cousins' visit was perhaps the best. On two of our outings we attended the opera and took lunch with the Lord Mayor of London. Most rewarding, in my opinion, was this: Albert and I were playing the piano and singing duets when Signor Lablache arrived for my lesson. He entered my apartments swirling a cape, his comical eyebrows executing a little dance. He had scarcely been presented to dear Albert when he burst out singing *Non più andrai,*" Figaro's aria from the second act of *The Marriage of Figaro*. Signor Lablache did that to tease me, for he knew I was not fond of Mozart's operas, and he considered the Austrian composer to be the greatest.

Albert appeared to agree with my singing teacher. "Signor, it has been my greatest pleasure to hear you in the role of Leporello!" he said, referring to Lablache's best-known role. Then Albert actually sang a bit of Leporello's famous aria, a long, humorous description of all the women that Don Giovanni had loved. So delightful!

It was a wonderful solo for a bass voice, and dear Albert was a tenor, which was completely out of character and made it VERY AMUSING indeed. He had us all laughing. Albert, so full of fun!

That very evening we were privileged to hear Signor Lablache and my other favorite singers perform at the home of Sir John and Lady Conroy. Naturally, Victoire and Jane were both present, but while Jane was her usual retiring self and barely noticeable, Victoire on the contrary seemed determined to attract as much notice as she could. She had taken to dressing most unappealingly, laying on far too much lace, too many ribbons, and a profusion of jewels and curls. Lady Elizabeth Conroy was as bland as ever, but Victoire seemed to take after her father and chattered on endlessly in a way that was NOT AT ALL AMUSING. I wanted to kick her, but as that was not possible, I smiled stiffly and uttered not a single word.

Alas, on the tenth of June the delightful visit came to an end, and my beloved guests prepared to return to Germany. We had our last HAPPY breakfast with this dear uncle and those beloved cousins, whom I loved so VERY, VERY dearly, much more dearly than any other cousins in the world. I loved Ferdinand and also good Augustus, but I loved Ernest and Albert _more_ than them. Oh yes, MUCH more!

Even dear little Dashy loved all of them, but especially Albert, who tossed him balls and played tug-of-war with his favorite toy.

"What shall you do now?" I asked them as they prepared to leave.

"We are on our way to London," Ernest replied.

"Then I will proceed to the University of Bonn for studies in philosophy, law, and economics," Albert said, adding with a smile, "with time left for fencing, I trust."

I embraced both of my dearest cousins most warmly, and at eleven o'clock they left us. I cried bitterly, very bitterly, when they left, but this parting was not so difficult for me as some of the earlier ones had been. *Perhaps I am growing up and have better control of my emotions,* I thought as I climbed slowly up to my rooms. I comforted myself that it was VERY likely I would see my dear uncle and my two VERY DEAR cousins again at some future time.

I wrote immediately to Fidi to tell her exactly how I felt about dearest Albert and dearest Ernest. They are so natural, so kind, and so well informed! So well bred, so truly merry in a childlike way, yet very grown-up in their conversation. It was delightful to be with them. I cannot say that I love one more than the other, because I love them both so VERY MUCH.

It was true, I did love them BOTH. But I also wondered how Albert in particular felt about me.

Life was excessively dull after the departure of Albert and Ernest, though I did try to improve the time. Uncle Ernest had given me a beautiful parrot, which I named Norris for the lovely castle where we often stayed on the Isle of Wight. I determined to teach Norris to talk, but my efforts to get him to say "pretty bird" were so far unsuccessful. In a very short time dear Albert had taught sweet little Dashy to roll over and to sit up and beg and to speak. Norris stared at me silently with a baleful eye. *No doubt Albert would have the bird fluent by now,* I thought glumly.

Daisy arrived during Norris's lesson and proposed an outing. "Come, my dear Victoria," she said. "We shall take a carriage to Hampstead Heath for a vigorous walk. It will do us both a world of good after so many days of dinners and concerts and balls."

"I'm in no mood for a vigorous walk," I protested. "The day is much too hot even for a not-so-vigorous walk."

"May I remind you," Daisy said firmly, "that Dr. Clark has emphasized the importance of exercise." She folded her arms and waited.

The good doctor had called on me nearly every day since my illness the previous November. Sergeant Owen still came three times each week with his Indian clubs. I ate more lightly and chewed more thoroughly, and I was no longer as plump as I had been. I could stay up half the night and dance every quadrille without tiring! "Dr. Clark has pronounced me the very picture of health," I argued.

"The picture remains good only when we continue to follow the doctor's orders," Daisy said. "And it will give us an opportunity to have a good talk."

I returned the uncooperative parrot to his cage and reluctantly prepared to accompany Daisy. The coachman left us off and was instructed to wait for us at Highgate Ponds. I was relieved that it was just Daisy and I and two footmen; no Lady Flora Hastings, no Lady Conroy, not even Mamma. We set off at a brisk pace. It was always a challenge to keep up with Daisy, who was much taller than I.

"Now," said dear Daisy, "I'm going to speak to you quite openly, as I have been instructed by your uncle Leopold."

"Is this about Albert?" I asked.

"It is. You liked him well enough, did you not?"

I nodded.

"The foreign press already has you engaged and planning a wedding. But Leopold wants it clearly understood that no marriage is possible at this time, nor is there to be any announcement of an engagement. All of that must wait until you are at least eighteen, you understand."

"I understand," I said. *Good*, I thought, much relieved.

I had been thinking about dear Albert a great deal since his visit. Though we never spoke of it, I was aware—and I was sure Albert was, as well—that behind the scenes our families were executing an elaborate dance they no doubt intended to end eventually in our marriage. I loved Albert, truly I did, but I was not <u>in love with</u> him. I thought of the conversation I had once had with dear little Maggie, my maid, who had told me what it was like to be in love. *When my Simon holds me in his arms and kisses me, I think I'm going to melt—just like butter.* I had no such melting-butter feelings about Albert. Of course he had not kissed me—that would have been highly improper. Nor did I <u>want</u> him to kiss me. I did not intend to marry for a VERY long time.

I had also been thinking about Queen Elizabeth, who had never married. I did not approve of many things she did—for example, ordering the execution of her cousin, Mary, Queen of Scots. But Elizabeth had immense power, and she ruled for a very long time without any need for a consort. Could I not do the same, if I chose?

In one of our long talks, in which Uncle Leopold and I had discussed the qualities of a good ruler, I had brought up the subject of Elizabeth and posed the question: "Was she able to remain powerful because she didn't marry and refused to say if she ever would? Or might she have been a better, more compassionate ruler if she *had* married?"

"Difficult to say," my uncle had replied. "But if she had married and produced a living heir, the course of history would have been considerably altered."

"In what ways?" I'd asked, prepared for a serious lesson.

Leopold had smiled broadly. "For one thing, you would not be the future queen of England. When Elizabeth ordered the execution of Mary, Queen of Scots, and named Mary's son, James, as heir to the throne, everything changed. You are descended from Mary, not Elizabeth."

The lesson was clear: If I did not marry, someone else would provide the future heir to the throne. My future subjects might not approve of that.

I thought of that conversation now as I walked beside Daisy, who began speaking about Albert. "It is most important that you feel that your mind is made up about Albert. Your uncle fears that some other young man might be forced upon you— one of the Oranges, for instance."

"What dull boys they are! Two great lumps!"

"Many a princess has been turned away from her heart's choice and coerced into marriage with a great lump—or worse. Leopold desires that you find a choice and anchor yourself to it. Those are his words."

"Mamma would prefer Albert—he is her nephew! She loves him, I'm sure!"

"Your mother does love him," Daisy agreed. "But if Sir John should decide someone else is better suited to his purposes— not yours—his influence over the duchess is very strong. Leopold calls him 'Mephistopheles,' the devil himself."

"Well then, we must make sure the devil does not get his due."

Dark clouds had rolled in. Rain would come soon. We spoke no more about Albert, but hurried toward the place where our carriage was waiting.

"My dearest uncle," I wrote later that day, "I must thank you most sincerely for the prospect of great happiness you have contrived to give me in the person of dear Albert. Allow me, then, to tell you how delighted I am with him, and how much I like him in every way. He possesses every quality that could be desired to render me perfectly happy at some time in the distant future."

I sent the letter to Mamma for her approval before I sealed it. I considered the matter settled.

Chapter 18

THE KING'S BIRTHDAY, 1836

Mamma and I received an invitation from King William to come to Windsor for celebrations of Queen Adelaide's birthday on the thirteenth of August and to stay for the king's eight days later. But there was a problem: Mamma's own birthday fell on the seventeenth, squarely between the two royal birthdays.

"This is my fiftieth birthday and worthy of a special celebration, and I've planned a party at Claremont," she said. "We shall decline the queen's and attend the king's."

I knew that refusing the invitation to the queen's birthday was a mistake and a very rude one, but there was no way to change Mamma's mind. On the thirteenth we were on our way to Claremont.

Little lanterns had been set all round the gardens for Mamma's party, and we dined on the terrace with dancing afterward. Two days later we left Claremont for Windsor.

King William had gone to London to officially end the current session of Parliament. Around ten o'clock that evening the king arrived at Windsor, plainly very tired and out of sorts. Nevertheless, he greeted me cordially. "My dear Princess Victoria!" said the king, taking both of my hands in his. "What a very great pleasure to see you here! My only regret is that I do not have the honor of your company more often!"

He turned to Mamma and made a low bow. Suddenly his mood changed. "Madam," he said in a voice loud enough for everyone to hear, "I have just come from Kensington Palace, where I discovered to my extreme displeasure that apartments have been taken possession of without my consent and contrary to my commands." He glared at Mamma. "I will not tolerate such disrespect."

Mamma grew extremely pale. The king was speaking of our apartments. I didn't understand why. What had my mother done? Had she really gone against the king's wishes? Queen Adelaide called for the musicians to play and tried to calm the angry king. Mamma, too, was angry, but she pretended that the rebuke had nothing whatever to do with her.

I did not dare to say a word to Mamma, but prayed for the evening to conclude and hoped that would be the end of it. Later Daisy explained to me what had happened: Mamma had asked the king for permission to move into the new suite of rooms, and the king had refused. She had simply gone ahead and appropriated the seventeen rooms *without* his permission. "Your mother believes it entirely appropriate for the next queen of England to have better accommodations," Daisy said.

The next day, after the king's rebuke, went VERY badly indeed.

A hundred guests attended the king's birthday dinner. Mamma was seated on one side of the King; I sat opposite. One of the king's *bâtards*, the very pleasant Lady Amelia, had been seated close to Mamma, which surely upset her. After dinner Queen Adelaide proposed a toast, and we all drank the king's health and long life. The king rose creakily to his feet to give a response.

"I trust in God that my life shall be spared for nine months longer," he said. "I should then have the satisfaction of leaving the royal authority to that young lady"—he pointed to me— "the heiress presumptive of the crown, and not in the hands of a person now near me to be surrounded by evil advisors." He stared angrily at Mamma, who sat open-mouthed in stunned silence. His speech turned into the most awful tirade. "I have been grossly and continually insulted by that person," he roared, "and I shall no longer endure such disrespectful behavior. I complain particularly of the manner in which that young lady has been kept away from my court, prevented from attending those events at which she should have been present. This shall not happen again! I am king, and in future I shall command that the princess appear at my court, as it is her duty to do."

During this terrible scene I began to weep, tears streaming down my cheeks. Never had I suffered such deep embarrassment. How could Mamma have defied the king's order? The new quarters were lovely, but were they worth this humiliation? And why did the king choose to rebuke Mamma in front of a hundred people?

By the end of his speech, King William was red-faced and fairly shouting. He stalked out of the ballroom, waving his arm at poor Queen Adelaide to follow, which she did, eyes averted.

The guests, aghast, seemed immobilized. The whispering had begun. Mamma rose with as much dignity as she could muster. "Come, Victoria!" she commanded, her face flushed scarlet. "I will not stay here to endure another insult. We shall leave at once." I obeyed.

Mamma was outraged, and no amount of calming words from others could soothe her wounded pride. She called for our carriage, but in the end she was persuaded that the hour was very late and it would be better to delay our departure from Windsor Palace until the next day. In silence, we retreated to our rooms.

The journey back to Claremont on the morning after this horrid evening was long and silent. I sulked and kept to myself, avoiding not only Mamma but also Victoire Conroy, who had been a witness to the whole thing. I counted the days until the arrival three weeks later of my dearest uncle Leopold. Aunt Louise could not accompany him, for she was expecting another child, but she had sent me several lovely dresses made by the finest dressmaker in Paris.

As soon as I was alone with my uncle, I poured out my misery, describing the scene at the king's dinner. "Now I will not be permitted to attend any of King William's drawing rooms," I complained. "He so much wants me there, and I *should* be there—it's my duty! He said so himself!"

Uncle Leopold listened, pacing up and down and shaking his head. "The king has a nasty temper," he said. "He once upbraided me at a dinner for drinking water instead of wine. It appears the old king is given to public outbursts, saying things that he ought not to say. On the other hand, my sister has behaved most appallingly in disobeying the king's order—or ignoring it, which is the same thing. And that puts you in the middle, dear Victoria."

My uncle understood perfectly, but there was little he could do to remedy the situation. And we had so many other important subjects to discuss! He changed the subject, asking to hear every little detail of the visit from my two VERY dearest cousins, Albert and Ernest, though I had written to him all about it. "But I want to hear the words from your own lips," he said.

I reported all the things we said and did during my cousins' visit, not omitting the fact that Albert could scarcely keep his eyes open after dinner. "It was my only disappointment," I told my uncle. "I enjoy dissipation, and Albert does not."

Uncle Leopold laughed. "Aside from his tendency to fall asleep before ten o'clock, Albert is a fine young man," my uncle said, "but I must emphasize that he is indeed young. My good friend Baron Stockmar has taken him in hand, and when Albert is not engaged in his studies at university, the two will travel together—gaining polish, as we say, so that he can slide easily into the role that awaits him. One is not born knowing how to be a prince consort, any more than one is born knowing how to be a queen. One must be formed properly to take one's place."

I felt agitated, and my face grew hot. It was one thing to talk about Albert, and quite another to talk about marrying Albert. *I am not ready for this!*

"I agree that Albert is a fine young man—and so VERY handsome," I said, my voice a trifle unsteady. "But my mind balks at the notion of a 'prince consort.' Indeed, I cannot even talk about the subject of marriage."

"Of course not, Victoria!" Uncle Leopold replied soothingly. "Nor for several years at least."

I was VERY MUCH relieved. "Now we must dress for dinner," I said, much calmer now and smiling. "Mamma is entertaining again, and I shall wear the lovely violet silk sent by my dearest aunt Louise."

I hated to see my uncle leave after his short visit. We enjoyed our shared silences as much as our important talks. He spoke so mildly, yet firmly and impartially. I could have listened to him speak on virtually any subject. His advice was always perfect, and I would often recall one bit in particular: "Royal persons are a little like stage actors; they must always make efforts to please their public."

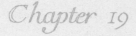

SPIDERWEB, 1837

A long winter stretched dully before me. My singing lessons with Maestro Lablache had ended and would not resume until spring. I finally succeeded in teaching my parrot, Norris, to say his own name, plus "pretty bird." My days were monotonous, and I yearned for some diversion, some gaiety. There was nothing.

In mid-February we left Claremont to return to Kensington. We came to a railway, where our carriages were stopped by a signalman. A train flew by, the steam carriage striking sparks as it raced along the iron rails, enveloped in clouds of smoke and making a loud noise. It was the first time I had seen a train, a curious thing indeed that gave us all a great deal to talk about.

I did wonder if King William had seized our apartments while we were gone, but he had not—dear Aunt Adelaide must have prevailed upon him. On the surface all was peaceful and quiet. I was able to enjoy music, opera, and theater. I resumed my lessons with Maestro Lablache. My studies with Mr. Davys continued, and dear Daisy and I read together. Still, the palace seemed caught in a web of ill feeling, the strong but often invisible strands spun between Mamma and King William; King William and Uncle Leopold; Uncle Leopold and Conroy; Conroy and Lehzen; Mamma and Lehzen; Lehzen and Lady Flora. I was the helpless fly trapped in the web.

My eighteenth birthday was coming. In a short time I would reach my majority and become my own mistress, unless Mamma somehow managed to intervene and delay it for three more years. I watched Sir John carefully, knowing that he was still determined to take the post of my private secretary. I was equally determined that he would not.

Mamma must have realized that I would not surrender easily, and she asked my brother, Charles, to come to Kensington to argue in Sir John's favor. I had never felt close to Charles, who was at school in Switzerland when I was born, and his recent visits had not made me feel any warmer toward him. Charles had a GREAT fondness for Sir John, and in my opinion anyone who championed John Conroy was to be viewed with deep suspicion.

Daisy and I discussed the situation endlessly. Like me, she did not look forward to Charles's arrival. She knew that Sir John had expressed hatred for her, and as a result of his influence Mamma nursed a bitterness against her old friend. Charles would certainly hear all about it. Daisy's own situation was precarious, but she was more concerned about me.

"Sir John sees a position as your private secretary as a way to establish his whole family at court," she said. "He wants a place among your ladies for Miss Victoire Conroy, too."

Miss Conroy as a lady-in-waiting? Unthinkable! The idea almost made me laugh.

"You must be prepared for the most awful pressure to be brought to bear on you," Daisy warned. "I fear that Sir John will find ways to force you to bend to his will."

"He will not succeed," I said. "I promise you that, dear Daisy."

But I really had no idea how my mother, my brother, and Sir John might conspire to force me. If only Uncle Leopold could help me! He was far away in Belgium, though he wrote encouragingly, "Be steady, my good child. Be not put out by anything."

I would have to manage somehow on my own.

Soon after Charles's arrival at Kensington he came to my rooms, full of smiles and good cheer. "May we have a word in private, dear sister?" he asked, with a slight nod indicating that I should dismiss Lehzen.

"The baroness can hear whatever you wish to say to me, dear brother," I replied.

Charles frowned and waited, no doubt hoping Lehzen would excuse herself and leave of her own will. But I caught her eye and she stayed where she was.

"Very well then, Victoria," Charles grumbled. "It has become my role to try to bring some sort of acceptance to this situation. I understand that there are tensions, resulting no doubt from misunderstandings. Let's not complicate those tensions with unnecessary stubbornness."

"I'm not being stubborn, Charles."

"Surely you understand how it would damage your reputation among your future subjects if they thought that you and our mother had had a falling out." He folded his arms and leaned close, his face only inches from mine. "The people want to see a warm feeling between mother and daughter. Ill feeling would surely upset them."

"Ill feeling has not been caused by *my* words or deeds," I told him firmly.

Charles heaved a deep sigh. "I am suggesting that if you were to accept John Conroy as your private secretary, the situation would right itself. Or, better yet, to recognize that you are indeed too young and inexperienced to rule. It would be for the good of the country, as well as for yourself, if you asked for an extended period in which a regency would be in effect until your twenty-first—"

"I will not consider such a thing," I interrupted.

Charles tried again. "It has been suggested that you must be coerced into taking Conroy into your favor."

"Coerce me!" I exploded. "Who dares to suggest such a thing? John Conroy has called me a termagant! Don't believe what Mamma tells you about him! Our uncle Leopold refers to him as Mephistopheles."

This was too much for my brother. "If you will not listen to reason, then the devil take you!" he shouted as he stormed out of my sitting room, slamming the door and leaving Daisy and me staring at each other.

The mood at Kensington did not improve. I would not speak to Mamma or to Charles. We received word that King William's health had been failing. Later we learned that he was rallying. Then, a week before my birthday, I was summoned to my mother's sitting room. Mamma and Sir John waited with

Francis Conyngham, lord chamberlain and senior official of the king's household. Lord Conyngham looked VERY ill at ease.

"Your highness," he said, "I have a letter addressed to you from his majesty, King William." He added with peculiar emphasis, "The king desires that it be handed to you and to no other."

"Very well. I thank you, Lord Conyngham." I glanced at Mamma and Sir John, wondering why they were here at all.

"Sir John Conroy insists that your mother be present when you read the letter," the lord chamberlain explained uncomfortably, and handed me the letter.

I broke the seal. In a weak and unsteady hand King William wrote that he had asked Parliament to grant me the sum of ten thousand pounds a year for me to do with as I wished, commencing on the day I came of age. I would have the right to appoint my own keeper of the Privy Purse to oversee this considerable sum. In addition, I had the right to appoint the members of my own household.

This letter meant that in just seven days, the twenty-fourth of May, my eighteenth birthday, I would indeed be my own mistress, able to choose my own ladies and pick my own servants. I could barely suppress a smile.

"The letter, please, Victoria," Mamma said, reaching for it.

I clutched the letter to my chest, shaking my head. Sir John took one menacing step toward me. "Give the letter to your mother, Victoria."

Gritting my teeth and throwing Sir John a scornful look, I did as I was ordered.

Mamma's face darkened as she read it. "This is an outrage!" she cried.

Sir John turned to the lord chamberlain, who waited stiffly. "Our thanks to you, Lord Conyngham, for delivering this letter to the princess. Kindly carry expressions of our gratitude to his majesty, King William."

The lord chamberlain cast me a long and, I thought, sympathetic look, bowed, and left the room. The door had scarcely closed behind him before the battle began.

"I am utterly humiliated," Mamma wailed. "The king obviously intends to insult me yet again, and he has succeeded. But I mean to tell you, Victoria, that it is not possible for you to be given such a sum of money for your own uses! You are not prepared to handle it discreetly—"

"I am to have a keeper of the Privy Purse to administer it, Mamma," I said, struggling to control my temper. I wanted to lash out at her but felt that nothing would be gained. "The king offers Sir Benjamin Stephenson." I extended my hand for the letter, in order to point it out.

"A thoroughly detestable man!" Mamma exclaimed, snatching the letter out of my reach.

Struggling to maintain calm, I suggested my tutor, Mr. Davys, for the post. "You could find no man more scrupulously honest than he."

"Absolutely not," Sir John cut in. "Out of the question."

"Why not?" I demanded, too loudly. Whomever I suggested would receive the same response: *no*. My restraint was slipping away. "Perhaps you will allow me to consult with Lord Melbourne on the matter," I said in one last attempt to bring reason to the table.

"The prime minister will doubtless go along with whatever King William wants," Mamma raged.

The argument went on and on with no one willing to bend. Mamma's fury increased, matched by what Sir John called my obstinacy—"A sign," he claimed, "that you are simply a stubborn child unfit to rule or do anything on your own."

I could endure no more. I was exhausted. It was the two of them against me. I fled to my room, too upset even to explain the reasons to dearest Daisy. I refused to go down to dinner and would not eat what Daisy brought up to me. I fell into bed very early and cried myself to sleep. I did not hear my mother come to her own bed, but woke during the night to the sounds of her tossing and turning and muttering to herself.

If I thought matters would improve, I was wrong. The next day I was summoned once more to my mother's sitting room. At first I refused to go, but then thought better of it. I needed to find out what new devilishness Sir John had concocted and then persuaded my mother to agree to.

They had composed a letter to the king—Sir John's ideas, taken down in my mother's words and by her own hand, like a dutiful secretary—and they presented the letter to me. "It is my wish," said my mother coldly, "that you copy this letter and sign it as though it were your own."

I stared at her, scarcely believing what I heard. "You want me to put my signature on a letter that is not my own?" I had not yet read the letter, but I could guess at its content.

"It will be your own, Victoria, the moment you sign it. There is nothing here with which you should disagree. You are well aware that due to your youth and inexperience it is essential that you remain in my care for the next few years."

There it was again: your youth and inexperience.

I read the words that my mother and Sir John had put forward as my own:

*I wish to remain in every respect as I am now,
in the care of my mother. In the matter of money,
I should wish whatever sum your majesty deems
advisable to be given to my dear mother, who always
does everything I want in financial matters and will
certainly put it to the best use for me.*

"I will not sign it," I said. "I disagree with nearly every word of it."

"Of course you will sign it, my dear Victoria," said Sir John smoothly.

Over the next hour, as I continued to refuse, Conroy wheedled, cajoled, ordered, and threatened. My mother wept crocodile tears as she reminded me that I owed her everything, everything, for the sacrifices she had made, for her endless devotion. In the midst of the heated argument, my brother, Charles, joined us. He sided with Mamma in reminding me how much she had done for me and with Sir John in berating me for my obduracy.

Now it was three against one.

Worn down at last, I gave in. I sat at my mother's writing table, took the paper and pen Sir John provided, and copied the letter. I signed it, placed my seal on it, and rose. "I shall have nothing further to say to either of you," I said curtly, tossing the pen aside. "Or to you, Charles," I added, and stalked out of the room as Sir John was summoning a messenger.

For several days I heard nothing. I was true to my word and

did not speak to my mother, to Sir John, or to my brother. I knew the king's health was fragile and that he was mostly bedridden, but I was almost certain the king realized that, though the handwriting was mine, the words and the sentiments were not. Much later, I learned in conversations with Lord Melbourne, the prime minister, that the king had indeed recognized the truth. In an attempt at compromise, he had suggested dividing the sum and offering six thousand pounds to my mother and the balance to me. Mamma did not tell me about this, but refused the compromise. She wanted it all.

My eighteenth birthday arrived, the most important one yet: I had now legally come of age. The dear old king had arranged a birthday ball in my honor on the evening of the twenty-fourth of May. I looked forward to sitting beside him at St. James's and having a private word with him, but that was not to be. He was too ill to attend and sent his best wishes. I realized that his time was indeed running out.

Crowds had gathered for a glimpse of me as I drove to the ball. Flowers and banners, one with my name spelled out in letters of ethereal blue, were displayed everywhere. I rode in the same carriage with Mamma and Daisy and my brother Charles's wife, Mary, and had to smile and wave at the crowd as though nothing untoward had happened. I had not spoken a single word to Mamma since I signed the letter, and I still refused to speak to her, creating a VERY awkward situation. She rode with her eyes averted and a fixed smile as we passed through the streets of London, packed with people who had turned out to celebrate the birthday of their future queen. Their cheers quite touched me, and for a time I could forget the raging battle. Dearest Daisy squeezed my hand reassuringly.

The roar of the crowd still ringing in my ears, I entered St. James's Palace as I had so many times before. My heart was heavy because the king could not be present, but I danced with many different partners and did enjoy myself enormously. Yet throughout the evening on what should have been a high point in my young life, I remained aware of John Conroy's fierce, unwavering gaze fixed upon me.

PART II

THE QUEEN

THE QUEEN, 1837

Being my own mistress brought me a measure of welcome independence. Though I felt keenly the unending pressure from Mamma and Sir John, I began to try my hand at exercising the rights belonging to an independent person. One of my first decisions was to dismiss the duchess of Northumberland. Lady Charlotte was a kind and pleasant woman and she had often been helpful to me, but I no longer required a governess. Appointing her had not been my idea; it was Mamma's and Sir John's. I composed a letter to the duchess, expressing gratitude for her punctual attendance even when it was at great inconvenience to herself.

Good-bye, dear duchess!

I sent a message to dear little Maggie asking her to come back, which she did gladly. I rejoiced to have Maggie in my service again, and she rejoiced to be with me, though we did not exchange confidences as we once had. Our lives had changed a great deal: Maggie had married her Simon and had an infant son, cared for by her sister, and I awoke every morning knowing that very soon I would become queen.

A few days after my birthday, I received a letter from Uncle Leopold, who wrote that he was sending Baron Stockmar, his trusted friend and confidant of many years, to Kensington to try to bring about an armistice between the warring parties. This was the same Baron Stockmar who was with my dear cousin Albert, now studying at the university in Germany.

It had been a year since Albert had visited Kensington with his brother and father, a year since Uncle Leopold had spoken to me seriously about a future marriage. In the beginning I had thought often of dear Albert, but, as the months passed, I thought of him less and less frequently. There were too many other matters to occupy my mind. I was more concerned with the problems Stockmar had to address at Kensington Palace.

Baron Stockmar was short, round, and altogether pleasant, and I took an immediate liking to him. If it was not possible to have my uncle himself at my side, I was grateful for his good friend's assistance. Soon after his arrival, the baron suggested that we go for a drive while we discussed the issues. We rode through the countryside in a light rain.

"The main problem," I told him, "is that Sir John Conroy demands an appointment as my private secretary. If not that, then as keeper of the Privy Purse, in charge of my money. I detest the man, and I've refused to promise him anything."

"This distresses your mother," the baron observed.

"It does, and she subjects me to constant harangues in an attempt to persuade me. She tells me and anyone else who will listen, 'I gave up my home and my kindred to devote myself to my daughter, the future queen.' It's her favorite speech. When that fails to move me, she calls on my brother, Charles, to press me. Conroy himself never quits his attempts to intimidate me."

Stockmar listened sympathetically as I passionately described Sir John's insulting conduct, adding, "Mamma allows him to bully me and does nothing to interfere. She's docile as a lamb in his presence and does everything he wants. They plague me every hour of every day."

I showed the baron my mother's most recent letter. She still resorted to sending me hectoring letters, even more frequently now that I refused to speak to her. Baron Stockmar produced a pair of folding spectacles dangling at the end of a satin ribbon, perched them on his nose, and read:

You are still quite young, though you believe otherwise. Remember that all of your successes have been due to your mother's reputation, not to your own talents. Do not be overconfident of your abilities, my dear Victoria.

The baron returned the letter, shaking his head. "I find it difficult to comprehend that the duchess clings to such a notion."

"Sir John has convinced my mother that I am immature—'younger in intellect than in years,' he tells people—and that I would never be able to govern without a strong private secretary, meaning himself. My brother, Charles, agrees with him, as he agrees with everything Conroy says. I've told Charles it's none of his affair. Uncle Leopold believes that Charles is a spy. He says it would be prudent of me to ask my brother to leave England."

"I'll do whatever I can to assist your highness, and I'll speak to the parties involved here to try to smooth the dissensions. But please understand that I have no real power. I cannot order them to do anything."

"I know." I sighed, and sank back against the leather seat. "I don't really want to have to banish my brother."

Baron Stockmar folded his spectacles and replaced them in his pocket. "The best I can offer is to advise you to stay the course, my dear princess, to hold out against those who would try to bend your will. Perhaps it won't be necessary to send Prince Charles away."

We drove on in silence. The rain was coming down harder, and I gave the coachman the order to turn back.

Stockmar continued, "I have spoken with the king's eldest son, George FitzClarence"—one of *les bâtards*—"who assures me that, though the king is weak, he is in no immediate danger. We all realize that his days upon this earth are numbered. I believe you will not have to endure this dreadful situation much longer."

We returned to the palace, where the baron was treated coolly by my mother and her ladies and, of course, by Conroy. Each day I awoke knowing that Mamma and Sir John had probably come up with another scheme to force me to do their will, and until the moment I became queen, Mamma and Sir John would continue their efforts to secure him a powerful position. I was determined not to grant John Conroy any position whatsoever. But had it not been for Stockmar's steadying hand during this prolonged nightmare, I would no doubt have broken.

"Sir John will not give up," I told dear Daisy as we walked one day in the gardens. A hawk circled lazily overhead. "He will somehow find a way to force me to sign a paper agreeing to something I do not wish to do."

Daisy shielded her eyes against a bright sky, watching the hawk. Suddenly it swooped down and snatched up a vole. The struggle was brief. Daisy took my arm. "I have a solution. We shall draw up a paper in which you renounce any promises you might be coerced into making," she proposed. "You will sign it, and I will witness it."

We rushed back to the palace and promptly carried out Lehzen's suggestion. Later, I told Stockmar what we had done.

"I'm glad you have," he said. "I applaud your spirited response to this distasteful situation. O'Hum should learn his lesson."

"O'Hum?"

"My disrespectful name for a man for whom I have little respect—our friend Conroy."

The baron's derisive nickname for Sir John amused me VERY MUCH. And the baron's approval of my action bolstered my determination.

The days trickled by like sand through an hourglass, not one passing without some new effort being made by Mamma and Sir John, or without my brother or someone else calling on me to mend the breach between my mother and myself. The news from Windsor was what might be expected as the poor old king approached the end of his life. A letter from my uncle Leopold acknowledged that I might soon become queen and must not be frightened of the prospect.

I wrote back immediately. "I am not in the least frightened. I look forward to the event, though I do not suppose myself quite equal to all that will be asked of me. I trust, however, that with good will, honesty, and courage, I shall not fail."

We were in a state of waiting. For a fortnight I did not go out in public. Mr. Davys no longer came to give me lessons. We knew what was about to happen. I felt very calm, very quiet.

On the morning of June nineteenth Daisy proposed going out for a drive. She called for a carriage, and I sent a message to my brother's wife, Mary, inviting her to join us with her sweet children whose chatter served to distract us. Though I was at odds with Charles, I bore his wife no ill will. Fidi's husband, Prince Ernst, had come from Germany to console Queen Adelaide, his cousin, so soon to be widowed. Ernst arrived at Kensington after lunch, bringing word from Windsor that the king was not expected to live through the day. The tension was so great and my emotions drawn to such a heightened state that I burst into tears.

At seven Daisy and I went down to dinner. On my eighteenth birthday I had told her, laughing, that I was now of age and no longer needed to hold her hand as I descended the two flights of stairs, and since then I had gone down unaided. But on that evening, Lehzen offered her hand, and I accepted.

As I expected, Mamma and Sir John and his wife and daughters were present. I acknowledged them but did not engage them in conversation and left immediately upon finishing my meal. I read while dear Maggie was silently undoing my hair, said my prayers alone, and went early to bed.

How odd it was, still to be sharing a bedroom with Mamma under such strained circumstances! I slept soundly, dreamlessly, until six in the morning when I heard Mamma's voice.

"Victoria."

I opened my eyes and saw Mamma standing over me. I knew the reason.

"Victoria, you have important visitors. The Archbishop of

Canterbury and Lord Conyngham are here, and they wish to see you."

I flung on my dressing gown, and with Mamma and dearest Lehzen hovering nearby, went QUITE ALONE into my sitting room where the two gentlemen waited.

"Your majesty," they said gravely, and knelt before me. "We have come from Windsor," said the lord chamberlain. "It is our sad duty to bring you word that his majesty King William is no more. He expired this morning at twelve minutes past two. You are queen."

I had known for years that this day would come. Now it had. Somehow I knew exactly what to do. I held out my hand, and each man kissed it. I thanked them for coming, and they left.

I am queen, I thought as I stood alone in my sitting room and let the awareness and the magnitude of my new station settle over me like a benediction. *I am queen*.

The twentieth of June was only one day short of midsummer, and it was already bright, though still very early in the morning. Mamma was waiting for me in our bedroom, nervously pacing. As she stepped forward, I stopped her. "Mamma, please grant me the first request I make to you as queen. Let me be by myself for an hour." Without waiting for her reply, I walked past her and firmly closed the door of my dressing room. For an hour I sat alone, simply wishing to experience in solitude the flood of thoughts and feelings.

Dearest Daisy had already called for Miss Skerrett, a tiny woman of middle years who had been seeing to my wardrobe. Skerrett had the proper mourning clothes laid out for me, a plain black gown trimmed in white at the neck and wrists. After a tearful Maggie had finished doing my hair, I took the time to write a few letters, a rather long one to Uncle Leopold, signed, "Your devoted niece, Victoria R"—the R for Regina, queen, the first time I had signed with my official signature—and a short note to dear Fidi, "You are now the sister of a queen," signed V. R.

An hour had slipped by, and it seemed wise to go down for breakfast. Good, faithful Baron Stockmar was waiting for me. He knelt, like the others, and kissed my hand, and sat with me while I ate my usual boiled egg and buttered toast. "Lord Melbourne will come at nine o'clock, your majesty," he told me. "Your uncle Leopold urges you to retain him as prime minister."

At the appointed time, the prime minister appeared. Lord Melbourne was a large man in his later years, still quite handsome with some white in his hair, thick black eyebrows, expressive eyes, and a charming, graceful manner. I talked to him quite ALONE, as I expected to do with all my ministers. This was our first meeting, and I liked him immediately.

"I have taken the liberty of writing out a short speech for you to deliver at your meeting later this morning with your Privy Council," he said. "I hope it will be helpful to you, your majesty."

All my life I had listened to Mamma read speeches written in pompous language—words put into her mouth by Sir John—and I was happy to find that Lord Melbourne's prose was simple and direct and entirely suited me. Later, in my room, I practiced reading the speech aloud to Daisy.

"Perhaps a bit slower," she suggested. I read it again, following her advice, and she pronounced it perfect.

There was still time, before I was to meet with my council, to write a careful, thoughtful letter of condolence to Aunt Adelaide. Dipping my pen in the silver inkwell, I told Daisy, "I wish to assure her majesty the queen that she is welcome to stay at Windsor Castle for as long as she likes."

"Very kind," Lehzen said, but she reminded me that the proper form of address for my aunt was "the Queen Dowager."

"I'm quite aware of her changed status," I said, "but I would rather not be the first person to remind her of it. Poor lady, how very sad she must feel!"

At eleven o'clock I entered the Red Salon for my first meeting with the gentlemen of my Privy Council. In this grand chamber Mamma had announced Fidi's coming marriage to Prince Ernst, and here we had had the wedding breakfast. My chair, newly upholstered in rich red velvet, was a very LARGE chair and my feet did not quite touch the floor. Dozens of men, all somberly dressed, were waiting.

After I had read my speech, the councilors approached one by one, knelt, and swore his allegiance to his new sovereign. At the last my two elderly uncles tottered forward, their rheumy eyes shiny with tears, and bent their creaky knees. First came the ugly duke of Cumberland, followed by the eccentric Sussex, who lived surrounded by dozens of clocks.

I had a GREAT many things to do, and I was eager to plunge into my new duties. I passed the afternoon writing letters when I was not receiving visitors, people who would no doubt be of great help to me in my new life, and attending to several VERY important matters that I did not wish to delay.

The first was to order my bed removed from my mother's bedroom to my sitting room. As soon as it could be accomplished, I intended to have my own bedroom with Daisy installed in the room next to it.

The second was to order my dinner served to me in my sitting room. Though I had often been lonely, only rarely did I have the luxury of BEING ALONE. Now, for the first time in my life, I could be alone whenever I wished, and on this, the first night of my reign, I intended to indulge that desire without even dearest Daisy's company.

The third matter, to dismiss Sir John Conroy from my household and rid myself of him forever, would not be so easily accomplished. But I began by barring him from attending the Proclamation ceremony to take place the following day.

After I had luxuriated in my solitary dinner, Lord Melbourne called upon me for the third time that momentous day. Such a dear, good, and kind person! He seemed to understand what troubled me without my having to say much about it.

"I am determined to rid myself of Sir John Conroy," I told him, "and I have sent him a note informing him that he will not attend my Proclamation."

One of my prime minister's heavy eyebrows lifted slightly. "You are within your rights to exclude anyone you wish, your majesty. But it is wise to remember that Sir John does have his supporters—most importantly, the duchess your mother."

"Mamma will be angry. I don't care."

"I see." He hesitated. "Perhaps this is a discussion best left for another day."

Lord Melbourne wished me a pleasant night's rest and left me, and I went to my mother's room to bid her good night. I found her in a petulant mood. "I understand that you have banned Sir John from attending the Proclamation tomorrow," she said sullenly.

I expected it, and I was ready. I would not attempt to soften my words. "Not only do I not wish to see John Conroy at my Proclamation, I do not wish ever to see the man again."

"How ungrateful you are, Victoria!" Mamma cried. "You have declared that you will not have Sir John as your private secretary, though he has helped you with your correspondence all along. You have further determined that you will not have our kind friend as the keeper of the Privy Purse, though he is eminently qualified. And now you deny him even the courtesy of allowing him to attend such an important ceremony."

I planted myself in front of my mother, though she turned her head and refused to look at me. "Hear me out, Mamma. While I was meeting this morning for the first time with my Privy Council, Sir John was outside with Baron Stockmar, presenting him with a list of his demands. His demands, Mamma! This list was passed on to Lord Melbourne, who showed it to me. 'As a reward for my past services to the duchess of Kent and her daughter, Princess Victoria, now queen, I believe I should receive a peerage'—he wants the title of baron—'the red ribbon of the Order of the Bath, and a pension of three thousand pounds a year.' Baron Stockmar said the audacity of it quite took his breath away!"

Mamma dabbed at her eyes. "Surely Sir John deserves all of these things for the service he has rendered to us!"

"Surely he does *not*. His demands are outrageous. Some other more appropriate offer will be made. And he will not attend the Proclamation tomorrow," I said, adding firmly, "nor will his friend Lady Flora. Not after the way she has spoken so ill of dearest Lehzen."

"But just this once—"Mamma whimpered, and when she saw that I would not be moved, she became angry. "Take care, Victoria!" she said, shaking a warning finger. "Take care that you do not allow Lord Melbourne to become king!"

For a moment we glared at one another. "Good night, Mother," I said shortly.

I retired to my own bedroom, and that night <u>for the first time in my life,</u> I slept ALONE!

BUCKINGHAM PALACE, 1837

As was the custom, I remained in retirement at Kensington Palace until after dear King William was laid to rest at Windsor on the eighth of July. Less than a month after my accession as queen, I left Kensington and moved into my new home: Buckingham Palace. I did have some feelings of regret at leaving poor old Kensington, where I was born. So many important things in my life had taken place there: Fidi's wedding, pleasant balls and delicious concerts, visits from dear relations—I had met dear Albert there! On the other hand, I had endured too many painful and disagreeable scenes at Kensington that I preferred to forget.

Buckingham Palace had gone through various stages of enlarging and rebuilding during the reigns of three different kings. It was only now ready for occupancy. I toured the halls and galleries, accompanied by the steward—there are more than seven hundred rooms, and he feared I would get lost. I was VERY MUCH PLEASED with the royal suite, its high ceilings and cheerful windows. After the tour, I made certain that Mamma's apartments would be located in another part of the palace, and arranged for dearest Daisy's bedroom to adjoin mine.

I should have known that the battles with my mother were not over. In the past I had been obliged to do whatever Mamma decided. But now I was my own person, and she was clearly not prepared to acknowledge that.

On my first day in my new home, Baron Stockmar, who would also have quarters at the palace, offered me a piece of advice: "Your majesty, may I respectfully suggest that you invite your mother to walk with you in the palace gardens, so that the public may see you amicably together. King Leopold fears that your antipathy toward the duchess—whatever its cause—will not be taken well by your subjects. They want to see a proud mother with her happy daughter. If it were felt that you had caused a breach in that sacred relationship, it would do your reputation untold harm."

This was what my brother, Charles, had told me. It was easier when the advice came from Baron Stockmar.

I also remembered what Uncle Leopold had once told me: *Royal persons are a little like stage actors; they must always make efforts to please their public.*

"Very well," I told Stockmar. "I shall do as you say."

That afternoon, I sent Mamma a message asking her to join me in the gardens. As soon as we set out on the path near the lake, with dear little Dash frolicking round us, a crowd began to gather nearby, waving and calling out greetings. Dashy raced about, exploring every corner, appearing to be quite happy in his new home. Mamma was less so.

As we strolled arm in arm, pausing now and then to admire some bright bloom or a butterfly's lazy swoop, Mamma again beset me with complaints.

"I was most distressed at dinner last night—our last at Kensington Palace!—when I was seated below the late king's sister at the table," she said. "I found it quite insulting."

"It was proper that she should take precedence over you, Mamma," I reminded her. "The princess is entitled to sit closer to me at the head of the table."

"She would not take precedence if you were to give me the rank of queen mother, as I have requested."

"As you have *demanded*," I corrected her. "You are not entitled to that rank, as you well know, because my father was not king. It would do you no good to have it and would no doubt offend my aunts."

Mamma chose to ignore my explanation and continued undeterred. "Furthermore, I find it highly offensive that you have actually invited some of the king's *bâtards* to dine with you. You know how strongly I disapprove of them."

"They were my guests, not yours. You may be as offended as you like." I dropped her arm and moved away from her.

She turned the subject to Sir John, as I expected she would. "You seem intent on persecuting that good man. Now I understand that you do not intend to invite Sir John to the Lord Mayor's banquet in your honor at the Guildhall. You must remember that I have the greatest regard for Sir John, and I, for one, am thankful for all he has done, even if you are not."

We were in full view of a growing crowd of women and

children, watching us from a respectful distance. If my mother continued to berate me I would be unable to contain my anger much longer. "This conversation must end at once, Mamma," I told her, my throat tightening and my fists clenched. "We shall return to the palace and speak of this no more, for I will not change my mind about John Conroy. Now smile, please, and let's gather a few blossoms to give to those lovely children peering in at the gate."

This was not the end of it. Having Mamma's apartments remote from mine helped the situation, but it was not easy to convince my mother that she could no longer simply walk into my rooms whenever she wished.

"It is my desire that you come only when I have invited you," I told her, "or, should you wish to speak to me, that you first request permission."

My mother stared at me, open-mouthed. "You are still my daughter," she said, her voice shrill. "And you expect me to ask permission to speak with you?"

"I am your daughter, but I am first and foremost the *queen*," I reminded her.

I reported this scene to Lord Melbourne. "I can now expect to receive a series of scathing letters from my mother," I explained. "Some will be about what she perceives is her due—where she believes she should sit at the table. But I imagine most of them will be about Sir John Conroy and the debt of gratitude owed him. She still hasn't given up on that. She insists that I must receive him and his entire family at court, and I insist that I shall not. How can she expect me to invite him after the detestable manner in which he behaved toward me when I had fallen ill? The two of them badgered me day after day to sign a paper promising him an important post!"

"May I offer my advice, your majesty?" Lord Melbourne asked.

"Please do, sir!"

"Allow me, as your prime minister, to reply formally to the duchess's letters. Then you can ignore the matter and let the blame fall on my shoulders. They are quite broad enough."

I gladly accepted his advice, though I did recall my mother's angry words: *Take care that you do not allow Lord Melbourne to become king!* And that was how she would regard this.

Still more trouble was brewing: Mamma had run up a large debt and, with Sir John no doubt whispering in her ear, she asked for an increase in her income. I turned the matter over to the cabinet minister in charge of finances, who offered to pay whatever debts she had incurred before I became queen. She rejected this generous offer. Her income was increased, though I felt certain she would soon overspend. The problem, I believed, was that Sir John was siphoning off a good part of it.

With Lord Melbourne's advice, I made a decision about Sir John's future. He would be elevated to baronet—ranked below a baron but above a knight—and awarded a sizable pension. O'Hum, as Stockmar called him, remained a member of Mamma's household, because there was no way to get rid of him. Only Mamma herself could do that, and I was certain she would not.

A New Life, 1837

I was delighted with my new life. I now had my own money; Parliament voted to grant me a very large Privy Purse for my own purposes, plus a generous allowance for the expenses of my household, and I had the income from several royal properties. I had become, almost overnight, a very rich girl. I could do as I wished.

I began by appointing the members of my household. The most important was dearest Daisy, who remained closer to me than my mother had ever been. She was always perfectly discreet, disappearing when Baron Stockmar or Lord Melbourne or any other official visitors came to visit, reappearing when I was again alone. Not surprisingly, she was in a fine mood, having triumphed over her old enemy, Sir John.

While I studied lists of highborn ladies, nearly all of them the wives or daughters of my ministers, dear Daisy sat nearby, knitting stockings for one of her many nieces and nephews in Germany. I commented on each of the ladies, and we discussed their various qualifications for the post. Soon I had named a dozen ladies of the bedchamber and eight bedchamber women, all to be paid for their services and assigned periods during which they stayed in the palace. I also named a number of maids of honor, young girls who received no payment but were promised a gift of one thousand pounds when they married, if they wed with my consent.

The most coveted appointment was mistress of the robes, whose duty was to accompany me to all ceremonies and who had the privilege of riding in my carriage whenever I traveled to and from my royal palaces. I awarded the golden key, symbol of this exalted position, to Lady Harriet Gower, duchess of Sutherland. Lady Harriet was a tall, handsome woman who had married a much older man when she was seventeen and was now the mother of six delightful children. Despite the difference in our ages, we quickly became fast friends. But I was determined that I would not permit friendship to excuse lax discipline among my ladies, and when Lady Harriet arrived half an hour late at dinner one evening, I lectured her in front of everyone.

"I trust this will not happen again, madam," I said.

Lady Harriet's cheeks colored a deep red. "I beg your pardon, your majesty," she said, and promised that it would not. Later I received a letter of apology from her, explaining that she had again fallen pregnant and had felt quite ill. "I shall not permit my own physical weakness to interfere with the execution of my duties," she wrote, and naturally I forgave her.

Most of the gentlemen of my household were already in

place, having served King William, and I saw no reason for them not to continue to serve me. One new appointment was the royal physician; to this post I named Dr. Clark, who had restored me to health after my serious illness the previous year. When I summoned Dr. Clark, he asked with a sly smile if I had been dutifully continuing to exercise with my Indian clubs. I confessed that I had not, and offered a number of excuses.

He said kindly, "You will find many new exercises to develop the strength of your mind, but I beg you, your majesty, to continue to develop the strength of your body as well."

I indicated that I would try to follow his advice, but I did not promise. Fortunately, he didn't ask if I had followed his prescription to chew each mouthful thirty times. Possibly, he knew what the truthful answer would be.

Dearest Daisy declined to become the head of my royal household, telling me, "It would please me simply to stay on as your dear friend and advisor, just as I always have, but with no official title." I agreed, but gave her an invented title, lady attendant. She took over many of Sir John's former duties, such as answering routine letters. I trusted her far more than I had ever trusted him!

My life was a whirlwind. During my first weeks as queen I was constantly occupied and happy to be so, receiving foreign ministers as well as cabinet members in my audience room, signing papers at my writing table, and spending hours each day with the charming Lord Melbourne. He patiently explained to me many of the workings of government of which I was still quite ignorant, though my tutor, Mr. Davys, had done his best to prepare me.

"You will not rule as some of your predecessors have done," Mr. Davys had said. "Queen Elizabeth had absolute power. She could order a queen's execution, as she did her cousin Mary's. Today the power to make laws lies with Parliament. But you will have enormous influence. Your power is of a different sort. Your subjects are quite enchanted by their new queen—young, fresh, vivacious—just what our nation has yearned for, for a very long time."

I had thanked my old tutor for his confidence. Now Lord Melbourne took over my instruction, adding to it daily—even hourly!

In July I would preside at the prorogation of Parliament, the ceremony bringing an end to that year's session. But something worried me: Lord Melbourne had told me that new elections to Parliament were required. "Always held following a change of monarch," he explained.

Lord Melbourne's Whig party was in power; but the outcome of the election was not a certainty. "We've been losing our majority in recent years," he cautioned. "But I think we shall hold steady for the foreseeable future."

"But if we should not?" I asked uneasily, for my sympathies were entirely with the conservative Whigs.

"If the Tories should take the majority, then you shall have a new prime minister."

I could not imagine how I would endure the loss of dear Lord Melbourne, and I was nearly ill with worry over the outcome. What a relief, then, when I could write to Uncle Leopold, "I'm thankful to say the vote was rather favorable." Lord Melbourne would remain by my side.

On the day of the prorogation, Skerrett and Maggie helped

me into a gown of white satin embroidered in gold. Maggie arranged my hair to accommodate my gold coronet. Diamonds glittered in my ears and on my wrists. Dear Daisy fastened a crimson velvet robe trimmed in ermine round my shoulders.

I rode to the House of Parliament in a gilded carriage drawn by eight white horses. The Yeomen of the Guard in their crimson tunics, knee-breeches, and flat, black hats strode ahead of me past cheering crowds, and the band played "God Save the Queen" as I entered the House of Lords and was escorted to my throne. I read my speech, again written by dear Lord Melbourne, and it was over.

A day in the life of a queen, I thought contentedly, waving and smiling at my subjects as my carriage rumbled over the cobblestone streets. I loved every bit of it, though I was happy to be rid of that heavy, fur-trimmed robe when I reached the palace, and Dashy bounded out to greet me carrying his favorite red rubber ball.

A Year of Changes, 1837–1838

The first summer of my reign was the pleasantest I EVER passed in my eighteen years. Nearly every day I went out riding with Lord Melbourne at my side. I had nearly forgotten how much I enjoyed going at a canter and challenging the others to keep up with me. There were many long walks in the gardens, pleasant evenings playing whist—everyone's favorite card game—and engaging in agreeable conversations with dear Lord Melbourne. The more I knew him, the more I liked and appreciated him.

Late in August, the entire court left Buckingham Palace for Windsor. The queen dowager had moved from the state apartments to private quarters in another wing. At first I could not help feeling as though poor King William and dear Aunt Adelaide might turn up at any time, but once settled into my apartments, with dear Daisy occupying the adjoining rooms and Lord Melbourne installed nearby, I felt quite at home. On rainy days, of which there were many, my ladies and I discovered that we could get up a lively game of battledore and shuttlecock in the Grand Corridor, with the marble busts and gloomy family portraits as witnesses.

What a happiness to welcome Uncle Leopold and Aunt Louise for a visit! They were both looking so very well, though Aunt Louise had grown quite fat. I was VERY pleased to see how well my uncle and my prime minister got on together. I had many interesting conversations with both of them, and I was aware that I had been learning SO MUCH and still had much left to learn.

The days flew by, and it was a sad moment when I had to say good-bye once more to my dearest aunt and uncle. But there was no time for weeping, for I was scheduled to review three army regiments. Dressed in a dark blue riding jacket trimmed with scarlet collar and cuffs, the Windsor colors, and mounted on my horse, I returned the soldiers' salutes, putting my hand to my cap as the officers did. I inspected the lines and watched the men perform complicated military maneuvers, and for an hour or two I felt just like a man, ready to fight at the head of my troops.

I was happy enough to return to Buckingham Palace, but that happiness soured quickly. Mamma, who had seemed in better spirits during Uncle Leopold's visit, renewed her campaign to convince me to allow Sir John's attendance at the Lord Mayor's banquet.

"I implore you, if you cannot find it in your heart to *like* him, at least forgive him and do not exclude him!" she wheedled. "For the sake of your poor mother!"

I told her for the VERY LAST TIME that I would not grant him permission. Once again, my mother and I were not on speaking terms. I decided the only way to stop her constant pleas on his behalf was to speak directly to Sir John. My brief notes to him hardly seemed to make plain my intention: Sir John Conroy no longer had any part in my life. Therefore, I sent him one last message, asking him to call upon me in my audience room at fifteen minutes before nine o'clock in the morning. Lord Melbourne always arrived promptly at nine. I could accomplish what I wished in a quarter of an hour.

Sir John appeared with his usual confident swagger, smiling broadly, and bowed. "How do you do, my dear Victoria? Pretty well, I hope!" he greeted me jovially—and much too familiarly, I believed—as though we were old and dear friends.

I glared at him coldly. "The proper form of address is 'your majesty,' Sir John."

His smile remained fixed. "Of course, your majesty. Forgive me."

Taking a deep breath, I addressed him in my most imperious tone. "I have summoned you here, Sir John, in order to make perfectly clear to you that you will not be invited to the Lord Mayor's dinner, to my coronation, or to any other event, either public or private, at which I am to be present. You are not welcome at my court." His smile faded. "You may be my mother's friend, but you are not, and have never been, my friend," I told him.

"What have I done to offend you, your majesty?" he cried, obviously shocked at my tone as well as my words. "I have devoted my life to the service of you and your family! Does that count for nothing?"

"You are an ambitious man, Sir John, and since my earliest childhood you have used my mother's position and her unfortunate situation to advance your own position and your family's. Now that I am queen and of age, you can no longer manipulate the duchess or browbeat me. You've requested the title of baron and a large pension as well. These are denied. I suspect, Sir John, that if a full investigation of your financial affairs were undertaken, certain irregularities might be discovered." I sat back and observed as Sir John's usually smug expression vanished. His jaw dropped and his lip twitched. His hands were trembling. I was gratified to see that I had made my old enemy as uncomfortable as he had so often made *me*. "I wish you and your family a pleasant retirement, Sir John. Now, I bid you good day."

There was a long silence. I turned my attention to a sheaf of papers on my writing table. I heard the door of the audience room open and close, and I nearly wept with relief. When Lord Melbourne arrived moments later, I could tell him with assurance that Sir John Conroy was now truly gone from my life.

I rode to the Guildhall accompanied by Lady Harriet and two of my ladies, and was seated at the high table with the Lord Mayor. Above me hung a huge banner proclaiming "WELCOME, V. R." Below me sat hundreds of guests, Mamma and Daisy among them. Following Daisy's advice, I had eaten a few a bites of bread and butter before leaving the palace, to curb my tendency to eat too much and too fast.

"God Save the Queen" was played, my health was drunk, addresses given and responses made. When at last we returned to the palace at the end of a very long evening, my ladies complained of fatigue. I was not in the least bit tired. I had been the center of attention, all eyes upon me, and I gloried in it!

Daisy read to me while Maggie was undoing my hair. After Maggie had gone, Daisy put away her book and we sat up until long after midnight, discussing every detail of the banquet, from the ladies' gowns and feathered headdresses to snatches of overheard conversation.

"Everyone talked of your perfection," Daisy said proudly. "The elegance of your bearing, your poise and confidence, your clear, beautiful speaking voice when you responded to the addresses. They are delighted to find themselves with such a charming and proper little queen."

"*Little* queen?" I asked. "Do they remark on my stature?" For years Uncle Leopold had encouraged me to grow taller, as though this were something I could accomplish through my own determined efforts.

"They do, and they adore you for it. The evening was another triumph for you, Victoria," Daisy assured me.

"No Sir John! No Lady Conroy, no Misses Conroy! That's the great triumph." I yawned and climbed into my bed. "I haven't seen Victoire since I became queen, and I don't miss her in the least."

"You must feel rather sorry for her, though. Poor girl, she always believed she would have a prominent role in your court, possibly as a lady-in-waiting or as a maid of honor. But now she has nothing."

I sat bolt upright. "I don't feel a bit sorry for her. I've always hated her father, and I'm sure she knew it. How could she ever have believed she had a future in my court?"

"She believed it because that's what Sir John promised her."

"Now she knows that he was wrong," I said, and lay down to sleep.

"Victoria," Daisy reminded me sternly, "even a queen must not forget her prayers."

"You're right," I said, getting out of bed and kneeling. "But don't expect me to ask God to bless any of the Conroys."

Over the next several months I worked diligently to learn my duties as sovereign of a great nation. I leaned heavily on Lord Melbourne. There was still much that I simply did not know, but there was no topic I could not discuss easily with my prime minister, no subject on which I could not question him. Lord Melbourne imparted his knowledge in a kind and agreeable manner—even on matters of a delicate nature, such as my tendency toward plumpness.

"Gentlemen of the royal family have been inclined to acquire excess weight. This was true of your father and your uncles," he pointed out.

"Mamma's, too," I added, for she had become QUITE stout. "It would help if I would grow taller," I said rather wistfully. "Several inches would do. Everybody grows but me."

Lord Melbourne replied, smiling, "I think you are already grown."

As the winter wore on, the cold increased, the snow lay deep, and the River Thames froze over for the first time since before I was born. I thought of the gypsy family I'd met the previous winter while we were staying at Claremont. Just before Christmas, I had been out walking with Daisy, Lady Flora, Lady Conroy, and Victoire, and we had come upon a family of gypsies camped by the side of the road. A woman with untidy hair black as a raven's wing stepped out of one of the frail canvas tents, accompanied by a swarm of little children, about six in all, clinging to her dingy green cloak. The mother's face had a beautiful simplicity, and she talked to us easily and politely. As we conversed, I took careful note of this picturesque little group, and when we returned to our house I made a watercolor portrait of the scene.

The next time we passed that way, the woman again came out, accompanied by several others, to tell us very proudly that on the previous day their sister had given birth to a son. The gypsy women offered us the honor of naming the baby, but our ladies refused. Had I been my own mistress then, I would have asked that the child be named Leopold in honor of my uncle, whose birthday happened to be the day the infant was born.

When we told Mamma about the family, she ordered nourishing broth sent for the mother and a scuttle of coal to warm her and her infant until she was recovered from childbirth. That night it turned very cold and began to snow. A week later the gypsies were gone without a trace. I thought of them now and wondered how they were faring, and resolved that as queen I would do whatever I could to help those in need.

The people's fascination with their "little queen" frequently interfered with going out in public. At the theater I was usually called to come forward in the royal box between acts to hear the audience sing "God Save the Queen." Crowds clamored for me when I was spotted at a concert. Wearying though it often was, I did love it!

In this busy new life I learned the pleasure of an hour or two spent quietly with a book. As a child I had been restricted to books Mamma deemed uplifting. But that winter I read my first novel, *The Bride of Lammermoor* by Sir Walter Scott. Lady Harriet had spoken of it very favorably, and I sent for a copy.

When Mamma learned of my choice, she voiced her disapproval. "Such reading will do you no good and may even do you harm, my dear Victoria," she said through pursed lips. We were on one of our obligatory rides through the palace park that were so important to my public image: the loving daughter of a devoted mother. Our conversation did not match the image.

"I do not find the novel harmful in the least," I replied tartly. "According to Scott, it is based on a true story. I find it full of truths."

"It would be wise of you to accept a mother's advice, as a daughter should," she snapped.

"And it would be good for you to remember that I am of age and perfectly capable of making up my own mind. That includes the right to reject your advice on matters of literature."

We endured a mutual silence until we had returned to the palace and gone our separate ways.

Next I began to read Charles Dickens's *Oliver Twist* in serial form, and found myself absorbed in the story of the boy thieves and their desperate lives. "I consider Mr. Dickens a great author," I told Lord Melbourne even before I had reached the final chapters. "I should very much like to meet him."

But Lord Melbourne did not share my view of Dickens or of his novel. "It's all about workhouses and coffin makers and pickpockets. I don't like those things in reality, and therefore I don't wish to read about them," he grumbled.

Literature was not our only source of disagreement. I was

quite excited by the development of the railroad, but when I mentioned to Lord Melbourne that I yearned to travel somewhere—anywhere—his reaction startled me. "I will not allow a railway to be built within fifteen miles of my house!" he said. "Those monstrous machines are bad for the country! I shall not be happy until every mile of track is torn up and turned to scrap."

Not wishing to argue with dear, stubborn Lord Melbourne, I dropped the subject, but hoped secretly that I might yet have an opportunity to ride on one of those monstrous machines.

There were, naturally, serious issues to contemplate, and I consulted Lord Melbourne on a number of smaller matters as well, such as the inadvisability of receiving divorced women at court. "I am determined to do everything *correctly*," I told him.

"Good idea to set the proper tone for the court right from the start," Lord Melbourne agreed. "Divorced men are not tainted by their status, as women are."

So, no divorced women at court.

During a visit to Windsor Castle, two of my maids of honor wished to walk out on the terraces. I decided that unmarried ladies of my court could not do so unless they were accompanied by a chaperone. I explained to the abashed young ladies, "It's simply a matter of propriety."

"Of course, your majesty," they murmured with bowed heads.

"I would expect that you never do anything to reflect poorly on yourselves, your position, or the reputation of the court," I told them.

"We understand, your majesty."

I observed several of the girls rolling their eyes. They were about the same age as I, but they would bear watching.

CORONATION, 1838

At my birthday ball on the twenty-fourth of May, I opened the dancing with my cousin George, as I had so many times before, though we still did not very much care for each other. I delighted in breaking with tradition by eating my supper <u>standing up</u> in the ballroom and chatting with my guests. It amused me to note the disapproving frowns on the faces of the elderly ladies, who seemed to think I was doing something <u>shocking</u>.

I had not danced for <u>such</u> a long while, and I felt so very merry and HAPPY to do so again. I danced all the quadrilles but of course no waltzes, considered too intimate to be danced by an unmarried lady. But as the sun was peeping over the horizon, I ended the night with a vigorous English country dance that left us all laughing and gasping for breath.

There was one great disappointment: Lord Melbourne was not there, and I missed him VERY much. Lady Harriet was absent as well, having sent an excellent excuse: the birth a week earlier of her seventh child, a fifth daughter, to be named Victoria.

My life had settled into a predictable routine. Except on mornings after a ball when I had not retired until sunup and slept late, I rose at eight. After going over my schedule for the day, I went down to breakfast. Sometimes, when I felt that I must, I sent word to Mamma to join me. I much preferred the company of Lord Melbourne, who could be SO amusing.

We took our breakfast from a large table laden with platters of sprats, cod, eggs, broiled kippers, deviled kidneys, haddock, and pork pie, and a gleaming molded jelly wobbling in their midst. I limited myself to a single boiled egg and buttered toast. Lord Melbourne and I then retired to my sitting room and set to work. Among other important items requiring my attention was my coronation, fixed for Thursday, the twenty-eighth of June. Parliament had voted to set aside a very large sum of money for an array of celebrations throughout coronation week. Planning had begun months earlier.

For days before the actual event, the whole city was in an uproar. Crowds of visitors were pouring into London from all over England and Scotland, and from the Continent as well. Fidi and her husband, Prince Ernst, had arrived, and so had Uncle Ernest, dear Albert's father (but not Albert!). I was VERY disappointed that custom would not allow dearest Uncle Leopold and Aunt Louise, as crowned heads themselves, to be with me.

On the afternoon before the ceremony, Lord Melbourne escorted me in a carriage through the teeming streets to Westminster Abbey with the idea of trying the thrones for size, reminding me that I sometimes found myself sitting on chairs that were too high and left my feet dangling.

"Are we not to have some sort of rehearsal?" I asked my prime minister as we walked through the vast nave of the church, where workmen were hanging banners of crimson and gold along the gray stone walls. "There are so many parts to it that there's sure to be some confusion."

"Don't worry," said Lord Melbourne, waving off my concern. "These bishops are accustomed to the most elaborate ceremony. It's their life work. You can depend upon them to guide you."

That night I slept little—not due to excitement or nervousness, but because large guns had begun booming in the park nearby. By seven o'clock I was up and peeping out the window at the throngs that already surrounded the palace. Skerrett had been there since daybreak. While I was still in my dressing gown and my hair was doing, Daisy read aloud the order of the various parts of the ceremony.

Under Skerrett's direction, the maids dressed me, tightly lacing the corset over my chemise and pantaloons, rolling the white silk stockings over my knees and fastening the garters, tying the petticoats round my waist, lifting the white satin gown over my head and hooking it up the back. Maggie settled the gold coronet on my head.

After the maids had finished, Fidi and Charles and Uncle Ernest came to my dressing room. While I studied my reflection in the glass, Fidi and Daisy draped the ermine-trimmed robe on my shoulders. My sister's eyes met mine, reflected in the looking glass; she blinked away tears. Dear Daisy pressed her fingers to her lips and turned away. By ten o'clock I was ready. My brother and my uncle helped me climb, with my heavy train, into the gilded coach, and I drove off with Lady Harriet. It was a fine day.

The procession wound slowly through London's major streets, to afford the people a glimpse of their queen. The cheers were deafening, and the crowds far exceeded any I had ever seen. An hour and a half after leaving Buckingham Palace, I arrived at Westminster Abbey.

My eight trainbearers were waiting, young ladies in white satin trimmed with pink roses. The mother of one of the girls had ordered their dresses without consulting the other mammas. Now some of the girls complained that they could not manage my eight-foot train and their own trains at the same time.

"Do your best, dear ladies," I told them, "for we are about to begin."

Trumpets blew a fanfare and we started the long, solemn walk down the aisle. Hundreds assembled in the great vaulted space of the abbey observed my progress. Noblemen displaying their decorations and titled ladies in dazzling jewels filled the stands. Clergy in gorgeous white and gold vestments waited by the main altar. I could feel occasional tugs on my robe as the girls struggled with my train; Lady Harriet, walking behind them, muttered instructions.

We should have practiced this, I thought.

The organ resounded and the voices of the choir soared in the anthem traditionally sung at coronations: "I was glad when they said unto me, We will go into the house of the Lord." My heart fluttered a little and my breath came quickly as I made my way toward my throne.

The ceremony was so long and complicated that at many points I hardly knew what I was expected to do. Worse, despite what Lord Melbourne had said, many of the clergy seemed not to know either—when I was to change from one robe to another, when the crown was to be put on my head, when I was to be handed the orb. Mistakes were made. The archbishop, who was to place the coronation ring on my little finger, instead forced it painfully onto the ring finger; I nearly cried out, and later I had to soak my hand in ice water to remove the ring. One of the bishops lost his place in the prayer book and had to go back and start over. When he handed me the orb, a golden sphere set with precious gems, it was much heavier than I expected, and I nearly dropped it.

Once the crown was on my head—too heavy and too tight, bringing on a throbbing headache—I sat on my throne. One by one, the members of the Privy Council mounted the steps, approached the throne, and knelt, swearing to become my "liege man of life and limb and of earthly worship." When my good Lord Melbourne knelt, I grasped his hand with both of mine, and saw that his eyes were filled with tears. Then came Lord Rolle, eighty-two years old and dreadfully infirm. When he attempted to ascend the steps with the help of two ministers, he slipped through their grasp and rolled down to the bottom. Unhurt, he was lifted up and made a second brave attempt. To prevent another fall, I rose and walked to the top of the steps, a gesture that brought applause.

Near the end of the long ceremony, I looked up toward the box where I knew dearest Daisy was seated, and we exchanged smiles. Next to her sat Baroness Späth, who had come to London with Fidi to share in the triumph of this splendid occasion. I did not smile at Mamma, but inclined my head ever so slightly.

Weighed down by the purple robe of state, carrying the heavy orb, suffering under the tight crown, I climbed into my carriage and rode again through streets jammed with exuberant crowds. Eight hours after I'd left Buckingham Palace, I returned, now a crowned queen.

Needing desperately to do something that felt normal, I flung off my royal robes, ran up to my royal apartments, and prepared to give my beloved Dashy a bath. I was up to my elbows in a tub of soapy water when my sister arrived.

"Your majesty," Fidi said, and dropped a low curtsy.

I leaped up and threw my wet arms around her. "Oh, Fidi!" I cried. "It was such a day! Do you think it went well? The bishops couldn't find their places, some of the gentlemen were tripping over their robes, the archbishop nearly broke my finger when he mashed the coronation ring on the wrong one. And poor Lord Rolle!"

"You couldn't see what was going on behind you," Fidi said. She imitated Lady Harriet's haughty manner as she stalked up the aisle in her role as mistress of the robes. We laughed together like naughty children. "And two of your younger maids of honor were twittering between themselves throughout the service as though they were in a drawing room. You must speak to them about their deportment."

"Yes, it's true." I sighed. "But do you think, on the whole, even with the blunders, that it went well?"

"Victoria, everyone is *so* happy with their queen! Ernst has been out in the streets since we arrived, and he tells me that people from every station are talking about you, your dignity and grace. 'Our little Vic' they call you, with great affection."

I fastened Dash's jeweled collar round his neck. "Not *everyone* is happy," I said.

"You mean Mamma? But she is so proud of you! She was moved to tears when the crown was placed on your head. This was the moment she's lived for, for so many years."

"She and Sir John. She still depends on him for everything. I've always hated him, and I always will." I released Dash, who bounded away in search of his rubber ball.

"She told me that you have exiled him and his family from everything. It pains her deeply."

I turned to my sister. "Fidi, you don't know the pain that man has caused *me*. You can't expect me to forgive him for all that he has done."

Fidi took my hand in both of hers. "No, I don't expect that. But perhaps we could both join Mamma tonight to watch the fireworks."

I agreed. On the evening of my coronation, I stood with the rest of the family on Mamma's balcony while colorful wheels and fiery fountains blazed across the sky. The Conroys were not present. But on this most glorious day of my life, my mother and I exchanged scarcely a word.

Chapter 25

SCANDAL, 1839

The coronation was over. Fidi had gone back to Germany, and her departure left a hole in my life. Lord Melbourne had begged to be excused for a fortnight. He had been required to carry the excessively heavy Sword of State at the ceremony, and the effort had apparently taken its toll. He seemed extraordinarily tired, exhausted from all the events leading up to the coronation as well as the seemingly endless ceremonies of the day itself.

For days he was absent, not only from our morning meetings and afternoon rides, but also from dinners, where I always counted on him to sit beside me and entertain me with his amusing anecdotes. When he did recover and eventually returned to my company, Lady Harriet sat to his left at dinner, as etiquette required of the mistress of the robes, chattering unstoppably and drawing his attention away from me, where it properly belonged.

Somehow my life had lost its brightness. As I thought back to a year earlier at my Proclamation, the zeal I held then for my new duties and my new life, I wondered what had happened to that joyous enthusiasm. When my dear uncle Leopold and aunt Louise came for their long awaited visit in August, I sensed that my relationship with my uncle had undergone an unmistakable change, and I did not like it.

Uncle Leopold continued to offer advice: I should devote several hours each day to my duties, receive my ministers only during certain hours, delay all decisions until the day after the matters were proposed. Useful advice, certainly, but I was now a crowned queen and I no longer needed to have even so kind a person as my uncle telling me how to conduct my affairs. Did he think that he must rule the roost everywhere? Apparently he did, and when he learned that I passed many of his letters on to my ministers—particularly Lord Melbourne—he thought ill of it and said so. How irritating!

This, then, was my mood when he brought up the subject of marriage to Prince Albert. I refused to discuss it. "I have only lately achieved my independence, and I cherish it," I told my uncle. "I'm in no hurry whatever to give it up."

Uncle Leopold tried to reason with me. "Your cousin Albert has been groomed from boyhood to be your consort. According to Baron Stockmar, Albert would like to have some indication from you of your intentions toward him. I believe he deserves that, Victoria."

"My cousin Albert will simply have to wait," I said firmly, "and you may tell him that."

My uncle was not pleased—I could see that—but I didn't care. Nothing more was said on the subject of marriage and

Albert, and after a rather unsatisfactory visit, Uncle Leopold and dear Aunt Louise returned to Belgium. I was glad to see them go.

I was often very cross. Sometimes I felt unwell, so lethargic that I did not even want to get out of bed in the morning or read one more dull report from one more boring minister. Each time I stared into the looking glass, I could not help noticing that I was growing MUCH TOO PLUMP. I voiced my complaints to my dear Lord Melbourne, but instead of the sympathy I had come to expect from him, I got some rather unwelcome advice:

"Your majesty, if I may say so," he began, "I believe that you eat too much and exercise too little. It would be good for you to drink less ale and a bit more wine. Perhaps if you were to walk more in the open air, you would find yourself invigorated."

This was not what I wished to hear. My personal physician, Dr. Clark, had made similar suggestions, which I had rejected.

"I very much dislike walking," I told Lord Melbourne peevishly. "It makes me more tired than I am already. Besides, I get stones in my shoes, and they hurt my feet."

"Perhaps the solution is a different pair of shoes, your majesty," said Lord Melbourne. "A pair of sturdy boots might do it."

I rejected this suggestion, too. "My cousin Ferdinand says that his wife, the queen of Portugal, stomps round the palace gardens in her daily exercise program, and she grows fatter than ever."

Lord Melbourne merely nodded and raised one dark eyebrow.

"And speaking of looking very fat," I went on, feeling that a change in the direction of this conversation was in order, "have you taken notice of late of Lady Flora Hastings? Her figure looks so distended that not even tightening her laces seems to help."

"I have noticed, yes. Is it fat, do you think?"

"Is there something else that one might conclude?" I asked, noticing his tone.

"Difficult to say, your majesty." That was all I could get out of him.

It was no secret that I had disliked Lady Flora since the day my mother brought her into the household as my chaperone. She no longer served in that role, but now took her place among Mamma's ladies. Lady Flora was a VERY GOOD friend of Sir John and could be counted upon to repeat to him everything she heard. Further, her sharp tongue had too often been used to belittle my dearest Daisy. Lady Flora made SUCH unkind remarks about my loyal friend, even suggesting that her aromatic caraway seeds were used to disguise an overindulgence in ale.

I observed Lady Flora closely when she next appeared at dinner, taking her accustomed place near Mamma. Surely it could not be true! Yet to my eyes her condition was unmistakable. Now what was to be done about this shocking situation?

After dinner I put the question to Daisy, "Does it appear to you that Lady Flora, an unmarried lady, is with child?"

"It does indeed," she said. "I have discussed the matter with Lady Tavistock."

"Then you had best tell me what you've heard."

Lady Tavistock, my senior lady of the bedchamber, had confided to Daisy that Lady Flora had consulted with my own Dr. Clark, claiming that she was not well. He prescribed tincture of rhubarb and other remedies for intestinal disturbances. When her condition did not improve, Lady Flora asked for a further consultation.

"But when the good doctor asked her to remove her stays and permit him to lay his hands on her abdomen, she refused to allow it," Daisy said. "And then she wept and claimed that Lady Tavistock and Lady Portman and the other court ladies were gossiping about her."

For the moment there seemed to be nothing I could do. I counted on Lady Flora admitting to her grievous wrongdoing and leaving the court. But this did not happen. Lady Flora's belly continued to grow in size. No one could possibly look at her and have any doubt that she was with child. Yet she refused to confess it. Lady Tavistock took it upon herself to discuss the matter with Lord Melbourne, who then reported to me.

"The ladies are convinced that Lady Flora is pregnant," he said, "and they insist that something must be done to protect their purity."

I well understood the importance of shielding the ladies of the court from any hint of improper conduct. For this reason, I insisted that my maids of honor be chaperoned in every sort of situation, so that there was no possibility of damage to their reputations, which would then reflect badly on mine. I had always been suspicious of the friendship between Sir John and Lady Flora. Rumors were accepted as fact that the two had traveled together unchaperoned in a post chaise when Lady Flora had gone to visit her family in Scotland at Christmas. If they had been so indiscreet then, there were undoubtedly other occasions as well.

"What must be done, Lord Melbourne?" I asked. "I've discussed the matter with Baroness Lehzen, and we too have no doubt that Lady Flora is, to use plain words, with child. We are quite sure of the horrid cause of Lady Flora's plight—that monster, Sir John Conroy."

I could not allow Lady Flora to dine with me or to be among my guests. Such a thing was impossible—surely she understood that! The situation must be resolved without delay.

Dr. Clark urged her to confess her wrongdoing. She protested her innocence and at last agreed to an intimate examination. She asked her own physician, Dr. Charles Clarke—he spelled his name with an "e"—to attend her, along with Dr. James Clark, my own physician. Both physicians agreed that no pregnancy existed. They certified that Lady Flora was a virgin.

Lady Portman, who had been present during the examination—though she kept her eyes averted—brought me the results of the doctors' examination.

"Thank God!" I cried, and I promptly sent Lady Flora a note telling her that I sincerely regretted all that had happened and asking her to call upon me. She replied that she did not feel well enough to do so at that time.

But the very next day the doctors admitted that they were still unsure. There was, in their view, a possibility that even with the evidence of their examination, Lady Flora might be carrying a child. The doctors expressed this revised opinion to Lord Melbourne, who told me. On the basis of this new opinion, I continued to believe that Lady Flora was with child, though as time passed it did appear that she might be ill.

Every effort had been made to keep the gossip within the palace walls, but that proved impossible; it seemed that all of London was talking of little else. The Hastings family was outraged. They blamed Lehzen for spreading the vile rumor. They blamed Lord Melbourne for doing nothing to prevent the slander. The press blamed the physicians for their misdiagnosis and demanded in print to know why I had not dismissed them. They blamed Lady Tavistock. They blamed Lady Portman. Most of all, they blamed me! And all because of that nasty woman, Lady Flora, whom I had never liked, not since her first days at court.

The one person who was not blamed was Mamma, who had stood loyally by Lady Flora and believed in her innocence.

My mother and I still had to appear together publicly to avoid any perception of antagonism between us. We barely spoke, and when we did, our conversation was usually filled with acrimony.

As we walked in the gardens one day in April—the affair was well into its fourth month of rumor and denial—Mamma said, "I do not understand how my own daughter could behave in such a heartless manner. Have you no compassion for the poor, sick woman who has been so badly maligned, through absolutely no fault of her own?"

"What do you mean, 'no fault of her own'?" I retorted. "What business had she to travel unchaperoned in the company of your great friend, Sir John? As I tell my ladies repeatedly, one expects a member of the court to be above the suspicion of any sort of compromised conduct."

"Once again you prefer to accept as truth the rumors spread by those who have reason to cast doubt on her virtue," Mamma snapped.

"I imagine that you refer to Baroness Lehzen," I said through clenched teeth.

Mamma kept her gaze straight ahead, her jaw rigid. "You may imagine whatever you wish, Victoria," she said bitterly. "As you like to remind me as often as you can, you are the queen of England, and I am nothing." She inclined her head slightly and swept away.

The whole sordid matter had brought back in vivid detail the memory of that moment long ago when I had glimpsed Mamma and Sir John in an embrace. I had not forgiven her. I <u>would</u> not.

I am right, I told myself, staring after her receding figure. *She is wrong and I am right.*

But my confidence was badly shaken, and I felt VERY sad. This was my LOWEST DAY since I had become queen.

Chapter 26

CANDIDATES, 1839

My bleak mood became even darker.

"I cannot abide having my mother living under my roof," I complained to Lord Melbourne. "It's like a serpent dwelling in one's house. You can't imagine the terrible scenes I've endured with her and Sir John, and I don't wish to describe them. Now she blindly insists upon the total innocence of Lady Flora! Perhaps Mamma would be willing to move to another palace," I suggested hopefully. "Back to our old apartments at Kensington, for example. That might even please her—the Conroys are still there. And if not there, somewhere close by."

"Impossible, your majesty," replied the prime minister with the arched eyebrow I had come to know so well. "As an unmarried woman, you may not properly live alone."

"I would not be living alone, Lord Melbourne," I argued—very reasonably, I thought, though I was by now quite out of sorts. "Baroness Lehzen would be with me, as she always has been.

The ladies of the bedchamber: Lady Tavistock, Lady Portman, Lady Charlemont, Lady Lansdowne"—I ticked them off on my fingers—"and all the others would be here, according to their schedules. And of course, my mistress of the robes is here whenever her children can spare her. That is hardly 'living alone.' "

"Properly, you must have a lady of equivalent rank in residence, madam."

"My mother is duchess of Kent," I insisted stubbornly. "That's scarcely equivalent in rank to the queen, though she did want her rank raised to queen mother, which of course I refused."

Lord Melbourne sighed. "There is really only one solution to the problem, my dear Queen Victoria. If you may not live unchaperoned in your unmarried state, then it follows that you must be married."

I glared at him. "That is out of the question."

Lord Melbourne shrugged. "Out of the question for now," he said. "But perhaps not for long."

I had not wanted to bring up the subject, but perhaps it couldn't be avoided, and this was as good a time as any. I drew a deep breath. "Uncle Leopold urges me to marry my cousin Albert," I said. "He writes to me, not once but several times, that it is his greatest wish."

"And what have you told him?"

"That I do not wish to marry—Albert or anyone else. Certainly not now. Perhaps not ever."

"Marriage is a very great change, a very serious thing indeed," Lord Melbourne said agreeably. "What has King Leopold responded to your statement?"

"That we should revisit the question at a later time."

"An excellent idea," said Lord Melbourne. "But perhaps that time is coming sooner than rather than later."

I truly had no desire to marry. None whatsoever! In fact, I dreaded the idea of marrying. I was so accustomed to having my own way that I could not imagine yielding to anybody. The only positively <u>good</u> thing I could see about marrying was that it would allow me to remove Mamma from my household. Having her there was <u>perfectly awful</u>! She intruded constantly, popping into my apartments when I was in the midst of VERY serious business, though I had asked her NOT to do so. But would a husband, a consort, be any <u>less</u> intrusive, really? Was there any guarantee of that?

We ended our discussion of marriage for that day. Later, when I was in a less vexatious mood, Lord Melbourne proposed, and I agreed, that we would have a calm and objective deliberation on the subject. We sat side by side at my writing table and went over a list of potential consorts.

"How does one even know if one can bear to be with a person one has never seen or spoken to?" I asked. "The queen of Portugal married my cousin Ferdinand without ever having set eyes on him."

"A serious question," he replied. "But one cannot be certain of that even if one has been acquainted with the other person for quite some time."

We pondered the name at the top of the list: *Prince Albert of Saxe-Coburg-Gotha.*

Lord Melbourne admitted that he was not a great partisan of Albert. "Cousins are not very good things," he said. "Someone from outside the family offers less chance for jealousies to arise. Besides that, Albert is a Coburg, and they are not at all well liked abroad. The Russians positively hate the Coburgs, and the English, of course, dislike all foreigners."

I was quite aware of the English attitude; my mother was also a Coburg, the sister of Albert's father, and her German-ness had made life difficult for her in England. It was nearly impossible, though, as we went down the list, to think of ANY PERSON who <u>would</u> be a "good thing." Certainly not one of those two oafish creatures from the Netherlands whom King William had favored. There were no men of appropriate rank anywhere in Europe who would do. Marrying a subject was simply out of the question, for that would make him my equal—though I could not help thinking momentarily of Alfred Paget, my excessively handsome equerry who accompanied me whenever I went out riding. He sat a horse with such easy elegance, his smile was so brilliant, his eyes the deepest shade of blue. . . .

"Everyone wants to see you married," Lord Melbourne was saying, drawing me away from thoughts of Paget's blue eyes and back to the list in front of me. "But no one can agree on who it should be. There are those who insist it should be an Englishman, and those who say it must be anyone *but* an Englishman."

I tossed aside the pen with which I had been jotting little notes as we worked our way through the field. "Then I suppose we are back to Albert," I said grudgingly. "But not yet. Not until I have seen him again. And not for several years—three or four, at a minimum. In the meantime, he needs to improve his English. I noticed certain weaknesses during his visit. And his French as well."

I was VERY definite about that, and dear Lord Melbourne quite agreed.

But that still did not solve the problem of what to do about Mamma in the meantime.

Chapter 27

CRISIS, 1839

The very thing I dreaded above all else actually came to pass. On Tuesday, the seventh of May, I received a note from Lord Melbourne; a vote had been called in Parliament on a colonial issue, and the Whigs had lost the necessary majority. Lord Melbourne was forced to step down. Dearest, kind Lord Melbourne, no more my prime minister!

Distress overwhelmed me. I was a poor, helpless girl, clinging to Lord Melbourne, as close to me as any beloved father, for protection and support. In one blow ALL, ALL my happiness was gone, my happy, peaceful life utterly destroyed. There would be no more riding out together once we had gone over the work of the day, no more of his amusing conversation at dinner, no more comfortable evenings of chess or whist. It was all finished! I could not bear it!

Dear Daisy knelt beside me and held me in her arms as she

had when I was a young child, stroking my hair and trying to comfort me. But I was inconsolable. I could not stop crying.

Late that morning after the vote was taken, Lord Melbourne came to my sitting room, seeming so very solemn and tired, as though he were in mourning. He stood with his back to the window, regarding me so sadly, and I took his dear hand in both of mine and looked up at him. "Don't forsake me!" I cried, and clung to his hand.

He gave me a look of affection and pity, and finally he managed to say, "No, never."

He led me to a chair, and we sat side by side, gazing at the pattern in the carpet as though it offered some solace. After a silence during which I strove to calm myself, Lord Melbourne said, "You must try to be as collected as you can, and act with great firmness and decision."

I nodded, still weeping, and through my tears promised that I would.

When he got up to leave, I was unable to let go of his hand, pleading, "You will come again this afternoon, will you not? And stay for dinner?"

"It would be improper for me to dine with you while the opposition is forming a new government," Lord Melbourne explained.

I began to protest the unfairness of being deprived of his company by those STUPID Tories whom I disliked so intensely, but he put a finger to his lips to quiet me. "Your majesty, I am about to advise you on an important matter, and I ask you to act on it, even though you don't like it. I suggest that you send for Sir Robert Peel, who served as prime minister when the Tories were last in power and is likely to do so again." Without allowing me to interrupt, he continued, "You may find him rigid and awkward in his manner, but I assure you, he is a very able and gifted man. You must show that you are ready to place your confidence in him and his administration." Lord Melbourne kissed my hand, said, "God bless you, madam," and left.

Oh, it seemed utterly impossible! I collapsed again in unstoppable tears.

I could neither eat nor sleep, but the following afternoon I braced myself and sent for Sir Robert Peel. He arrived in full court dress: black tailcoat, white satin waistcoat, a ceremonial sword at his side. I received him in my audience room—NOT my private sitting room where I always saw Lord Melbourne.

"I am ready to receive your majesty's commands for the formation of a new government," Sir Robert said stiffly.

I found him such an odd, cold man, so dreadfully different from the kind and warm manner of Lord Melbourne. Sir Robert seemed shy and rather embarrassed, and I felt a bit sorry for him and made an extra effort to treat him with great politeness. But there was one issue I was determined to make clear between us from the start, and that was the matter of my household. Lord Melbourne had warned me that Peel might ask me to dismiss my ladies of the bedchamber, most of whom were wives and daughters of Whigs, and to replace them with ladies whose connections were with the Tory party.

I told the man now standing uneasily before me, "I trust, Sir Robert, that none of my ladies will be removed."

Sir Robert nervously adjusted his cuffs. "I assure you that nothing will be done without your majesty's knowledge and approval," he said.

This answer did not fully satisfy me, but I nodded and said, "Very well then," and allowed him to leave.

I was determined that <u>nothing would be done</u>, period, and when Sir Robert returned I was ready to do battle, should the need arise. At first it did not. He suggested several changes in ministers, and I did not protest, though the ones he proposed were not gentlemen I regarded highly. Then he cleared his throat. "Now madam," he began, "about your ladies."

I spoke up before he could say more. "I shall not allow any of them to be taken from me."

Sir Robert appeared startled. "None of them, madam?" he asked uneasily.

"None. Not a single one."

"Your majesty, you do understand that many of your ladies are married to my opponents," he said, looking distressed.

"I know very well to whom my ladies are married, but it matters not one whit, for we never discuss politics."

"I am not asking you to replace all of your ladies—just some of the senior ladies. The duchess of Sutherland, for example, is known to be very active in Whig politics."

"The duchess of Sutherland will remain as mistress of the robes," I informed him. "I am quite familiar with English history, and I know that previous queens have not been required to change their households when there was a change in government."

"Madam, I beg your pardon, but previous queens have been the wives of kings, and you are a reigning queen."

"Irrelevant, Sir Robert," I said coolly. "My ladies stay. All of them."

He stared at me, his eyes bulging. "I respectfully suggest

that the public needs to see some sign of your confidence in the new government. Replacing a few—I repeat, *a few*—of your ladies would demonstrate your confidence and allow us to go forward."

"And I, sir, respectfully decline."

After a long silence—uncomfortable, I thought, for him, though not for me, for I knew I was in the right—Sir Robert bowed and excused himself.

I skipped gleefully to my writing table and dashed off a triumphant note to Lord Melbourne.

> *I was very calm but very decided. You would have been so pleased to see my composure! The queen of England will not submit to such trickery. If this was an attempt to see if I can be managed like a child, it has failed! Keep yourself in readiness, for you may soon be wanted.*

I sealed the letter and sent it off, confident that Lord Melbourne would applaud my firmness. But he immediately replied, sounding a note of caution.

> *It is better to negotiate than to refuse to do so. I feel I must warn you that your defense of your rights could have some very serious consequences. It may be unconstitutional.*

I did not wish to hear this, and I would not back down. "They want to treat me like a girl," I told Daisy, "but I will show them that I am queen of England."

"Absolutely right, my dear Victoria," she agreed. "Remember—far better for a queen to be thought high and decisive than to be thought weak. You must stand firm!"

When Sir Robert returned later that afternoon, nothing had changed. He again humbly requested that I give up some of my ladies. And I told him I would not.

I waited nervously to see what would happen next, and passed another night with little sleep. Early the next morning, Lord Melbourne was announced and ushered into my sitting room.

Lord Melbourne was smiling broadly. "You have carried the day, madam! Peel was unable to form a government without your support. He has resigned his commission."

"And you are once again my prime minister?" I asked.

Lord Melbourne bowed. "At your service, your majesty."

Yes, yes, yes! I had triumphed! Lord Melbourne was back in my life and at my side, much more securely than before.

I celebrated my twentieth birthday with a dinner at Windsor, followed by a ball. Among the guests was the <u>excessively</u> handsome Grand Duke Alexander of Russia, a delightful man only a little older than I. For that one evening I may have even been a little bit in love with him. Dancing the mazurka with the Grand Duke was SUCH fun! We were all so merry! I danced all night and did not get to bed until three o'clock in the morning.

My mind was once again happy. I never enjoyed myself more.

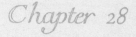

BLAME, 1839

I had demonstrated my determination to Sir Robert and to Parliament and congratulated myself on my victory. But I soon learned that my trials were far from over. As I went out driving in the park, I was greeted with stares instead of cheers and even a few rude shouts of "Mrs. Melbourne! Mrs. Melbourne!" What were they suggesting? That I had some improper relationship with my prime minister? It quite took my breath away. I learned that even Baron Stockmar had expressed disapproval of what I had done. But I had succeeded in keeping the ladies in my household, and I had dear good Lord Melbourne at my side for many hours each day. I was more determined than ever to stand firm. There would be no weakness in this quarter!

To keep up appearances, I breakfasted each morning with my mother, after which we walked out together briefly. I spoke to Mamma as little as possible, but she had not stopped speaking to me.

"I have received Sir John's letter of resignation," Mamma informed me. Her voice trembled. "Because of your cruelty and selfishness, he and his family are leaving England. I tried very hard to persuade them to stay here, but they are firm in their decision. They go first to Germany, and then on to Italy." She dabbed away tears, which I chose not to notice. "I shall miss them dreadfully."

I, on the contrary, thought this was a cause for rejoicing, though I said nothing.

"Sir John and his wife and children have been my real family for twenty years," Mamma went on. "You would not be where you are now, Victoria, were it not for that good man."

I broke my silence. "What are you saying, Mamma—that I would not be queen? How can he possibly take credit for that?" I demanded. "He and his horrid Kensington System, as he was pleased to call his attempts to bully me!" We kept on walking, eyes straight ahead, not daring to look at each other.

"He worked very hard to be sure you got the proper kind of training to prepare you for the responsibilities that are now on your shoulders. And which, from the look of things, you are still too young to handle properly," she said sharply. "You would have been better to rely on the advice of Sir John as your private secretary than on your beloved Lord Melbourne, who has allowed you to make a fool of yourself with this bedchamber business."

I refused to speak to her further, and we finished our walk in silence. By mid-June Sir John—that monster, that demon!—and all the Conroys were gone.

"Perhaps now you and your mother can heal your differences," Lord Melbourne suggested.

I was not so hopeful. "I dislike her," I told him. "That will not change."

Even after his departure, Sir John's shadow continued to haunt me in the form of Lady Flora Hastings. I unshakably believed that the two had behaved scandalously. Lady Flora was not recovered from her supposed illness, and I suspected that she might actually have been pregnant, no matter what explanation the doctors had concocted. Mamma and I were obliged to continue the empty ritual of our daily walks, and my mother used these outings as an opportunity to place the blame for Lady Flora's illness at my feet.

"Lady Flora is dying, Victoria!" Mamma insisted. "I see her every day, I spend hours by her bedside. Her fever remains very high, and she eats next to nothing. Meanwhile, Baroness Lehzen with her fine airs and rouged cheeks and your Saint Melbourne continue to spread rumor and innuendo about a pure and innocent woman who is utterly without fault." The more Mamma spoke of Lady Flora, the angrier she became. She was spitting out her words, her voice shrill. People strolling by paused to stare at us. Even Dashy, who accompanied us, looked alarmed.

"Stop it, Mamma!" I hissed. "You are an embarrassment! And it is not I, nor dearest Daisy, who has always shown me love when you have not, nor Lord Melbourne, the kindest, gentlest man in the world—none of us is responsible for Lady Flora's unfortunate condition. It is Sir John Conroy, who undoubtedly had his way with her, just as I suspect he did with you!"

Shocked, Mamma stopped in her tracks and stood still,

mouth open, eyes wide in disbelief. Dashy and I continued determinedly along the path, leaving Mamma to make her way back to the palace alone. I was shaking. I had said too much, I knew. But there was no way to take back my words. They had been left unsaid for too long.

I had planned to entertain at a ball at Buckingham Palace at the end of June, but Lord Melbourne advised me to postpone it out of consideration for Lady Flora.

"I don't believe she's so very ill," I said sourly.

"Nevertheless, it would be very awkward if she were to die," Lord Melbourne said. "There might even be a call for an inquest to determine the cause of death and to hold responsible those who denied the seriousness of her illness. The Hastings family is up in arms. They are looking for someone to blame."

"It is not my fault!" I insisted. "They can look elsewhere." But at Lord Melbourne's urging I did decide to postpone my ball. Others, however, saw no reason to delay their pleasure, and that evening I attended a ball to which I had been invited, and I enjoyed myself excessively.

A week later I received a letter from Mamma. I refused even to read her messages but passed them on to Daisy, who let me know if there was something that I absolutely had to know.

"Lady Flora is near the end," Daisy reported. "The duchess begs you to visit the dying woman."

I sighed. There was no way to avoid it. "Very well, then. I shall go."

It was terrible, very much worse than I expected. I found poor Lady Flora stretched on a couch looking as thin as anybody could, a mere skeleton, but her body very much swollen. There was a searching look in her eyes, but she spoke in a friendly manner and said she was glad to see me. "I am very grateful for all you have done for me, madam," she said, and that made me feel uncomfortable, for in truth I had done nothing at all for her.

I was most anxious to leave this upsetting situation as quickly as possible, and so I took her hand and said, "I do hope to see you again when you are better, Lady Flora."

She squeezed my hand and shook her head, as if to say, *I shall not see you again.*

And then I fled.

A week later, the fifth of July, Lady Flora was no more. The surgeon who performed a post mortem on her body found a large tumor on her liver, which is what had killed her.

He also declared that she was a virgin, though I still had my doubts. He may have said it simply as a comfort to her family.

That should have been the end of it, but it was not. The newspapers wrote about me as though I were responsible for Lady Flora's death, stating that I had gone dancing while she lay on her deathbed and railing that I should be filled with remorse but showed none. Those parts of the public who are easily led by the press added their voices of blame, claiming that it was my cruelty that caused her death. The Hastings family made clear their loathing of me. When I drove to the races at Ascot, two foolish, vulgar women in the stands loudly hissed at me. There were more shouts of "Mrs. Melbourne," making my cheeks burn with embarrassment. I could go nowhere in London without having insults hurled at me. Gentlemen did not lift their hats when I drove by, and I was told that when my health was drunk at dinners, the guests responded with silence.

The more I was hounded for my lack of remorse, the more strongly I denied any fault. But the damage had been done. My spirits, already low, sank lower. I took no pleasure in the duties that only a year or two earlier had given me such deep satisfaction. Nor did I find enjoyment in the entertainments I had always loved. I no longer cared to go out riding—my handsome equerry failed to charm me. I did not want to go anywhere or do anything. I hated even to leave my bed in the morning. Several times I shouted at poor Maggie when she was doing my hair and reduced her to tears. This went on for the weeks of summer, until finally the press and the public lost interest and turned their attention to other matters.

I had done nothing wrong! I was convinced of it!

Despite my innocence, a worm of guilt gnawed at my conscience. I was in no way the cause of Lady Flora's illness, but was it possible that I might have behaved differently toward her?

Dearest Daisy assured me, over and over, that I had acted correctly. "Lady Flora brought it all on herself by her conduct," she said. "Not her illness, of course, but the rumors and gossip. She was most indiscreet."

Dear Lord Melbourne offered a different view. "I must shoulder most of the blame for what has happened," he said. "I did not advise you as well as I should have. Much of this pain could have been avoided. But now we must take steps to get beyond it."

"What can be done?" I asked miserably. "I'm no longer their beloved little queen. All of that is gone! The world seems to me a very black place."

"Your best days are still ahead of you, Victoria," he said, choosing his words carefully. "You need to spend time with people who care deeply about you, to restore your confidence."

"And who would that be?"

I wished that Fidi were here. She would have known exactly what to say to me. She would have known it was that monster, Conroy, who was truly at the root of the trouble.

"Permit me to suggest that you invite your cousin Albert and his brother to come over for a visit, as King Leopold has been urging."

Lord Melbourne's suggestion took me by surprise. "My cousin Albert! Really, my dear Lord Melbourne, I have no wish to see Albert. The whole subject of marriage will undoubtedly come up, and I find it an odious one. I hate even having to think about it."

"Very disagreeable," Lord Melbourne said sympathetically. "A very serious question."

"I know that I said I would see him, but I'd prefer that the visit be postponed indefinitely. I am in no mood to contemplate marriage. Please, no Albert, not now—perhaps not ever."

"I understand."

"I would rather not marry at all!" I went on heatedly, thinking again of Queen Elizabeth, who had managed so successfully to avoid it.

"Now, that's a very different matter," he said.

Lord Melbourne was trying to soothe me, but I did not wish to be soothed. "Albert should understand that absolutely *no* engagement exists between us. I have made *no* promises to him, and I would not even contemplate making any sort of final promise this year. I have *great repugnance* at making such a drastic change in my life, and if marriage were even to be contemplated, it would not take place for two or three more years. I believe that was made clear."

"Quite so," said Lord Melbourne.

There the matter was left. In a letter to my uncle Leopold I laid out in great detail my reluctance to give any sort of assurance to my cousin or to anyone else. In fact, I wished the whole matter could simply be dismissed. But letters flew back and forth, the court moved to Windsor in mid-August, and despite my deep misgivings and vehement protests, plans moved forward for a visit that I would have given ANYTHING to avoid.

PART III

THE PRINCE

Chapter 29

PRINCE ALBERT, 1839

Albert and his brother, Ernest, would arrive on the tenth of October, a Thursday. I did not want them to come, and yet I did. In truth, I didn't know <u>what</u> I wanted. I felt very LOW and spoke harshly to my servants. Poor, patient Maggie again bore the brunt of my bad temper. I was cross even with Lord Melbourne when he made the mild suggestion that I might introduce a few Tories to Albert and Ernest while they visited.

"The devil take the Tories!" I cried. "There is not one I will tolerate under my roof!" I stalked out of the room, leaving Lord Melbourne looking startled and speechless.

What could have possessed me to speak so sharply to that <u>dear excellent man</u>, who was kindness and forbearance itself, and whom I loved MOST dearly!

On the morning of the tenth, I awoke feeling unwell and out of sorts. While I was out walking in an effort to clear my head, a note was delivered from Uncle Leopold; my cousins would arrive that evening. Somehow I got through the day, trying and failing NOT to think about what lay ahead. At lunch I could eat nothing, and by five o'clock I was ravenously hungry and sent for an egg and toast. When Daisy brought me the tray, I looked at the yellow yolk staring up at me and my stomach turned over.

"Then please eat the toast, Victoria," Daisy pleaded, whisking the offending egg out of my sight, "or you will be ill."

I did as she asked and felt a little better.

Maggie was waiting to help me dress and to do my hair. I had decided to wear the rose-colored silk gown sent by my dear Aunt Louise, but after studying my reflection in the looking glass I changed my mind. "The blue-striped taffeta, then," I told Maggie. Off came the rose silk, on went the striped taffeta. That did not look right either. "Perhaps the purple velvet?" I was nearly in tears. Albert and Ernest would soon be here, and I was not READY! Maybe I could send word that I had fallen ill and would see them the next day. "Oh, Maggie, I don't know what to *do*!" I cried.

"The rose silk suits you perfectly," Maggie said.

Off came the striped taffeta, on went the rose silk. My hair still needed doing.

I had been wearing my hair with two little puffs in front and a false braid like a crown on top, and I wanted something more sophisticated. Maggie suggested plaits coiled round my ears— "As Lady Harriet wears hers"—and I consented.

At twenty-five minutes past seven, Maggie fastened my pearl necklace and diamond earrings, and I drew on my long gloves and took one last anxious look at my reflection. I liked what I saw, but in any case it was too late now to change. At half past seven I stood at the top of the Grand Staircase and waited to greet my cousins. It had been three years since I'd last seen them, when I had just turned seventeen. A GREAT DEAL had happened in the past three and half years. In all that time we had not exchanged a single letter. I had not the least idea what to expect.

The Coburgs arrived, and in that instant everything changed.

Ernest looked quite pale after a stormy crossing from Brussels. Perhaps Albert did, too, but I failed to notice. All I saw as he climbed the marble staircase toward me was how BEAUTIFUL he was! Everything about him was so excessively handsome—his blue eyes, his pretty mouth, his exquisite nose, his delicate mustachios, his very slight whiskers, everything! Tall, but not too tall, and not at all fat, as I had thought on his earlier visit. He had been just a boy then, a few months shy of his seventeenth birthday, but now he was a man, with broad shoulders and a very fine waist. In those first moments there was nothing about him that did not please me. A smile spread across my face without my even trying. I could not help wondering what he thought when he had his first look at me—no longer a young girl but a woman and a queen.

The customary greetings were exchanged, but when Albert bent to kiss my hand, I felt—or imagined I felt—that his lips lingered there a bit longer than was quite necessary. I returned to my apartments while the visitors were settled in their quarters, and prepared for dinner. Lehzen was waiting for me, her eyes questioning.

"Oh, Daisy," I said breathlessly, "Prince Albert is superb! Just wait until you see him!"

A knock at the door interrupted before I could describe my

first impression, and a servant delivered a message from the princes: Their trunks had not yet arrived, and they did not have the proper clothes in which to appear at dinner. They offered apologies; their traveling clothes would not do. And so I had to wait until <u>after</u> dinner, which I thought would NEVER END, to have the chance to converse with him.

As the hours of our first evening together flew by, I discovered that Albert was clever, charming, intelligent, and thoroughly agreeable. He spoke English very well, and his French was even better than mine. The trunks had finally been delivered, and Albert's dress that evening was elegant—I particularly admired his red top-boots. He had with him a sleek and obedient black greyhound with a white muzzle called Eos, for the Greek goddess of the dawn. She never left his side and was the subject of some VERY lively conversation.

The next morning Albert played the piano in my apartments—Haydn symphonies!—and quite dazzled me with his musical ability. In the afternoon when we looked through an album of drawings together, I found his comments wonderfully acute and sensitive. After dinner that evening, we danced. Albert performed SO gracefully in the quadrilles, and I watched with a pounding heart as he waltzed with some of my married ladies. How I longed to be among them! It pleased me that on this visit Albert did not seem ready to fall asleep before the evening had scarcely begun.

I had not expected any of this. What I <u>had</u> expected was to find an amiable young man of average looks and average accomplishments. But Albert was not at all average! Albert was MAGNIFICENT!

But if Albert had changed, so had I. In a matter of weeks,

it seemed, I had become a completely different person. Where was that drab, unhappy girl of the past summer who had gone about sleepless and complaining, weeping and shouting, seeing the world as a dark and dismal place? She was gone! Gone forever!

After only one day, I was enchanted. Skerrett assembled a series of costumes for me, depending on what plans I might be making for the entertainment of my VERY delightful guest; Ernest had receded quietly into the background, and I had nearly forgotten about him. Albert and I walked together in the palace gardens, completely unconcerned that it was raining hard—a downpour—though the ladies trailing after us looked far from happy.

On Saturday we went out riding. I had acquired a new horse, a delightful creature called Tartar, dark brown and full of spirit with a springy, charming canter, and I thought Albert would enjoy riding him. For my own mount I took the pretty little chestnut mare, Taglioni, that I had won on a bet at Ascot with poor old King William. The rains had stopped, but the roads around Windsor were so deep in mud that my riding skirt was soon caked with it and Albert managed to get splattered all over. How we did laugh! I pulled my mare up close to Tartar and used my handkerchief to dab a bit of mud from Albert's dear face, gazing into his eyes as I did and feeling an almost overwhelming desire to kiss his sweet mouth. I knew that he was struggling with the same feelings. But we drew apart and continued our ride, arriving back at the stables sodden and looking utterly disreputable.

Mamma hosted another dinner, for which I wore the blue-striped taffeta, assured by Maggie that it was excessively complimentary to my figure. Dinner was followed by a game of whist and a great deal of conversation that would have seemed dull had I not been watching Albert so closely—he had such elegant manners!—and listening to every word. He spoke BEAUTIFUL English with only a slight German accent, which was SO delightful to my ear.

On Sunday everyone attended services at St. George's Chapel. I sat near dearest Albert, who enjoyed the music excessively. My uncle Leopold would have been proud to note that at the luncheon afterwards, I ate sparingly. Dearest Albert sat far down the table next to the old king's sister and two of his brothers, the dukes of Sussex and Cumberland, and I seemed to have lost my usual appetite, preoccupied as I was with stealing glances in Albert's direction.

In the afternoon we took our dogs, Albert's glorious greyhound, Eos, and my dearest Dashy, out for a run in the park. When we returned to the castle, Albert sat again at my piano and began to play some very pretty but rather melancholy music by Frédéric Chopin. This set the mood for a very DEEP conversation about the parents missing from our lives—his mother, who had deserted the family for a lover, an army lieutenant, when Albert was just five, and my father, who had died before I ever knew him. This led me to speak of my loathing for Sir John Conroy, but I stopped short of confessing my strained relationship with my own mother. We talked in hushed voices, leaning close, our hands not quite touching except occasionally by accident.

Dearest Daisy peered in, cleared her throat, and reminded us that it was time to dress for dinner. Albert rose and, smiling, told me that he and Ernest had been invited to go out shooting the next day at nearby Frogmore. I struggled to hide my disappointment at not seeing him for the entire day, but once accustomed to the idea, I decided to take dearest Albert's temporary absence as an opportunity to pour out my feelings to Lord Melbourne. Albert and I had spent just three days together, but I had no doubts whatsoever about what I wanted.

I wanted dearest Albert.

"I see that you have indeed come to a decision," said my prime minister before I had spoken a word. "But I would advise you to take a week to make up your mind finally."

"A week! I can't wait that long. My mind is already made up." I put my hands to my face—my cheeks were burning. "I love him, and I want to marry him."

"Ah," said Lord Melbourne, "that's a very good thing." He was as calm as though I had just told him I had chosen a new horse for my stables. "You'll be much more comfortable, I think. A woman cannot stand alone for long. You have made a very good choice. But when are you thinking of the marriage taking place?"

"A year?" I suggested tentatively, for that did seem like a VERY long time.

"Sooner than that, I think." He was so kind, so fatherly!

"Oh, yes! Much sooner! As soon as possible, then!" I twirled around giddily, unable to contain my happiness.

"Then you must tell the prince of your decision," Lord Melbourne advised.

"How do I do that?" I asked, suddenly serious. "In general such things are done the other way, aren't they? It's the man who proposes, but dearest Albert would never presume to propose to the queen of England."

Lord Melbourne merely laughed and said, "Just do it."

"Very well, I shall!" I cried, and I could not help throwing my arms round my dear old friend and kissing his cheek, though it was no doubt HIGHLY improper to embrace one's prime minister.

PROMISES, 1839

Albert and his brother returned from their day at Frogmore for dinner on Monday, but we had only a little time alone that evening. The whole company seemed involved in playing jackstraws—the straws were made of ivory—and Albert and Ernest both proved VERY dexterous. Knowing what I was about to do the next day, I was unusually clumsy. When we said our goodnights, dearest Albert gazed deeply into my eyes and squeezed my hand, and that gave me confidence that all would go well. Nevertheless, I slept scarcely at all.

Tuesday morning, after I had taken care of a few items of official business, I sent Albert a note, asking him to come at noon to the little room we called the Blue Closet. Maggie and I spent an hour trying on various dresses—I settled on one of palest pink—and doing my hair. I decided against wearing any jewelry but pearl earrings. I longed to tell her what was about to happen, but of course could not, though she may have guessed.

Maggie disappeared, and at precisely noon Albert was standing in the doorway. I was sure he knew why I had sent for him, but that made it no easier. We were BOTH so nervous, we were trembling!

Though all of our earlier conversations had been in English, we now spoke in German of the MOST inconsequential things. My heart was beating wildly, and I wondered if Albert could hear it. My mouth was so dry I could hardly say a word. Finally, though, I drew a breath and plunged ahead, speaking in English. "Dearest Albert," I said, barely above a whisper, "it would make me *too* happy if you would consent—"

He did not let me finish. He seized my hands in both of his and kissed my fingertips. "My dearest Victoria, there is nothing more I could wish than to spend the rest of my life with you!"

And then we were in each other's arms, embracing, laughing, kissing, weeping, and kissing again. Oh, to feel as I felt at that moment, loved by such an angel! Albert was SUCH perfection, perfect in every way. How I adored him! We embraced over and over again, and I knew with all certainty that this was the happiest, brightest moment of my life. It would be MADNESS to wait a year! If I could have married him that day, I would have, without question.

We parted then for an hour or two to dress for dinner, and naturally I flew to dearest Daisy and told her my DELICIOUS news. There were more tears of joy. When I recalled how wretched I had felt only a few weeks earlier—only a few DAYS earlier—I could scarcely believe this new happiness. But I pledged her to secrecy.

"I shall write to Uncle Leopold and inform Baron Stockmar,

but no one else is to know," I told her. "Not even Mamma, who as we know is unable ever to keep a secret."

Daisy embraced me and gave me her word, and we went down to dinner. Of course, she no longer held my hand, but on this MOMENTOUS day I reached for hers.

I could hardly bear to sit through several courses and the conversation afterward when my heart was bursting with joy. There was dearest Albert, handsomer than ever in the Windsor uniform. Each time our eyes met, we could not prevent ourselves from smiling broadly. Our secret must have been obvious to everybody.

"Please, dearest love," I said when the evening finally ended and we had escaped to the privacy of my apartments, "it would mean so much if I could have a little of your dear hair."

"Then you must find scissors and cut off whatever lock pleases you," dearest Albert said, laughing.

I called for Maggie, who supplied the scissors along with a bit of advice: "Cut from a place just behind the ear, not from the front," she said, trying to suppress a smile.

I did as she advised, but when Albert inspected the results, he did say he might not hire me as his barber.

After many ardent kisses we said good night and parted VERY reluctantly. Maggie had just finished helping me into my nightclothes when a letter was delivered. I broke the seal and read:

Dearest greatly beloved Victoria, how can it be that I have come to deserve so much love, so much affection? I believe with all my heart that

Heaven has sent me an angel whose brightness shall illumine my life.

My eyes swept down the page. There was more, and then the last line: "In body and soul ever your slave, your loyal ALBERT."

I read it again and burst into tears. Dear good Maggie, understanding everything without my saying a word, wrapped me in her strong arms. "I pray that your majesty will have every happiness," she murmured, "as I have with my Simon."

The next weeks were deliciously happy. I gave dearest Albert a little ring with the date engraved, 15th October 1839, a date that would be ever dear to me, and he gave me a little ring that matched it. We decided that we would marry on the tenth of February in the coming year.

In order to have two months at home in Coburg, dearest Albert planned to leave England with his brother on the fourteenth of November. As I had counted the days with dread before his arrival, now I counted the days until his departure, determined to savor each one. We spent every possible hour together, talking and talking—I had never imagined there would be so much to talk about with a future husband! He stayed with me while I attended to the stream of papers that never stopped appearing on my desk. We walked together and rode together, played piano duets and sang together. I could hardly wait to be alone with Albert, to kiss his sweet mouth again and again, to whisper my passionate love for him. I understood now what Maggie had told me so long ago when I'd begged her to describe to me what it was like to be in love, for I'd had no idea of it then. I remembered her words:

'Tis the most wonderful feeling! When my Simon holds me in his arms and kisses me, I think I'm going to melt—just like butter.

That was exactly how I felt when Albert kissed me, that I was going to melt—just like butter.

I wrote to dear Uncle Leopold: "I love him more than I can say. The days pass like a dream, and I am so much bewildered that I scarcely know how to write. I do feel <u>very very</u> happy."

It must have been evident to everyone that I was deeply, rapturously, in love. But it was not until a few days before dearest Albert was to leave for Germany that I finally went to Mamma's apartments to give her the news. She was seated at her desk, writing a letter—to Sir John, no doubt—and she glanced up, surprised to see me. Though we met daily in public, it was rare for me to visit her, and I had forbidden her to appear in my apartments without an invitation, which was equally rare.

"Dear Victoria, how good to see you here," she said, rising to greet me with a wary smile.

"Mamma, I've come to give you good news. I'm sure you will be very happy to learn that I intend to marry Prince Albert."

Mamma's smile warmed. "Oh, my dearest Vic!" she cried, tears springing to her eyes, and she reached out to embrace me. "Albert is such a dear, dear boy, and I know he will make you very happy." Then she held me at arm's length and said sharply, "But it was very ill of you not to tell me until now. The servants have been gossiping about it for weeks."

I felt my face flush at her reprimand. Perhaps she was right—it <u>was</u> ill of me. "We will be married three months from today," I said.

This was not the time to remind Mamma that she should begin making definite plans to move out of Buckingham Palace and to establish a home for herself elsewhere. That discussion would have to come later. It was sure to be unpleasant, and I could not bear any unpleasantness now. As soon as I could break away, I hurried off in search of dearest Albert.

One delicious night just before my darling was to leave for Germany, I held a ball in honor of my two cousins—I had seen scarcely anything of Ernest—and Albert taught me to waltz. Due to my station, I had never been permitted to dance encircled in a man's arms, but now that everyone knew we were to be married, no eyebrows would be raised by any but the oldest and most conservative ladies of the court. When the band struck up a tune in three-quarter time, Albert and I danced together, my first public waltz and my last dance as an <u>unmarried girl</u>.

I hated our parting. It would be a VERY long three months until I would see my beloved again. I thought I could not bear it, I felt SO wretched, but dearest Albert consoled me and kissed me <u>so</u> tenderly that I shed tears but did not break down in sobs as I so often had at partings. I loved him so ardently, so intensely, and I knew he loved me just as passionately and devotedly, and that he would return, and from that day on my life would be perfection.

Then he was gone, almost like in a dream, and in the meanwhile, there was much to be done in preparation for the wedding. Soon after he departed, he wrote from Calais:

I need not tell you that since we left all my thoughts have been with you. Your image fills my whole soul. Our days together flew by so quickly, but our separation will fly equally so.

A few days later I read these words:

Dearly beloved Victoria, I long to talk to you. Your dear picture stands on my table, and I can hardly take my eyes off it.

And this:

Love of you fills my heart. Where love is, there is happiness. Even in my dreams I never imagined I should find so much love on earth. My greatest wish is to walk through life, with all its joys and all its storms, with you, my dearest, at my side.

His letters, arriving almost daily, sustained me. I kissed the pages, danced off to share a line or two with dearest Daisy, and put the letters in a box by my pillow, to read and to kiss again and again.

Trouble, 1840

A week after bidding good-bye to dearest Albert at Windsor, I rode up to London to present a formal declaration of marriage to my Privy Council. I did not need Lord Melbourne's assistance in writing this speech; I felt perfectly capable of doing it myself. I could not stop my hands from trembling and the paper from shaking—it was rather an awful moment—but my voice was firm and did not betray my nervousness.

What would I have done without the advice of dearest Daisy? She agreed with me that the wedding should be held at Buckingham Palace and not at Westminster Abbey, where it would seem like a second coronation. I made list after list, deciding on which young ladies should attend me and who was to be invited to the ceremony and to the wedding breakfast—lists with many additions and crossings-out. But I was VERY firm and unwavering about one thing: <u>no Tories to be invited.</u>

In January, my household left Windsor and moved back to London. Buckingham Palace had been newly painted and gilded, and pretty flowered chintz curtains and furniture brought in. *This is where my dearest Albert and I shall live,* I thought, and I could not help smiling.

But my pleasure was soon blighted by the wretched Tories. In mid-January I opened Parliament and read a speech to the House of Lords. I was less nervous than I had ever been and thought it went well. Then, within a week, arguments had begun about the size of dearest Albert's household and his allowance. I had assumed that Parliament would provide my future husband with the annual sum of fifty thousand pounds, the same amount my uncle Leopold was promised when he married poor Princess Charlotte. But the despicable Tories claimed that the country was TOO POOR to provide my consort with so much. Even that nasty wretch, Sir Robert Peel, stood up and opposed it. They decided that <u>thirty thousand</u> was enough for Prince Albert!

Naturally, I was furious, and so was dearest Albert. "Those nice Tories have cut my income nearly in half," he wrote to me. "It is inconceivable that they could behave so insultingly to you and to me. I have little respect for them, and everyone here in Coburg is indignant at my treatment."

Making me even angrier was the suggestion by some in Parliament that Prince Albert might possibly have Roman Catholic leanings. As queen, I was forbidden to marry any but a Protestant. The duke of Wellington made quite an issue of it and was among those who opposed giving dearest Albert the fifty thousand pounds he deserved. Everyone fawned over him for his defeat of Napoleon at Waterloo, but I did not, for he was a wicked Tory. He said that the people deserved to know more about the German prince and be absolutely sure that he was a Protestant!

I vowed that I would not speak to the foolish old duke EVER AGAIN, and when I heard that he had fallen ill, I refused to visit him or even send a message.

"I beg you to reconsider, your majesty," said Lord Melbourne. "You must not be disrespectful to the duke, Tory or not. Wellington is considered a national hero. I suggest that you immediately send him a note to wish him well."

Reluctantly, I scribbled the note and dispatched it, telling Lord Melbourne, "I have done this as you requested, but I will *not* invite him to my wedding. It is *my* marriage, and I will have only those who are sympathetic to me and to Albert."

My contempt for the Tories deepened further over the matter of precedence for dearest Albert. I wanted to have him named king consort, but if that were not immediately possible, then certainly he should be given precedence over everyone except myself—meaning that, in any state procession, Albert should walk ahead of the royal dukes, my uncles.

When the Tories objected, I flew into a fury. "What monsters! They are scoundrels, capable of every villainy!" I raged while Lord Melbourne stood by, waiting for my anger to burn itself out. "Poor dear Albert, how cruelly they are ill-using him. Those Tories shall be punished! I shall have my revenge!"

Lord Melbourne, trying to calm me, managed to put his foot in his mouth in every way possible. He suggested that foreigners had always been a source of difficulties, and that remark made me crosser than ever.

Then, to my great surprise, the duke of Wellington reversed himself. Deciding that I had a perfect right to grant my husband whatever precedence I pleased, he persuaded others to concur. I got over my temper and decided that Wellington should receive an invitation to the wedding after all. But not to the wedding breakfast—that was simply asking too much.

Unsurprisingly, Mamma behaved badly too, complaining to any who would listen that her ungrateful daughter was threatening to order her out of her apartments in Buckingham Palace. Perhaps I should have had that conversation with her when I told her of my marriage. The matter might well have been settled.

These were trying times, but I had certainly not expected dearest Albert to make matters worse. Imagine, then, my chagrin when I received a letter from that very best of men stating that he wished to appoint the members of his household to include some Germans. And there was more to come.

"Also," he wrote, "it is very necessary that members of my household should be chosen from both sides, an equal number of Whigs and Tories." It was wrong, he said, for the Crown to favor one party over the other, and he planned to demonstrate that he favored neither.

I was shocked nearly speechless. Dear Daisy happened by as I was reading dearest Albert's letter for the second time. "I cannot imagine where he gets these ideas!" I sputtered, and waved the letter at her. "Read it and you will see why I am so upset!"

Daisy took the letter from me, read it slowly, and returned it. "How do you intend to respond, Victoria?" she asked.

"With great firmness," I said. "I do not intend to let my future husband and consort harbor the notion that he can simply do as he pleases when what he pleases is directly contrary to my wishes."

"Quite right," Daisy replied. "You must make that very clear to him from the start. You are the queen."

"That's right," I agreed. "I am the queen."

I wrote back immediately.

> *That will not do at all, my dear Albert. You may entirely rely upon me that the people around you will be of high standing and good character. Lord Melbourne has already mentioned several to me who are very suitable.*

I believed that I had put my case reasonably enough, and I considered the matter settled. To my consternation, dearest Albert did NOT agree. In fact, he disagreed quite forcefully.

> *I am very sorry that you have not been able to grant my first request, which I know was not an unfair one. Think of my position, dear Victoria: I am leaving my home and my friends and going to a country where everything is new and strange to me. I have no one to confide in but you. Can you not concede to me that the two or three persons in charge of*

my private affairs should be those I already know and trust?

I called for Daisy and showed her the latest letter on the subject. "What a stubborn man!" I exclaimed. "I had not expected to be challenged!"

Daisy smiled. "I have known you for a very long time, Victoria," she said. "I have complete confidence that you have an equal measure of stubbornness in your character."

"But I am right!" I insisted. "It has nothing to do with stubbornness. It has to do with the simple fact that I am right and Albert is wrong."

I sent off my reply.

My dearest and most excellent Albert, I fear you do not like it, but I am insisting upon this for your own good

Then Uncle Leopold interfered, taking Albert's part, which I refused to accept.

Back and forth our letters flew. I had expected letters expressing Albert's love and devotion, and though I received those as well and treasured them, I was stunned at his show of obstinacy. Why could Albert not see that Lord Melbourne and I knew best in this situation? I did yield to a small degree and allow the appointment of one German to a minor post, but I felt I was doing absolutely the correct thing when I prevailed upon dearest Albert to accept Lord Melbourne's private secretary, George Anson, as his own. At first Albert resisted—more of that German stubbornness! Finally he yielded, on the condition that Anson first resign his position with Lord Melbourne, and at last that matter was settled.

The days passed slowly, tediously—Christmas, the New Year, then the bleak days of January. I tried to hold on to the happiness that had once filled my heart to bursting but now felt cold and shriveled. *I love him*, I told myself. *My dearest Albert loves me. All will be well, all will be perfect.*

But in the meantime I was feeling quite <u>unwell</u>. My head throbbed, and again I suffered from sleeplessness. I wept to dearest Daisy, "Oh, my dear Albert is so unbending! He does not see that I know best in these matters. My advice must be taken, or he will be perceived as a foreigner, another German bringing his German friends with him, just as Lord Melbourne warned me."

"Ah, yes," Daisy said sympathetically. "I understand how Prince Albert feels. I have felt myself to be a foreigner here as well, and it is a difficult thing. But you are right, dear Victoria, you *do* know best, and you have Lord Melbourne to guide you. The prince must be grateful for that."

"But what if he's not?" I cried. "What if he's simply resentful?"

"Then he must get over it," Daisy said forcefully, "and you must remain firm."

WEDDING, 1840

It was SUCH a trying time! On the one hand I was caught up in the delightful duty of preparing for my wedding, enduring the final fitting of my gown, deciding on the dresses to be worn by my maids of honor, choosing the dishes to be served at the wedding breakfast. With Skerrett's help I ordered a number of new dresses and bonnets and gloves and riding clothes, in addition to silk stockings and underthings and the nightgown I would wear on my wedding night. It was all VERY time-consuming and would have been amusing as well if I had not begun to harbor many misgivings about marriage in general. Perhaps Queen Elizabeth had been right. How would she have handled a bridegroom who insisted on having his own way? No differently, I was certain. Elizabeth was never weak.

But what about dearest Albert? Who is this man I am about to marry?

On the seventh of February I received word that my dearest Albert and his family had arrived at Dover and that all of them, but Albert especially, were suffering the ill effects of a rough crossing. Our wedding was to take place in three days, scarcely giving us time to become reacquainted, and my nerves were on edge.

Lord Melbourne, in our last private meeting before my marriage, tried to reassure me. "It's right to marry, it's most natural. Difficulties may arise, but they arise from everything."

And what if those difficulties cannot be overcome?

The next day at four o'clock, I waited anxiously at the door of Buckingham Palace to welcome my future husband. The moment I saw my beloved Albert's <u>dear, dear</u> face, all my doubts and worries were immediately put to rest. We embraced again and again, and as soon as dearest Albert had settled into his rooms, we began to talk over the particulars of our wedding day.

We also argued just a little, but very lovingly, about his insistence that the mothers of my trainbearers must be of impeccable character. Not just the girls themselves—that went without saying—but their mothers as well! This seemed to me to be overly strict. "I think one ought always to be indulgent toward other people," I told him. "If we hadn't been well brought up, we might also have gone astray."

Then we kissed, and kissed again, and joyfully counted the hours that remained until we would become man and wife in the eyes of God. Oh, I was so very, VERY happy!

Sunday evening was my last as an unmarried woman. Mamma did not think it proper to have an engaged couple stay the night in the same dwelling, but I reminded her that my "dwelling" had

750 rooms, and besides, the rule was foolish nonsense. Beloved Albert and I went over the marriage ceremony together and tried on the ring to be sure it fit. And he gave me a magnificent sapphire brooch as a wedding present.

When I lay down on my bed that night after some VERY long and heartfelt prayers, I thought, *For the very last time I shall sleep alone. Tomorrow my dearest, most beloved Albert will sleep by my side,* and drifted off to sleep.

I awoke in fine spirits on my wedding day, Monday, the tenth of February, to find that we had been blessed with thoroughly unpleasant weather—cold wind and lashing rain. While still in my dressing gown I dashed off a note to dear Albert: "Send word when you, my dearest loved bridegroom, will be ready."

Mamma came to my apartments with a lovely posy of orange blossoms, and we breakfasted together for the last time. I was not in the least unhappy about that, but Mamma seemed a bit tearful. Our conversation concerned, as always, only the most trivial of subjects—if the rain would stop before the ceremony, whether the trainbearers' dresses were sufficiently modest. Then abruptly my mother leaned close and took my hand. "My dear Victoria," she whispered, avoiding my eyes, "perhaps we should discuss what you may expect on your wedding night."

"Not at all necessary, Mamma," I told her briskly. "I have already spoken to the duchess of Sutherland on the subject, and she has told me *exactly* what to expect."

Mamma got the injured look she wore so often and said, "I would have thought that conversation might best be had between mother and daughter."

"Lady Harriet has borne seven children, Mamma. I think you may be assured that I have been correctly informed."

Lady Harriet had shown no reluctance whatsoever in her discussion of the subject. "I shall tell you what I plan to tell my own daughters when they are about to marry," she'd said, and proceeded to describe the differences between male and female anatomy, the function of these specific parts, and precisely how the joining of these parts was best facilitated.

"You may rest assured," Lady Harriet had continued, "that Baron Stockmar has instructed Prince Albert more than adequately. Stockmar was educated as a physician. You have nothing whatever to fear. But perhaps you have questions? You may speak freely and openly to me."

I hesitated. I did not tell Lady Harriet that I wasn't in the least fearful and in fact looked forward EAGERLY to the hour when my body would be joined with Albert's as passionately and as rapturously as our hearts, but I <u>was</u> fearful of the results of that passion: the possibility of conceiving a child. I thought of every horror I had ever heard of a young woman dying in childbirth, as Uncle Leopold's first wife, Princess Charlotte, had, and of the many babies born who had died very young, as Queen Adelaide's had, and Aunt Louise's too.

"I do have a question," I told Lady Harriet, who leaned forward eagerly. Shyly and with several false starts I asked, "Is there a way to prevent conceiving a child?"

Lady Harriet drew back, shocked and frowning. "My dear Victoria, please banish such thoughts from your mind," she ordered sternly. "People of quality do not resort to such measures, which most Christians regard as sinful and in violation of God's will. And you must remember that it is your duty to provide the nation with an heir."

My face grew hot with shame. "I only meant to delay conception for a time. A year at most."

"Impossible," she said and rose abruptly. "I beg your pardon, your majesty," she said, refusing to look me in the eye. "I fear that I can be of no further help to you." She fairly fled from my presence.

I sighed. There was no one else to ask—certainly not Mamma. Perhaps dearest Albert had raised the subject with Baron Stockmar. I did hope it was something we could discuss.

After my mother had gone, Maggie began doing my hair, brushing it smooth and looping it over my ears. When she had finished, I simply could not resist running to Albert's room to see him for the last time alone, as my bridegroom and not yet my husband. He seemed rather shocked to find that I had once again broken with tradition, but nevertheless was SO HAPPY to see me. We embraced and kissed and could scarcely bear to be parted, even for a little while.

Back in my dressing room, Skerrett and the maids were ready to begin: the corset laced up the back over my embroidered chemise, the white silk stockings fastened above the knee with garters, the layers of petticoats, and finally the rich white satin wedding gown with a very deep flounce of lace. A white wedding gown was not the custom, but I remembered that Mamma had always dressed me in white for my public appearances as a child. Though I disliked many of the habits my mother inflicted on me when I was too young to protest, I had grown to believe that a white gown set me apart as queen. Maggie checked my hair, fastened on the wreath of orange blossoms, and arranged the lace veil. Dearest Daisy carefully added the diamond necklace and earrings and the sapphire and diamond brooch, the deep blue stone the only note of color.

The wind had stopped, the rain had ceased, and the sun was

peeping hopefully through a scattering of fleecy clouds when I climbed into my carriage shortly after noon. With me were Mamma and Lady Harriet, who said she would not have missed this for the world but still avoided my eye. We were driven to St. James's. I had not been granted my wish to have the wedding at Buckingham Palace. Lord Melbourne had persuaded me that the chapel royal was more appropriate, shrewdly guessing that I had wanted a smaller chamber only in order to accommodate fewer guests—nearly all of them Whigs.

Crowds had turned out for my wedding day, though perhaps not so many as had jammed the streets around the palace for my coronation. I waved and smiled and they rewarded me with cheers.

My twelve young trainbearers, dressed in white with white roses and looking very pretty, waited nervously in the Queen's Closet. There was a flourish of trumpets, and then the organ began to play as my procession entered the chapel. Three hundred people (only the merest handful of them Tories!) were gathered to wish me well.

Lord Melbourne carried the Sword of State—he handled it much more deftly than he had at my coronation—and Uncle Sussex escorted me to the altar. All proceeded without mishap, except for the trainbearers who were continually tripping over their own feet. Dearest Albert waited at the altar. Dressed in the uniform of a British field marshal with scarlet jacket and white breeches and stockings, he looked SO handsome, SO dashing! Though I was trembling when I first entered, I now felt very calm and spoke my vows in a clear voice.

As I left the chapel on dearest Albert's arm, I did notice that Mamma looked disconsolate and distressed. Could she not manage to look happy for me on this, the most glorious day of my life? I shook her hand, but I stopped to kiss the powdery cheek of my dear aunt Adelaide before we proceeded to my carriage for the short journey to Buckingham Palace.

Dearest Albert and I had only half an hour to be alone together before we were to appear at our wedding breakfast. We were very quiet, simply gazing at each other, our hearts and minds at ease. I gave my darling a wedding ring, slipping it on his finger, whispering yet again my deep love for him.

"Victoria, my dearest wife, let us pledge today that there will never be a secret we do not share," Albert said in a voice rough with emotion, and I agreed, and we kissed and kissed until my husband had to remind me, "Dearest love, we really must go down to join our guests."

We celebrated our marriage with the most elegant breakfast my cooks could devise. The centerpiece was a magnificent wedding cake that measured three yards around and required four men to carry. I was content with a few bites of cake and a small glass of wine. My desire was not for food or drink—it was to be alone without interruption with my beloved Albert.

After the breakfast I changed into my traveling dress, white silk trimmed with swansdown, and Albert came up to fetch me downstairs. We took leave of Mamma, this time with an embrace that was perhaps warmer than either my mother or I had expected, and at four o'clock we drove off. Albert and I alone, and SO delightful! We did not have a grand new coach but a rather plain one, with just three other coaches and a few post horses following. Darkness had already fallen, but the crowds that turned out along the roads to cheer for us were so great that we did not reach Windsor until eight o'clock.

We changed our clothes again—dearest Albert dressed in his Windsor uniform—and had a simple dinner in our sitting room. The servants were VERY discreet and disappeared until dearest Albert rang for them. I was nearly ill with a headache, no doubt the result of the strains of the past few days, and could eat nothing but had to lie down on the sofa after the meal had been cleared away. I NEVER, NEVER spent such an evening! MY DEAREST DEAREST Albert sat on a footstool by my side, and his excessive devotion and affection gave me feelings of love and happiness I had never even hoped to have. He clasped me in his arms, and we kissed each other again and again. His beauty, his sweetness and gentleness—really, how can I ever be thankful enough to have such a <u>husband</u>? To be called by names of such tenderness I had never heard before was bliss beyond belief. Oh, this was the happiest day of my life!

And so began our life together.

MARRIAGE, 1840

Our very first real argument burst like a summer storm on the day after our wedding. We rose early, my headache completely gone. At breakfast dearest Albert insisted on opening my boiled egg for me, tapping the shell delicately with the same skillful hands that had touched me so delicately the night before. NEVER had an egg tasted SO delicious! We made plans to go walking after lunch, and my beloved Albert played the piano in his room while I sent off invitations to a few people for dinner that evening. When I'd finished, I joined him, sitting down beside him cozily.

"It's the usual custom, is it not, for newly married people to stay four to six weeks away from society?" dearest Albert asked, in a tone suggesting that was how it should be for us as well. "To become better acquainted and to settle into their new lives," he went on.

"That is impossible, my love," I said. "We aren't like other people." I began paging through some piano duets and propped Schubert's "Serenade" on the music rack. "Here, shall we try this, darling?"

"We can try it once we've finished this discussion," he said and closed the music book. "I think we should stay here at Windsor for a fortnight at least, Victoria."

"Three days, dearest Albert," I told him firmly, reaching out to caress the cheek of this most excellent man. "You forget, my dearest love, that I am the sovereign and that the business of the country can stop and wait for nothing."

"Victoria, I do not forget for a single moment that you are the sovereign. But perhaps you have forgotten that I am the husband, and that I should have a say in this. In my opinion, we need more time together, alone, at least a week without Lord Melbourne and Baroness Lehzen—"

"I don't think you understand the matter, my love," I interrupted, perhaps a bit too forcefully. "It has nothing to do with Lord Melbourne or dearest Daisy. Parliament is sitting, and something occurs almost every day for which my attention is required. It's quite impossible for me to be absent from London for a week, let alone a fortnight. Three days is a long enough time to be away from my duties."

"All right, three days. You are already inviting people for dinner for one of them and have planned a ball for another. Could we not have it just we two, tête-à-tête?"

"Dearest, it's only ten people, very delightful, a nice little party! The ball is larger, it's true, but it will be *such* fun, my first ball as an old married lady! Oh, tell me you're not going to be a *stick* and fall asleep just as everyone is feeling so merry!"

My husband looked at me wearily. "Very well, then—as you wish, Victoria."

He <u>did</u> seem tired. I felt sure this little gathering for dinner would brighten him up, but when he disappeared sometime after midnight, I went upstairs and found him fast asleep. The next night, after the ball, was the same. Still, I was <u>so</u> happy to lie beside him and gaze at him as he slept in only his shirt, his face so pure and angelic, his bare throat so beautiful, so perfect, that I could not resist kissing it until he awoke and drew me close. It did seem that our bodies were made for each other. Lady Harriet's description had been accurate as far as it had gone, but now I understood <u>exactly</u> what Maggie meant about "melting, just like butter."

On the third day I organized another ball and danced a lively galop with my husband, and on the fourth day we returned to our apartments at Buckingham Palace, where my darling would have his own rooms next to mine, and my dear little bed had been replaced by one that was VERY large and VERY grand.

The nights—oh, those blissful nights! They were far too short, and the VERY, VERY happy days seemed to <u>fly</u> by. I was SO much in love with my husband, and I knew that he was in love with me. There was never quite enough time to spend walking with him in the palace gardens, with his greyhound, Eos, stepping primly by his side and my little Dashy literally <u>dashing</u> in every direction. Dearest Albert tried to teach me the names of every growing thing and demanded a kiss when I could not remember them—my memory became remarkably poor! He often took my hand in public, which made me blush with pleasure. When we were alone, it was dearest Albert who undid my laces and rolled down my stockings, Albert who removed the pins from my hair and let it fall over my bare shoulders. I teased him that I now had an official <u>undresser</u>.

I had always known that we had differences. But I soon began to discover just how MANY differences and how strong those differences were. My dearest Albert was not at all fond of dinners and balls and concerts that lasted far into the night, after which I loved to step out onto the portico of the palace as the sun rose behind St. Paul's Cathedral. Albert much preferred quiet evenings of reading and music, game after game of chess, and early bedtimes. I enjoyed the city; Albert felt more at home at countrified Windsor than he did in lively London. His interest in the natural world greatly exceeded mine.

There were other, far more serious differences. I had made up my mind not to involve my husband in political matters—perhaps this was owing to the suffering I had endured at the hands of Sir John—and I made it a point always to meet with Lord Melbourne alone. I refused to discuss affairs of state with dearest Albert, and I became irritated when he presumed to offer advice or to do anything that suggested to me he might consider himself my co-ruler and entitled to share my authority.

"I have learned from my brother that Queen Maria da Gloria of Portugal has made your cousin Ferdinand her king consort," Albert informed me stiffly. "He determines which visitors may see her, and then they may do nothing more than kiss her hand. He takes over from there."

"The English are not at all like the Portuguese," I explained patiently. "My people are very jealous of any foreigner who interferes in their government."

We argued—again. I lost my temper—again. I rushed weeping to dearest Daisy.

"Of course you are *quite* right, my dear Victoria," she said, as I expected she would. "You are the sovereign, and your husband is simply your husband, nothing more. The prince must learn this. But perhaps you are not handling his missteps in the best possible way." When I was calmer, she continued, "If my memory is correct, even as a little girl you were given to outbursts of temper. Do you remember your Good Behavior Book?"

"You made me write in that book every time I threw a tantrum or stamped my foot or spoke impertinently," I said with a rueful smile. "Are you suggesting that I need a Good Behavior Book now?"

"No, I'm not recommending that. But I *am* suggesting that losing your temper is not the way to control Prince Albert. Dear Victoria, I believe that you can accomplish that goal very easily if you flatter and cajole him. Stand firm, my little love, but sweetly!"

I made every effort, but still I found myself snapping at dearest Albert, refusing to listen to even his mildest suggestion on the most trivial matter. One day he snapped back, "I see quite clearly that I am only the husband, and not the master of the house."

"Because it is *my* house, not yours!" I shouted at him, forgetting dear Daisy's lesson entirely.

The argument grew more heated. He stared at me for a moment before he turned and stalked out. I leaped up and followed him, still shouting, "Albert! Albert!"

He ignored me, went into his room, shut the door, and BOLTED IT. I pounded on it furiously.

"Who is there?" came a peremptory voice on the other side. "The queen of England!" I cried.

I expected the door to be opened at once, but there was only silence. The door remained closed. I pounded even more furiously than before. Again the stern voice called out, "Who is there?"

And again I roared, beside myself with wrath, "The queen of England!"

Then a third time, but this time less harsh: "Who is there?"

I paused, my lips quivering. Then I replied in a completely different tone, "Albert, it is your wife, Victoria."

The door was immediately opened. We looked at each other, tears in our eyes, rushed into each other's arms, and kissed and kissed again. So much in love!

And then, only a <u>very</u> few weeks after we were married, I discovered that I was carrying a child.

I should have been happy to find myself with child—that was the natural thing and what everyone expected—but I was <u>not</u> happy. Far from it! I was utterly dismayed and out of sorts, because this was the very thing I had dreaded. I had tried just once to raise with my beloved Albert the possibility of delaying such an important development, asking him rather timidly if Stockmar, a trained physician, had offered any advice on the matter.

"It is against the laws of nature and the will of God," dearest Albert said. He seemed nearly as appalled as Lady Harriet had been.

"Yes, yes, of course, my love," I said, though I was not at all certain of God's views of the matter and had prayed night and day to be left free for at least six months. My prayers had not been answered, so perhaps dearest Albert was right.

"It is simply beyond me that anyone could ever wish for such a thing to happen," I wailed to dearest Daisy, who was the first person I told. "Especially at the beginning of a marriage."

"But, my dear Victoria," Daisy said, "the prince must be over-joyed. And the duchess, I'm sure, is delighted. King Leopold, too, and Lord Melbourne! Your subjects will be pleased beyond imagining to know that an heir is on the way."

"I haven't told any of them," I said crossly.

"No one? Not even your husband?" Daisy exclaimed, clearly surprised.

"Not even Albert. He'll only make a fuss. Or Mamma either."

I saw very little of my mother since I had moved her out of Buckingham Palace to a handsome house on Belgrave Square that she complained was too small.

"Then it shall remain a secret between just the two of us," dear Daisy promised, "until you are ready to share your good news."

Eventually, of course, I *did* tell dear Albert, and he *did* make a fuss, but of the nicest kind, calling me by the sweetest of names, until I let it slip that I had already talked it over with Daisy and she was making plans for the royal nursery. His mood changed abruptly, storm clouds swiftly covering the sun. He regarded me with narrowed eyes, tapping his finger against his upper lip in a way that NEVER FAILED to irritate me. "You have already discussed this with Lehzen? Before telling me?"

"Yes," I said, lifting my chin and meeting his unwavering gaze. "And she will take charge of the nursery."

"Victoria, she is already meddling in the running of the household and making a hash of it," Albert said sternly. "She can hardly be expected to do better if she is in charge of the nursery. I forbid it."

"*You* forbid it, Albert? YOU? You have no authority to do anything of the sort."

Another row had begun, only one of many in the months that came after.

Parliament passed a Regency Bill, naming dearest Albert as regent in the event that I died, leaving a child as heir to the throne. The vote of confidence did wonders for his mood. My mood improved, too, as my time approached. I had my husband's writing table moved into the same room with mine, and my reliance on him increased day by day.

On the twenty-first of November 1840, a dark, dull, windy, rainy day with smoking chimneys, I gave birth to a baby girl. She was to be christened Victoria Adelaide Mary Louisa. I had always enjoyed children from about the age when they had begun to talk, but I did not much care for babies, their wailing and froglike squirming, and I was happy to turn her over to the care of a nurse. Mrs. Southey had been most highly recommended by the Archbishop of Canterbury. It was dearest Albert who doted on our infant daughter from her earliest days and called her Pussy, a name we all adopted.

Albert and I celebrated our first anniversary in February, and our little princess royal was christened. Her father was delighted with her behavior through the ceremony. "Our Pussy seemed immensely satisfied at the lights and brilliant uniforms, for she is very intelligent and observing," he noted with satisfaction.

I was once again VERY happy! If only things could have remained as they were—so idyllic! But alas, they did not. Every day, it seemed, dearest Albert managed to find fault with something dear Daisy had said or done. And Daisy behaved in the manner of a jilted lover, deeply jealous of Albert.

"My dear Victoria," Daisy said to me more than once, "the prince no doubt is a loving husband, but he cannot know you as well as I do—I who have been with you since your birth, who heard your first words and watched your first tottering steps! No man can boast of that! And he cannot begin to know what we two endured at the hands of Sir John Conroy."

Naturally, I agreed with her—how could Albert possibly understand what it had been like for me? Had it not been for dearest Daisy, I might not have had the strength to resist Sir John's—and Mamma's!—insistence that I name him my private secretary and give him immense power. "You have always been my closest confidante," I assured her, "and you always shall be. I remain devoted to you."

The friction between Daisy and Albert was a constant irritant. But matters grew still worse.

I was pregnant again.

Oh, how I hated it! I complained bitterly to Lady Harriet, my mistress of the robes and the mother of a brood of seven. "I can enjoy nothing, not travel about or go about with my husband. If I could have waited at least a year, it would have been very different!"

Lady Harriet smiled, unperturbed, apparently forgetting our conversation the day before my wedding. "It's the sad lot of women," she said, patting my hand. "One can only make up one's mind to endure it. And just imagine, my dear, what delight you will bring to the kingdom when you have a son."

More disruption was to come. Late that summer—I was at the stage where I felt as awkward as a cow—the Whig government fell. Lord Melbourne was out of office. I felt completely bewildered, hardly able to believe that my excellent Lord Melbourne was no longer my prime minister. After four years of seeing him almost daily, the parting affected me very deeply. But with my dearest Albert at my side, I was finally able to accept Sir Robert Peel in that role. The crisis that had been so very difficult before was now averted when some of my ladies resigned their positions in the bedchamber and new ones were appointed. Things went along reasonably well. I even found myself becoming quite fond of Sir Robert after all, a state of affairs I could not have imagined.

Lady Harriet was proved correct. When Edward Albert was born on the morning of the ninth of November 1841, the country went mad with joy, singing "God Save the Queen," firing off salutes, and hoisting signs that read, "God Save the Prince of Wales."

My mother was overjoyed. So was my husband. I was simply relieved.

Bertie was strong and robust from the start, but our poor, dear little Pussy, who had been so healthy and fat, now turned sickly. I was much worried. Dearest Albert came to believe it was the fault of dear Daisy, who had taken over the supervision of the nursery in spite of his objections. He called her a crazy, stupid intriguer and even ordered her out of the palace; she refused to go, telling him that he had no right to give such an order, that it was the queen's house and not his. We argued over this, and our words were intemperate. Albert accused the doctor, the nurses, and especially Lehzen of doing harm to the child; I shouted in defense of both Daisy and the doctor. Albert wrote me a furious letter, telling me that I could do what I wished, but if our daughter died, it would be on my conscience, and in a flash of temper I screamed that he could murder the child if he wanted to. We both behaved shamefully. Pussy recovered and again thrived—we now called her Vic—but the battle raged on.

Albert had begun to loathe dear Lehzen, and the more he criticized her, the more I took her part.

Something had to be done. Then came Baroness Sarah Lyttelton, who had served as one of my ladies since I became queen. A widow with five grown children, Lady Sarah had earned my respect and Albert's confidence, and we decided to make her superintendent of the nursery. She brought about a complete change in the way the children's care was managed. She was SO calm, SO patient and sensible, even in the face of our fat little Vic's horrible screaming fits.

"I wonder how our daughter came by that temper," dearest Albert said mildly.

"I can't possibly imagine," I replied, also mildly, and we both burst out laughing.

Dear Daisy immediately found much to disparage about this estimable woman, and her quiet attacks on my dearest Albert increased in intensity. She had, I admitted, become a trial to us both. It was finally decided that my oldest and closest companion since childhood needed to leave. I quite agreed that it was best for her, and certainly best for us, but I could not bear to speak to her. I left it to Albert to make the arrangements for her return to Germany, where she would live with her sister.

"In over twenty years," Lehzen reminded him in an unsteady voice, "I have never once taken a day's leave."

"I thanked her for her selfless devotion," Albert told me later, "and for all she had done for my dearest wife, who would remain forever grateful."

"Did she say anything more?" I asked sadly.

My dearest Albert shook his head. "No. Nothing more."

One morning in September 1842 I stood watching a tall, erect figure in dark traveling clothes climb into the handsome coach-and-four I had ordered as a parting gift; I had also approved a generous pension. Daisy did not come to bid me adieu, and I did not send for her. I think neither of us could have endured the pain of saying good-bye. But as the carriage rolled away, I saw her press her face to the window. I raised my hand in farewell, and so did she.

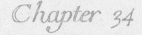

The Secret Picture, 1843

Shortly after Albert and I celebrated the third anniversary of our wedding, I sent for the artist Franz Javer Winterhalter to paint my portrait as a birthday gift for my beloved Albert's twenty-fourth birthday. Winterhalter had done earlier portraits of me, formally posed in a court gown with my hair done up, wearing diamond necklaces and earrings, all very proper.

This one is QUITE different. No court gown, no diamond jewelry, no queenly profile. My hair is loose, falling over my bare shoulder. I am wearing only a simple locket, and I gaze off to my left, my lips slightly parted. This is the way Albert sees me, and only Albert sees me, when we are alone. I am not a queen in this portrait. I am dearest Albert's wife. The painting is to be a surprise and to remain a secret. It is for no other eyes but his.

A new infant, our third, sleeps in the royal nursery: Alice, born on the twenty-fifth of April. A month later I attended a ball in celebration of my twenty-fourth birthday. Since then the artist has come nearly every day, and we retire to his rooms—first at Buckingham Palace, now at Windsor Castle—where he has set up his easel. Winterhalter is German, and in the past when I posed for him we spoke together in his language through the long hours. But not this time. I have asked him to let me sit in silence with my thoughts.

"I shall leave orders that I do not wish to be disturbed," I told him. "I wish to use these hours to recall the most important events of my life."

That is when I allowed my memories to drift back over my life, back to Sir John Conroy, when I was still a child.

At first Winterhalter was concerned that my reveries, as he called them, were unpleasant, for my brow furrowed and my mouth often became grim.

"I was thinking of a man I used to despise," I explained with a laugh. *Mamma knew that I was never fond of him, though she did not suspect how much I despised him.* "Perhaps I should think instead of my singing lessons with Luigi Lablache."

The man I despised has returned to England and retired to his rural estate, Arborfield Hall, in the country west of Windsor. How Sir John must have laughed when he learned that his old enemy, Baroness Lehzen, had been sent away! I have not forgiven him; I have simply decided to forget him.

There are some things I would rather forget but cannot. One was my refusal to honor Sir Robert Peel's quite reasonable request to replace some of my ladies of the bedchamber. I was too young and inexperienced to see that he was right, and my pride and stubbornness nearly brought on a constitutional crisis.

Another incident I'd rather forget is my treatment of Lady Flora Hastings. I felt no remorse at the time, believing myself blameless and her guilty. I recognize now that I was wrong on both counts. I ill-used her, in part because she, in her turn, had ill-used Lehzen, to whom I was completely devoted. That was no excuse for my cruelty, and I do very much regret it.

In the months following Lehzen's departure, I have come to realize how sorely trying it must have been for dearest Albert to endure her constant carping. I blame myself for my blindness, and I shudder to think what my beloved Albert had to go through. We never speak of it.

There has been another change that I did not anticipate. When I was first recovering from the birth of our Pussy, dearest Albert went every evening to dine with Mamma, who of course is his aunt as well as his mother-in-law. They grew fond of each other, and after Baroness Lehzen was no longer present to stoke the fires, Albert began to patiently repair the breach that had opened between my mother and me. He persuaded me to give her Clarence House, only a short walk from Buckingham Palace, as well as Frogmore House near Windsor. Comfortably settled there, she visits my children nearly every day—never interfering, but simply delighting in them. I have come to look forward to those visits. For the first time in many years, my dear mamma has a loving daughter who welcomes her into her life.

These sittings are coming to an end; Winterhalter says he will finish the portrait within a fortnight. I, too, have finished my reveries. Sir John long ago lost his power over me. Lehzen, once so dear to me but at the end such a trial, has gone away, though we do exchange letters. Lord Melbourne is still a dear friend, but no longer indispensable.

And I—I am the most fortunate of women. My three children grow more enchanting each day. I have the devotion of
my beloved Albert, SO good and SO beautiful. We labor side
by side at the hard work of governing the realm. Sometimes we
argue—my temper is still short—but our passion for each other
burns more brightly than ever. That is the secret of my secret
picture.

V. R.

THE VICTORIAN AGE

NOTES FROM THE AUTHOR

Victoria was queen for nearly sixty-four years, the longest reign of any English monarch. Though she had no direct power in a constitutional monarchy—she reigned, but she did not govern—Queen Victoria had enormous influence at a time of great expansion of the British Empire, all those vast areas in pink (originally red) on the map of the world. Her name defines an age.

Fortunately for historians, Victoria began, at the urging of her mother, to keep a diary when she was thirteen, and it was a habit she kept throughout her long life. But the entries in these diaries were written with the knowledge that they would be read—by her mother and her beloved governess, Baroness Lehzen, and later by those who might have an interest in the life of a queen. They were not private. We can only guess at what she was really feeling at the most critical times of her young life—until Prince Albert entered her life. Suddenly she was wearing her heart on her sleeve, her great love and passion for her husband splashed across the page. As a diarist she employed a dramatic style throughout her life, liberally sprinkling her entries with LOTS OF CAPITALS and underlining furiously, sometimes three or four times. Victoria's diaries have provided much of the inspiration for this book.

I have long been interested in the young princess in the years before she became her own mistress, as she put it, and then queen, and could free herself from the dark forces that ruled her life. I've included here additional material on her family history and the background of many of those around her.

Queen and Consort

Victoria and Albert adored each other, but their fights became legendary. Tempers flared on both sides as the balance of power shifted from one to the other. Albert complained to his friend, Baron Stockmar, "Victoria is too hasty and passionate for me to speak of my difficulties. She will not hear me out but flies into a rage and overwhelms me with reproaches and suspicions, lack of trust, ambition, envy, etc. I can either keep silence and go away, or I can be still more violent, and then we have scenes, which I hate."

Queen Victoria gave birth to nine children. Twenty-six of her forty-two grandchildren married European royalty or members of noble families from one end of the Continent to the other, so that Queen Victoria became known as "the grandmother of Europe." Among her many grandchildren was Tsarina Alexandra of Russia, the mother of Anastasia.

When Prince Albert died at the age of forty-two, his passing plunged Queen Victoria into profound grief from which she never fully recovered. The queen went into deep mourning for the rest of her long life.

Heir to the English Throne

When the thirteen American colonies declared their independence, King George III ruled England. He was happily married to a German princess, Charlotte, and the couple produced nine sons and six daughters. The eldest son, George, was created Prince of Wales, and when George III began to descend into madness, the younger George was named prince regent to rule in his father's place.

King George pressed the prince regent to marry his cousin, Caroline of Brunswick. The pair soon detested each other and separated after the birth of a daughter, Charlotte, in 1796. The prince regent took a number of mistresses; his favorite, Maria Fitzherbert, bore him several illegitimate children. His one legitimate daughter, Charlotte, was the heir to the throne.

Princess Charlotte of Wales was a rebellious young woman. When her father tried to compel her to marry William, prince of Orange, Charlotte fled. Eventually she returned to her father's house, still refusing to marry the "detested Dutchman." Instead, she fixed her sights on the handsome German prince she had met at a party, Leopold of Saxe-Coburg. Finally overcoming her father's opposition, Charlotte and Leopold were married in May 1816. Soon Princess Charlotte became pregnant, and England excitedly awaited the birth of the future king or queen. On November 5, 1817, a stillborn boy was delivered. Hours later, Charlotte, too, was dead.

The English line of succession had suddenly come to an end. King George III had fifty-six grandchildren; almost unbelievably, none of them was legitimate. Fifty-six *bâtards*, and not one eligible to inherit the throne.

Edward, duke of Kent, the fourth son, was in line for the crown after his older brother, the prince regent, father of the dead Charlotte; after Frederick, duke of York, who was childless (not counting his illegitimate children by various mistresses); and after William, duke of Clarence, all of whose children were illegitimate. Edward had been living in Paris with *his* mistress when he learned of the death of his niece, Charlotte, and her baby. The childless Edward decided to find a wife and marry for the sake of the succession. His fondest hope was to become the father of the future monarch of England.

The English Duke and the German Princess

Edward had met Charlotte's newly widowed husband, Prince Leopold, and liked him. Leopold had a sister in Germany, and Edward thought she might make him a suitable wife. With his equerry, Captain John Conroy, the fifty-year-old duke of Kent set off for Amorsbach, Germany, to woo Princess Victoire, a thirty-one-year-old widow with two children: Charles, age eleven, and Feodore, called Fidi, who was ten.

It was a successful trip. Edward's proposal was accepted, and on May 29, 1818, the duke and the dowager princess were married. Princess Victoire, now the duchess of Kent, was soon pregnant. Determined that the baby must be British-born, the duke, who was always entangled in debt, begged and borrowed enough money to transport his household to England.

The family left the castle in Amorsbach at the end of March 1819 in a caravan of carriages organized by Captain Conroy. The duke drove his open carriage with the duchess beside him. The duchess's lady-in-waiting, Baroness Späth, followed in a second carriage with Princess Feodore and Louise Lehzen, her governess. Prince Charles was away at school in Switzerland and did not accompany them. A caravan of various vehicles, crowded with cooks, maids, valets, and footmen, and the duchess's little dogs, made its way across Germany and France on roads so rough that Lehzen claimed her bones were badly rattled. When the group reached Calais, the royal yacht took them across the channel to England. Everyone on board was seasick on the crossing. Nearly a month after leaving Amorsbach, they arrived at Kensington Palace in the country outside of London.

A month later, on the twenty-fourth of May, 1819, a baby girl was born. "Plump as a partridge," the duke boasted about his infant daughter. "A model of strength and beauty combined!"

Naming the Baby
The duke and duchess of Kent discussed possible names for their little daughter. Her mother suggested naming her Georgina, in honor of her uncle George, the prince regent.

Her father disliked that suggestion, because he disliked his oldest brother. He preferred to name her Victoire, for his beloved wife.

Her mother then proposed Alexandrina, for her godfather, Tsar Alexander of Russia.

Her father offered a lengthy compromise: Georgina Alexandrina Victoire, adding Charlotte Augusta as well for good measure. Her mother agreed, and the list of names was sent to the prince regent, who had the right to decide the little princess's name.

For several days the baby's father received no reply, except to be informed that the christening must be a private affair with only a handful of invited guests. The walls of the Cupola Room at Kensington Palace were draped with crimson velvet. A christening font made of gilded silver was brought out from London. The Archbishop of Canterbury stood surrounded by a small group of important people. Holding the infant princess in his arms, the archbishop asked the baby's name.

Finally the prince regent spoke up. "Alexandrina," he said, adding that he would not permit his name to be used. The baby's mother began to weep, and her father grew red in the face. The prince regent glared at the parents and then agreed that the infant should have her mother's name, but it must not come before the Tsar's.

The archbishop poured water over the baby's head and named her Alexandrina Victoria. The baby's nurse shortened her name, calling her Drina. When she was a few years old, the little princess insisted that she be called Victoria. From then on, she was Princess Victoria.

Family Tragedy

The duke of Kent decided it would be healthier for his wife and daughter to spend the winter by the sea. He and his equerry, Captain Conroy, traveled to Devonshire on the south coast of England and settled on a house in the village of Sidmouth.

The duke's household moved to Sidmouth on Christmas Day in the midst of a fierce snowstorm. The rooms were small and dark and very cold, and the wind blowing off the sea rattled the windows. The duke fell ill, and on January 23, 1820, he died, leaving his wife saddled with debt. The duchess's brother, Leopold, came to her rescue and helped move the household back to Kensington Palace. Days later King George III died, and the prince regent ascended the throne as King George IV.

The Advisor

The duchess of Kent, widowed for the second time, had little money and spoke no English. She needed help with her day-to-day affairs, and her late husband's equerry was only too ready to advise her. John Conroy, a Welshman of Irish ancestry, had made a military career, married a general's daughter, and fathered six children. A handsome man of great charm and even greater ambition, he induced the distraught duchess to name him her comptroller, placing him officially in charge of her financial matters.

In time, King George IV was persuaded to create Conroy a knight, and the captain became Sir John.

The Governess

Louise Lehzen was Princess Feodore's governess and accompanied the duke and duchess of Kent on their journey to Kensington. After Feodore no longer needed her, Lehzen became governess to Princess Victoria, who began to call her Daisy.

The governess to a member of the royal family was usually herself of noble birth, but Lehzen was of humble background, the unmarried daughter of a Lutheran minister. When the duchess of Kent's older sister, Queen Antoinette of Württemberg, came to visit, she refused sit at the same table as Lehzen, who was seated there with Victoria. To give Lehzen the proper rank, King George IV agreed to create Lehzen a baroness of Hanover in Germany; in addition to being king of England, he also held the title King of Hanover.

But Sir John Conroy never let Baroness Lehzen forget that she was a foreigner, her title was foreign, and she still had no rank in England.

Lord Melbourne

William Lamb, later to become Lord Melbourne, married Lady Caroline Ponsonby when she was nineteen and he was twenty-six. The marriage at first was an extremely happy one. But Lamb was ambitious politically, and Lady Caroline, beautiful, talented, and well-educated, felt neglected. When she was twenty-seven, she had an affair with Lord Byron, the famous poet. They made no attempt to keep their relationship a secret. The poet tired of Caroline after a few months and broke off the affair, going on to attachments with other women. Caroline continued to pursue Byron, creating a scandal. Lamb, ever the gentleman, took his wife to Ireland, hoping she would forget Byron.

Even after William and Caroline Lamb had separated, he stood by his wife through years of mental instability and declining health. He was by her side when she died in 1828. That same year, he inherited his father's title as Viscount Melbourne and a seat in the House of Lords. King William IV appointed him prime minister, a position he held when Victoria became queen. She depended heavily on his guidance during the early years of her reign and regarded him as a father figure.

Prince Albert

Prince Albert was the son of Ernest, duke of Saxe-Coburg and Gotha, elder brother of the duchess of Kent and King Leopold. Albert's mother, Princess Louise, was sixteen when she married Ernest. They divorced when Albert was five years old; his mother eloped with an army captain who had been her husband's stablemaster, and the duke forced her to leave her two children behind. She was prohibited from ever seeing her children again. Though Albert was raised by two affectionate grandmothers, his separation from his mother at an early age deeply affected him and probably made him a rather rigid and moralistic man.

Albert worked devotedly for years for his adopted country, but was not especially popular with the English people, whose dislike of foreigners, and especially Germans, turned them against him. Victoria's wish to create him king consort was never realized, but after seventeen years as simply Prince Albert, he was titled "His Royal Highness the Prince Consort."

Albert's health suffered in the last two years of his life. He died at Windsor Castle on December 14, 1861, at the age of forty-two, with his beloved wife and five of their children by his bedside. The illness that caused his death, originally thought to be typhoid fever, is not definitely known and may have been attributable to other diseases.

Queen Victoria lived for another thirty-nine years. When she died at age eighty-one on January 22, 1901, she had ruled the British Empire for nearly sixty-three years and seven months. She was succeeded by her son, Bertie, who ruled as Edward VII.

Timeline

1817—Princess Charlotte, daughter of King George IV, dies, leaving
English succession open

1818—Edward, duke of Kent, marries German widow Princess Victoire,
mother of Charles and Feodore (called Fidi); family moves to
Kensington, England

1819—On May 24, a daughter is born; on June 24, christened
Alexandrina Victoria

1820—On January 23, the duke of Kent dies; his equerry, Captain
John Conroy, becomes advisor to the duchess of Kent, Victoria's
mother

1824—Fidi's German governess, Louise Lehzen, becomes governess to
Victoria

1828—In February, Fidi marries Ernst Hohenlohe-Langenburg and
moves to Germany

1830—King George IV dies; William, duke of Clarence, succeeds;
Victoria is next in line of succession

1831—Victoria's first public appearance at court

1832—Victoria, age 13, begins keeping a journal

1833—Victoria, age 14, begins royal progresses arranged by John Conroy

1834—Fidi's first visit in 6 years; Lady Flora Hastings becomes Victoria's
chaperone

1835—Victoria, age 16, confirmed in Church of England; suffers severe
illness

1836—visit from German cousins Ernest and Albert, for Victoria's 17th
birthday

1837—tension with mother and John Conroy increases; Victoria turns
18 and comes of age; on June 20, King William IV dies, and
Victoria becomes queen; meets with Lord Melbourne, prime
minister; moves to Buckingham Palace; appoints her attendants

1838—On June 28, Victoria crowned queen

1839—Victoria's early reign plagued with crises; in October, Ernest and
      Albert visit; Victoria in love, decides to marry Albert
1840—On February 10, Victoria and Albert marry; on November 21,
      their first daughter, Victoria, is born
1841—On November 9, their first son, Edward Albert, is born
1842—In September, Victoria's longtime friend, Baroness Lehzen,
      returns to Germany
1861—On December 14, Prince Albert dies at age 42
1901—On January 22, Queen Victoria dies at age 81

BIBLIOGRAPHY

Hibbert, Christopher. *Daily Life in Victorian England*. New York:
    American Heritage Publishing Company, 1975.
———. *Queen Victoria: A Personal History*. Boston: Da Capo Press,
    2001.
Hudson, Katherine. *A Royal Conflict: Sir John Conroy and the Young
    Victoria*. London: Hodder and Stoughton, 1994.
Mitchell, Sally. *Daily Life in Victorian England*. Westport, Conn.:
    Greenwood Press, 1996.
Plowden, Alison. *The Young Victoria*. London: Weidenfeld and
    Nicolson, 1981.
Strachey, Lytton. *Queen Victoria*. London: Chatto & Windus, 1921.
Vallone, Lynne. *Becoming Victoria*. New Haven, Conn.: Yale University
    Press, 2001.
Victoria, Queen of Great Britain, 1819–1901. *The girlhood of Queen
    Victoria; a selection from Her Majesty's diaries between the years
    1832 and 1840*, vol i. & vol ii, edited by Viscount Reginald Esher.
    New York, Longmans, Green & Co.; London, J. Murray, 1912.

Interesting Websites to Visit

For more about England during Victoria's teenage years:
www.pbs.org/empires/victoria/history/index.html
For more about fashion in Victoria's time:
en.wikipedia.org/wiki/1830s_in_fashion
For more about food in Victoria's time:
www.victoriana.com/victorianfood/
For more about Victoria's coronation, ladies-in-waiting, and other royal
attendants, visit Yvonne's Royalty Home Page:
users.uniserve.com/~canyon/index.htm
For more about Victoria's wedding:
www.queenvictoria.victoriana.com/RoyalWeddings/Queen-
Victoria-Wedding.html
To read Lytton Strachey's 1921 biography of Queen Victoria online:
womenshistory.about.com/library/etext/ls/bl_lsqv_02.htm
To find out more about important people in Victoria's life, look them up
on Wikipedia:

Her mother: see *Princess Victoria of Saxe-Coburg-Saalfeld*

Her half brother, Charles: see *Carl, 3rd Prince of Leiningen*

Her sister, Feodore (Fidi): see *Princess Feodora of Leiningen*

Her uncle, Leopold: see *Leopold I of Belgium*

Her prime minister, Lord Melbourne: see *William Lamb, 2nd
Viscount Melbourne*

Melbourne's wife: see *Lady Caroline Lamb*

Her mistress of the robes: see *Harriet Sutherland-Leveson-Gower,
Duchess of Sutherland*

Her chaperone: see *Lady Flora Hastings*

Her dearest Daisy: see *Louise Lehzen*

And to find out more about Sir John Conroy, read this article:
www.turtlebunbury.com/history/history_heroes/hist_hero_
conroy.html